P9-DMG-315

THE
SECLUSION

JACQUI CASTLE

This is a work of fiction. Names, characters, organizations, places, events, and incidents are either products of the author's imagination or are used fictitiously.

Copyright © 2018 Jacqui Castle
All rights reserved.

No part of this book may be reproduced, or stored in a retrieval system, or transmitted in any form or by any means, electronic, mechanical, photocopying, recording, or otherwise, without express written permission of the publisher.

Published by Inkshares, Inc., Oakland, California
www.inkshares.com

Edited by Matt Harry and Kaitlin Severini
Cover Design by CoverKitchen
Interior design by Kevin G. Summers

ISBN: 9781947848511
e-ISBN: 9781947848337
LCCN: 2017962692

First edition

Printed in the United States of America

RO454479158

Dedicated to
my grandmother Patricia Webb Ahearn
June 26, 1937–May 27, 2014
and
my mother, Suzanne Ahearn Regan

Unite this Nation
Through storm and drought
Sister North and Brother South
Sturdy; strong
Built to last
Shelter us from troubles past
From adversaries
Far and wide
All dangers on the other side
Give us hope;
Fill us with awe
With pride we serve the Board, the law
In your shadow
We will be
Secure for all eternity

—"Dedication to the Walls"
(Composed in 2031 by the Board)

CHAPTER 1

THE WALL LOOMED OVER ME.

The first time I laid eyes on it, I was in awe of its vastness—an iconic monument, stretching to the horizon in either direction. As strong and secure as its sister up north. Ten feet wide by thirty feet high by 1,954 miles long. We were told a substantial portion of it also went below ground, but for security reasons we weren't given the exact details. "The devil lies in the details," the Board was fond of saying. "Leave the devil to us."

It was widely agreed that the Walls were our greatest achievement. They were a statement to the world, twin barriers that declared our country a safe zone, free from the corruption of the outside. Growing up, we were shown videos of that corruption—other nations that had succumbed to violence and famine and political upheaval. I would sit on my father's lap, his long, steady arms wrapped around me, as we watched news feeds featuring the children of those countries. Children who had been bombed by their own leaders. Children who wandered demolished cities, starving and covered in chemical sores. Their ribs stood out like xylophone keys. The sight of them made my stomach queasy. Then the videos would cut to the Walls, and I would feel relief that I was protected from such horrors. Relief, and pride.

The first day I stood in the shadow of the Southern Wall, I wished my father could have seen it with me. What would he think? Would he be as entranced as I was? But, unfortunately, he was, like most citizens, not permitted to go near the barriers. Security reasons, the Board told us. Details.

Now, four years later, visiting the Wall had become a semi-regular part of my routine. Working beneath its shadow. The sight of it still amazed me. This thing that held us all together, that kept us safe. The vastness of it must be like seeing the ocean for the first time. Blood rushing, skin tingling. Beholding something far more powerful than you will ever be. But instead of fear, there was a sense of calm. Clarity. The overwhelming sense of a connection to something beyond oneself.

The Southern Security Barrier had been built sixty-eight years prior, making it older than most manufactured products in circulation. I had a fondness for older things. Artifacts, fossils, physical antiquities that had stood the test of time. And this Wall had stood longer than anything or anyone I'd known.

Some still wished to see for themselves what was on the other side. Radicals and malcontents. They refused to believe, or perhaps they hoped, that the videos the Board showed us weren't true. Maybe it was too painful for them to accept that the only thing waiting outside was a violence-ridden wasteland, that we were the last vestiges of civility.

Whatever the reason, a handful of these radicals occasionally tried to challenge the Wall or the Board. But every time, quickly and justly, they were captured and charged with treason. Cameras had been mounted every few feet, and the surveillance drones circling overhead captured sufficient evidence. Civilian eyes almost never saw this evidence firsthand, not unless an example was to be made. We were told the radicals—and there were less of them every year—were taken to military bases to repay their debt to the country. There, they would be rehabilitated into proper patriots. *Redeemed.*

I closed my eyes and rubbed the middle of my forehead. If you asked me, I'd say they got off easy. We'd all seen the videos of life on the outside. Why anyone would choose that over the security the Board provided was beyond me.

I gathered my amber hair, peeling the resistant sweaty strands from my neck and securing them with a band I'd grabbed from around my wrist. The freckles on my wheat-colored arms had darkened from the intensity of the spring sun. Beads of sweat on my forearms magnified certain freckles the way dewdrops magnify seeds inside a flower. I brought my arms down and wiped them off on my shirt.

The freckles were also on either side of my nose. They made me look younger than my twenty-two years, and I was self-conscious of that fact. "You know you can get rid of those," people had told me when I complained about them. Despite finding them annoying, and a hurdle to being taken seriously, I continued to opt out of the medical enhancements much of my generation enjoyed.

I lowered myself onto one knee, driving a cylindrical soil probe into the earth. Pressing a button, I heard the bore whir downward until the required depth of twelve inches was attained. After removing the probe, I examined the rusty soil inside. It was dark only slightly near the base. Still too much benzene. My finger scraped the soil, transferring the sample into a vial. The briny scent of the freshly stirred dirt settled on my tongue, and I licked my dry, cracking lips.

After packing away my sampling kit and slipping the vial into one of my pockets, I eyed my hands. Dirt lined my nails and nestled into the creases on my knuckles. My gloves were folded neatly in the probe kit, but I rarely used them. Though the toxicity levels at the site were perilously high during the last round of testing, I relished the sensation of dirt on my fingers and took my chances. Instead I grabbed sanitizer and a cloth out of my backpack and scrubbed.

Turning my attention back to the Wall, I noticed a clump of mayweed growing near the base. I shook my head. Just like the radicals. Some things kept trying, no matter the conditions. I carefully plucked it from the ground, then went on to clear the rest of the weeds from nearby fissures, tossing the pieces to the side. As I did so, I unearthed a piece of hornblende biotite granite, which I wiped off and put in my backpack for my collection. My open palm stroked the freshly revealed surface of the Wall.

When I rose, I noticed a dark shape slowly inching its way up the concrete barrier. I stepped back to get a better look. It was a lizard, a gecko probably, about six inches in length, tail curled against its back. I had a fondness for lizards, and every once in a while I would find one scurrying outside my apartment or spot one on my walk to work.

"Hey there," I said warmly. "Nice place you have here." We locked eyes for the length of a heartbeat, blue and lizard green connecting, and then it turned and scrambled over the Wall, leaving me behind. I sunk back to my heels and let out a sigh. Another radical who didn't appreciate the bounty of our country.

"Stay where you are," an authoritative voice boomed behind me. I froze, my eyes still focused on the gray barrier. I hadn't even heard anyone approach. "Hands above your head and turn around slowly."

My heart was suddenly up inside my throat. I'd been questioned by a Compo numerous times before—we all had been—but somehow it never got any easier. The hair on my arms stood upright as I interlaced my hands behind my skull. I began to pivot, making sure to turn slowly.

No sudden movements. Don't startle him. I knew the man behind me commanded respect, and I also knew that it didn't take much to convince a Compo to activate his or her weapon. Being shot with a pacifier was a prospect that frequented my nightmares. But deep down, I knew the fear was necessary. Fear protected, fear ensured survival. Fear was the evolutionary instinct embedded in each of us, the instinct that told us to freeze when we heard a rattlesnake, or halt when we came to a cliff's edge. Yes, the Board used that fear, but it was worth the price. Security was our reward.

The narrow, lambent eye of a directed-energy weapon pointed toward my neck. Clutched by the firm hand of the Compo, our shorthand for compliance officer. A crisp, standard-issue walnut-toned uniform whispered against his leathery, aging skin. A helmet in a matching shade crowned his brow, and a translucent face shield extended over his eyes.

I'd never met him before; his face was new. Plump and rust-colored, it resembled a beet picked too soon and left on the ground to wither in the desert sun. He towered a head above me and stood close enough that my fingertips could brush the weapon if I just reached out. I visualized myself doing so. An absurd response, given the circumstances, but my imagination didn't always cooperate with logic. Would it be hot from the mid-May sun? I didn't know much about the inner workings of the directed-energy weapons, but from what I'd witnessed in the past, his proximity was gratuitous. His weapon had a firing range of at least sixty feet. Would his close quarters result in more pain? A lump traveled down my throat and settled in my chest.

"Unauthorized persons are not to be within a hundred and fifty feet of the barrier," he said in a dry, hoarse voice. The dusty air had that effect.

I swallowed the surfacing lump farther down my parched throat. *He's just doing his job. Like you practiced, go on—answer him.* I recited my response, the response we were taught to give if questioned while on assignment.

"I apologize for any inconvenience, sir. Patricia Collins, Tier 3, authorized by the Natural Resource Department. I'm here collecting a monthly soil sample."

On his face shield I could faintly detect subtle, glimmering images. *What information is he viewing?* I wondered. He hadn't scanned me yet, so it was likely recent footage from the surveillance cameras nearby. Sweat beaded on my forehead, beckoning me to wipe it off. I resisted.

"It doesn't look like you're working. Pacing back and forth like that. Soil samples take what? Five minutes to collect? Where's your ideation device, miss? Why isn't it on your wrist?" A pinprick of blue light flickered on my neck, mirrored back to me in the Compo's face shield. The pacifier was aimed and ready. Its burnished surface sparkled mesmerizingly in the light. For a second I forgot the pain it could cause. But only for a second.

"The work is dusty, sir," I replied, doing my best to steady my voice. Compos put their lives on the line daily. For all he knew, I was the dangerous one; the least I could do was cooperate fully. "I sometimes put it in my pocket when I work somewhere particularly dusty. To keep it protected. I can get it now if permitted to reach into my pocket." He eyed me cautiously, weighing his options as his focus darted between me and whatever information he was viewing within his shield. My muscles tightened another notch.

"One hand. And make it slow."

I nodded slightly, and then slowly reached one hand down and into my pocket. I wrapped my fingers around my ideation device. When I pulled it out, something else fell to the ground. My eyes squeezed shut as I prepared for my worst nightmare to realize itself. Why, why wasn't I more careful? But the pain didn't come.

Not yet.

"What is that? What is that?" he said, his voice swelling, and he shoved the pacifier forward so the barrel was only inches from my throat. The blue dot grew larger on my neck. "Answer me right this second."

The words came out more forceful than intended. "Soil, soil, it's just a vial of soil, sir." The shaking in my voice could not be held. "It—it was in my pocket also. Please, it was just an accident." I breathed in the dusty air in short, shallow breaths. Thoughts of my father, my mother, and of my best friend, Rexx, flashed through my brain, intermixed with the image of the beet-red face in front of me. *I'm one of the good ones. You must know that.* I dared not speak next, but I hoped he could read the truth on my face.

"Just stay where you are," he said as he took several slow steps backward. "Kick it over this way. No sudden movements or I shoot." I detected a hint of nervousness in his voice, as if I'd dropped an explosive device and not a vial of dirt. That bit of tension, it opened the space closing in around me. His unease gave me the room to regain an ounce of control.

I nudged the vial of soil with the toe of my boot, rolling it toward him.

"Just stay right there. Don't you move." He kept the pacifier pointed as he stooped down, grunted, and eyed the vial curiously. The national emblem, prevalent on almost all manufactured products, was imprinted on the side, followed by a series of numbers that would not be recognizable to an untrained eye, but that I knew to be a location code and date. He reached the hand containing the soil out toward me, indicating I should hand him my device as well. I placed my device in his outstretched fingers. *This is almost over,* I reminded myself. *He's here to help. He's here to help.*

Eventually his puffy face relaxed, and he lowered his weapon and clipped it in a compartment on his uniform. Oh, thank the Board.

"It looks like your work here is done, Miss Collins. I expect you'll be departing now. I just need to scan you." He stepped forward, unclipped a handheld scanner from one of the compartments on his uniform, and grabbed the back of my hand, pinching it between his gloved thumb and index finger. A little too tightly.

My stomach dropped as he scanned my dorsal chip. Great. The event was now in my file. He compared the results on his scanner with the name on my ideation device, also known as an ID, then handed back my belongings.

"Thank you, sir."

I quickly scooped up the rest of my work gear and shoved it into the department-issued slate-gray backpack that accompanied me everywhere during the workweek. The national emblem split apart as I unzipped the rear panel to put the soil probe into its case, then reconstructed itself as the zipper was guided back into place. I slung the backpack over one shoulder and clipped it across my chest. The familiar pressure, the weight of the strap against my heart, soothed me, like a friendly pat on the shoulder.

The Compo retreated a bit, but I could feel his eyes still watching me as I hurried away. My feet crunched through the thick, low-lying brush. The quickest route to my car was straight on through.

Once there was a comfortable distance between us, I exhaled in relief. That was a close call; what the hell was I thinking? Pacing around the Wall and drawing attention to myself. I knew better. Get in and get out. I knew better, and yet I'd given a Compo reason to be suspicious. To go as far as to question my motives.

I hurriedly crossed the wide buffer zone between the Wall and the developed sector of town. All trees and high-growing plants within three hundred feet of the barrier were routinely clear-cut to discourage escape attempts. The crunching under my feet quickened as I noticed a surveillance drone circling overhead, like a hawk eyeing a potential meal. *I'm not a threat; I'm a patriot.* Still, it circled. I looked back to where I'd come from.

The Compo was gone, and his vehicle was nowhere in sight. In the distance, beyond the Wall to the right, a mountain range was barely visible. From my current angle, the peaks stuck up from the Wall's edge like thorns on a rose stem.

The gentle breeze on my neck did little to stave off my rapidly rising body temperature. May had been dry that year. But, truth be told, no drier than most years I could recall. The earth beneath my feet cracked with thirst. I took the final paces to the car, a vehicle checked out from the Natural Resources Department. I swiped the back of my hand against the handle and heard a click, indicating my identity had been verified and my car was unlocked. I tossed my belongings onto the passenger seat. It swiveled slightly in response. Sinking into the driver's seat, I pressed my palms into my eyes. Even though I'd escaped the pain of the pacifier, my heart hadn't yet gotten the message.

My foot tapped the accelerator, humming the electric engine to life. The white steering wheel telescoped out into my hands from its resting place within the front panel.

The Natural Resource Department had twenty vehicles available for scientists to use when performing fieldwork outside of city checkpoints. Inside city limits, everything operated on a tight grid. People were seamlessly shuffled around using a mix of light-rail trains and unmanned capsule-shaped vehicles called SafePods. They looked a bit like lightning bugs on wheels, especially in the evening.

Most days I was grateful for the travel leeway provided by my occupation. I relished the reflective time afforded by my solitary drives to and from the city. And learning to manually operate a vehicle was a privilege few were granted.

But after my encounter with the Compo, I just wanted to be home. The car bumped and jostled as I drove down the largely forgotten road, swerving to avoid the largest potholes. There were no potholes within city limits—even the slightest crack in the pavement was reported and filled in immediately. Tucson was a model of maintenance and urban planning.

Ten minutes into my drive, my windows rolled up of their own accord, and a voice, friendly and familiar, issued from the speakers overhead:

"Air quality advisory. Moderate. Windows will now seal automatically. Oxygen is being filtered and recirculated. You may breathe normally."

My ID beeped as well. I didn't check it; the message would be similar. Glancing at the air quality radar map on the dashboard, I saw that the orange zone I'd entered would last about another five miles. Air alerts never specified the exact danger, as most citizens wouldn't understand the terminology anyway. But as a scientist, I liked to deduce which harmful substances encased my vehicle at any given moment. Looking out the sealed windows, I saw that the air had a slight flaxen hue. Ozone or sulfur dioxide levels were probable culprits, and particulate matter pollution (excessive dust) was also likely.

My vehicle left the alert zone just as it reached the outskirts of the urban center. My route wound me past factory farm compounds, and my nerves continued to buzz. Though I'd been questioned before, having my chip scanned was a first. I didn't know what to expect next. The Board granted Compos full license for their actions based on professional judgment of a given situation, and I knew I was lucky. I walked away unscathed, unpacified, and that was something, I told myself. Maybe he wouldn't report me further. The gnawing feeling that I hadn't heard the end of it chewed at my chest, though.

I crossed the checkpoint into city limits.

ENTERING TUCSON, ARIZONA GRID. PLEASE RETURN VEHICLE.

I leaned my head back against the headrest. The scene around me shifted drastically. My lips turned up in a smile. I was almost home. I just had to return the car, then hop on a SafePod. A rectangular flashing light ahead indicated a train was about to cross, so I pressed the brakes.

Large, shining billboards hovered in the sky above. One advertised an interactive holographic movie opening at the cinema that weekend, while another boasted of free two-hour drone delivery for cabinet and refrigerator items ordered by midnight.

A third billboard sported a glowing picture of a grand, sprawling conference table adorned with several sets of hands folded stalwartly on top. Though I didn't count them, I knew there were exactly thirty pairs. No faces. There were never any faces, or names. Beneath the table rotated a few well-known mantras. My lips moved as I silently recited the current one on display:

THANKS TO THE BOARD, WE ARE SAFE, WE ARE SECURE, WE ARE UNITED.

As I read the familiar words, my nerves finally started to calm. The effect was as instantaneous as if I'd been injected with a sedative. I felt my body sink deeper into the white bucket seat, my muscles relax, and my jaw loosen. I said it once more, this time out loud: "I am safe. I am secure."

After the train had passed, I glided over the seamless light-rail tracks, passing the children's dormitories where I'd spent my nights between the ages of five and eighteen. My gaze climbed to the fifth floor, the tenth window from the left. My old room, which I'd shared with five others in a row of beds spaced a foot apart. Mine was the farthest on the right, next to the camera. I wondered who was sleeping in my bed, and who was in Amara's. Wondered if they held hands across the space between them when something scared them in the dark. The thought, or another like it, had surfaced nearly every time I passed the building for the past four years. Once Amara had left, the memories shifted from comforting to piercing.

One block farther, a group of children huddled together on the sidewalk to my right, outside a café—waiting to be seated for dinner, I presumed. Enjoying their free time before they would be required back for evening ideology and lights-out. They looked to be ten or twelve. All smiles and laughter. One of the girls was fixing another's hair while a boy played with the dial on the bottom of her shirt, causing her tank top to ripple from purple to green. A group of Compos stood a dozen feet away, watching the children attentively. Ready to intervene if necessary. Adolescence was a delicate time, and it was imperative to ensure loyalty developed as it should. We were all tasked with weeding out potential traitors; it was our civic duty.

I continued through the city center, past a sports complex and a park dotted with plastic trees, then came to my office building. It rose out of the sidewalk like a long glass tooth, narrowing as it extended toward the sky. I pulled around to the back, to the car return hangar, and reached my arm out the window to swipe my chip. A wide garage door opened to reveal a room large enough to house twenty identical vehicles. The hangar shared the first floor with the gray-water recycling equipment and battery banks for the building. Ours was the only department in the whole forty-story building that was granted access to private vehicles.

Once the car was parked in its original space and had started charging, I grabbed my stuff out of the back and walked to the rear of the vast hangar. It always smelled like wet cement in there, even though the cement hadn't been fresh in decades. In the back corner, several long tubes descended from holes in the ceiling. A stack of transport cylinders sat on the counter underneath. I carefully packed the soil sample from the day into one of the cylinders, swiped my chip at a scanner mounted on the counter, then sent the sample up one of the tubes, where it would travel to the lab and be waiting for me in the morning.

I wandered out of the hangar to the sidewalk outside, pressed a button on my ID, and within sixty seconds, a SafePod pulled up and opened its doors for me.

The vehicle navigated through a planned community of Tier 3 apartment buildings and pulled up to the curb in front of a lumicomm post. The units on the end of the hooked posts reminded me of ladybugs ready to take flight—the solar film with coated lights cascaded outward like glistening wings, while the central rotating surveillance camera resembled the beetle's abdomen.

Thank the Board I made it. The white-hot air from less than an hour before had been replaced by a comfortable, pressing warmth. I grabbed my backpack and stepped out of the car. As I walked away, a chirping noise indicated no chip was detected in range, so the vehicle automatically locked behind me and then drove off. I stood with my eyes closed, grounding my feet into the pavement, letting the setting sun's last rays bathe my eyelids and cheeks. A few deep breaths under the safety of the familiar lumicomm displaced the residual anxiety I held after my encounter with the Compo.

You're home. You're safe. You'll do better next time.

I walked up the sidewalk, between two of the ten identical Tier 3 buildings, until I reached the outside of my lower-level apartment—a small one-bedroom with a mint-green door and a concrete slab for a patio out front. I'd had to request the lower-level unit when I'd moved in, but it was granted almost instantly. The higher units were more popular, and a high floor number was often worn as a badge of honor. Higher floor: better view of the city. But I had a reason for wanting the ground level.

A thin metal chair fit snugly on the slab next to three raised garden beds made of thick recycled plastic, the only ones in sight.

Letting my backpack fall to the ground, I bent over to pick a lavender sprig from the overgrown bunch nearest the chair and inhaled the aroma. My other hand briefly grazed the earth. I pinched a bit of soil and rubbed it between my fingers and thumb. Dry, sandy. With renewed energy, I turned on the faucet underneath my kitchen window.

"Good evening, Patricia!" my neighbor Harold said boisterously as he walked past. Harold was friendly, always sharing the weather outlook each morning and saying hello anytime he saw me out in the yard. He was in his late fifties—a short, squat man with pockmarked cheeks and a bald scalp that glistened in the last rays of sun.

I opened my mouth to ask how he was, but he was already silently saying his mantras and swiping his hand in front of his door to unlock it. No doubt wanting to relax after a long day at the office, where he managed a team of equipment technicians. I could see it right there on the faceplate by his door:

HAROLD THOMPSON
TIER 3
EQUIPMENT TECHNICIAN MANAGER

"Have a nice night!" I called after him. He gave a smile and a nod then slipped inside.

I turned my attention back to the watering.

My garden might be small, but it was a soothing, satisfying place for me. Nourishing vegetables that would one day nourish me—a perfect symbiotic relationship, though always too short-lived. Once the excruciating heat of summer began and the water restrictions set in, produce merely one week from maturity would shrivel and dry up. With summer often a lost cause, I tried to make the most of my spring garden. I watered until each patch of cracked and gritty dirt transformed into moist, dark soil. I felt as if the water were washing over me as well.

Gardening was an expensive hobby. The process that went into first stripping contaminated soil, then adding back in the nutrients needed to produce successful results made the end product cost more credits than most cared to part with. We were all given a specific allotment of credits that refreshed monthly, with quantity based on our tier. As I picked a strawberry, I took a moment to feel grateful for my Tier 3 employment, which afforded me such luxuries.

I quickly harvested more berries, several radishes, a few mint leaves, and one ripe tomato. Harold's door stood next to mine. When viewed together, they resembled the two front teeth on a smile made up of all the doors on the first floor of the cylindrical building. Hoping I wouldn't be interrupting anything important, I knocked on Harold's door. He answered quickly, smiling when he saw what was in my hands.

"To have with dinner," I said as I handed him a few radishes and the tomato.

"I don't deserve all of this, Patricia. Thank you. These look delightful."

"No problem. We might as well enjoy them before the heat kills everything."

After a few more pleasantries, I stepped over to my front door. My hand found the faceplate adorning the siding. Every home in America had one. It stated the name, rank, and profession of the resident.

PATRICIA COLLINS
TIER 3
NATURAL RESOURCE SPECIALIST

Below the text was an image as familiar, or perhaps even more so, than my own hand. The national emblem. The strong outline of an eagle, wings spread, and the words *Unified, Secure* in bold typeface along the base.

In a ritual we were all taught to follow before crossing the threshold, I placed my hand on the metal faceplate. It was warm from the sun. I lowered my head and said a mantra in my head:

The Board provides. The Board protects. I am grateful for the protection.

The routine was calming. On the rare occasions I walked in without saying the mantra, I felt distracted and antsy until I remembered to do it. Such was the product of countless training sessions I'd been required to attend in the dormitories and classrooms.

Inside, I tossed my belongings in a pile by the front door and headed into the small kitchen built into the front left corner of the open space. Scouring the cabinets for dinner ideas, I was left largely disappointed, but I kept at it. Part of me clung to the hope that if I just opened the cabinet a second time, the magical ingredients to concoct the perfect five-minute meal would appear. But I hadn't shopped in several days and my supplies were dwindling. So, no such luck. Eventually I opened a cabinet a third time and grabbed, from the far back, a pre-packaged meal.

The lucky winner was lasagna. *Containing twenty grams of American-farmed protein!* it declared prominently on the front of the package.

As my meal plumped in the rehydrator, I showered quickly, changed into some fresh clothes, and then returned to the kitchen. It was amazing the difference a shower could make. With my dust-free hair and skin, I felt lighter, both physically and emotionally. I flipped a switch on the counter and watched as liquid from the gray-water tank under the sink sluggishly filtered up and into a reservoir next to the switch. When it was done, I filled my favorite red cup, grabbed my meal, and with the type of sigh that only emerged at the end of a long day, I dropped myself with a thud onto the sofa. A bit of water splashed onto my clean pajama shirt. I wasn't always the most graceful.

I liked my home. The one-bedroom apartment wasn't as large as Tier 1 or 2 housing, or as spacious as the Tier 3 apartments a couple would be reassigned to upon marriage. But compared to the dormitories where I'd spent my evenings until four years prior, it was roomy. And, more important, it was all mine. Occasionally I'd rearrange the furniture to fit my mood, playing with the few options of the space. The Board allowed us to decorate our space however we saw fit, provided the fixed screens and cameras were not blocked.

My sofa sat against the wall underneath a floating shelf holding a few trinkets—digital frames that cycled through photos of family and friends, a row of gemstones and rocks I'd collected over the years, and a few decorative candles I almost never lit.

To my left, a fixed, rectangular screen about the size of a tabletop was mounted firmly against the wall. Every few minutes the image shifted. Currently it displayed a simple crimson background and the following words: *Patriotism is about character—honesty, moral courage, respect, and loyalty.*

Across from the sofa, another screen, wider than the other, matched the curvature of the wall.

I settled in for the day's mandatory viewing segment—a thirty-minute episode of *America One: Helping Our Nation Succeed.* It was a comforting nightly ritual, though the content of the segments varied greatly. After swiping my hand over the sensor on my end table, my identity was verified and the show began to play.

A quick announcement about the new silver economy auto-vehicles being put into rotation was up first. The models featured wraparound solar arrays, virtually seamless against the exterior style, allowing them to run 20 percent longer than last year's models. Next was a quick local promotion about the upcoming baseball game, including an enhanced fireworks experience, premiere seventh-inning entertainment, and copious amounts of snack food. Virtual recordings would be streamed for those who could not attend in person. I made a mental note to ask Rexx if he wanted to come over and watch.

Then the national emblem lit up the screen—the same one that appeared on everything from hotel chains to restaurant tables to toothbrushes to my own front door. The voice of an offscreen announcer introduced Aelia Ramey. A gorgeous, petite woman in her mid-forties, with an elegant crop of dove-white hair, appeared. I smiled at the familiar face, feeling almost as if a friend had sat down next to me on the sofa.

"Welcome, Americans! Today's topic is 'the Family Dinner Table.' We'll explore ten conversation topics that will bring you and your loved ones closer as you enjoy a family meal together. It's a great way to catch up before getting your child back in time for evening rituals at the dormitory." Behind Aelia, a family of three sat at their dinner table, laughing, smiling, and enjoying one another's company. It looked lovely.

"I suggest taking notes and keeping a list in the dining room for when the conversation starts to lag—you don't want to be left to your own wiles now!" Aelia said with an exaggerated laugh and a wink. Behind her, the on-screen mother showed us where she kept her list—on a reusable pad mounted to the dining room wall. "First up, we have the good, old-fashioned sharing of one's day."

The words *#1: Sharing Your Day* popped up on a floor-to-ceiling screen behind Aelia.

"Kids can share with their parents what they learned from their virtual instructors on subjects such as math, English, patriotism, and communication skills. This is a great time for parents to help children master the art of acceptable conversation! Older children can discuss preparations for their aptitude tests. Parents, you can share an unclassified overview of what you did at work today, and how your role helps make America the greatest, safest, most united nation on Earth." I beamed with a bit of pride, alone in my living room, for being part of the picture she painted. But behind the pride there was also shame. I promised myself to not let the events of the day happen again.

I took a nibble of my dinner, which was about as appetizing as sawdust, but made more palatable by the fresh mint, carrots, and radishes I'd sprinkled around the dish. "A second great topic of conversation is *the weather*," Aelia continued, accentuating the last two words as if she'd thought of them herself. "For example, you might say, 'It looks like our dry spell will continue' or 'That last flood ended sooner than expected.' Weather is an excellent conversation topic, and it's one that naturally changes daily. Rain one day and sun the next—why, the possibilities are virtually endless!"

I nodded, remembering multiple conversations I'd had about weather that very day.

"Number three!" Aelia gestured excitedly as a *#3* and the words *On-Screen Friends* were added to the list behind her. "What is going on in the lives of your favorite virtual characters? Discussing on-screen friends makes for a fun and entertaining way to connect with your family members. 'What do you think will happen in next week's episode?' Remember, all programming is approved by the Board for your enjoyment, and automatically filtered based on the age of the viewer! Just be sure that everyone watching has registered by swiping their dorsal chip."

She tapped the back of her hand. Dorsal chips were implanted within minutes of a child's first breath. On the day of delivery, the baby was removed, whisked away, and implanted before the mother ever woke up. A person's chip contained their whole identity—not just their name but a record of their work history, aptitude tests, medical requirements, and location. Without it, it was almost as if a person didn't exist. The thought made my stomach churn. Or possibly it was the lasagna.

Aelia continued through her list and my mind wandered, hearing words like *baseball* and *fashion* tossed out as potential topics of conversation. I thought about my parents and how I owed them a visit. All the while I kept my eyes on the screen and felt the living room's camera lens focusing on me. It was mounted in the corner, framed on each side by hanging plants. Living alone, the round glass eye brought comfort, knowing someone was keeping watch. I also couldn't help but feel sorry for the poor saps that had to review the footage of me eating dinner in my living room.

Eventually I heard the standard sign-off. "Thank you for making time to join me today. We are all one, united." Aelia smiled wider than I thought possible. Unlike me, her face was smooth and blemish-free. "I look forward to tomorrow, when we'll discuss going to the zoo, seeing the native and non-native animals, and how a 'native' sign signals there's more to learn! This is Aelia Ramey, and Board bless us all!"

Every night for the past four years, I had sat on my couch, watching the mandatory programing. I had welcomed Aelia Ramey into my living room. Before that I'd done the same, though I'd been in the rec room in the dormitories, or sprawled across my parents' living room floor, or on a sofa at a friend's house. Regardless of where we were, before the day ended, it was our patriotic duty to swipe our chips and watch *America One: Helping Our Nation Succeed.* It had been that way since before I was born in 2068, and it would continue that way long after I died. It was life.

The screen lit up one last time with the ubiquitous national emblem, then the screen faded to black and the program ended. Out of habit I scrolled through the other entertainment options, searching for something that would pique my interest. Sporting events to catch up on, the latest episode of a sitcom, a romantic movie, an invite from a friend to log in and play a holographic video game. After a few halfhearted attempts to engage, I called it quits. The day had worn me out.

I wolfed down the rest of my bland dinner, tossed my dishes in the all-in-one recomper (recycler, composter, and washer), and decided to call it an early night.

A fitful sleep waited for me—a regular occurrence resulting from what my parents deemed an "overactive imagination." I tried to keep it under control, but at twenty-two, vivid imagery continued to surface, like pockets of air released underwater. I tossed and turned, rearranging my pillows, throwing one leg over the blanket and then, moments later, back under it again. I fussed with the sweaty hair stuck to my neck, hoping it was somehow the missing link impeding my sleep. After some time, maybe minutes, maybe an hour, I finally dropped off.

Suddenly I was ten years old, surrounded by my classmates during a virtual classroom session. A large national emblem decorated the far wall from floor to ceiling. The other walls were covered with what was known as "educational encour-agement": childhood mantras, national slogans, and images of children as model patriots. In unison, we recited the pledge, then lowered our hands from our hearts and sat down in our chairs.

The screens embedded in the long desks in front of each row of children flashed to life. We put on our headphones, and all was quiet. In my dream I recalled how it felt—the posture we were taught to adapt to show we were paying attention, and the knowledge that if we slipped up, we'd be removed from our classmates and put into an isolated room with a single desk and chair until our punishment was complete. We were taught early to know the difference between the time for learning and the time for socializing.

Mathematics, technology, communication skills, and post-Seclusion history, patriotism, and ideology. Those were the subjects that filled our days. Everything that took place before the Seclusion (before the addition of the Northern Security

Barrier in 2030 sealed our country) was highly classified for our protection. Many topics were strictly forbidden. Un-American history was one of them; pre-Seclusion American history was another.

We sat quietly and listened to the same exact recording every ten-year-old in America was listening to that day, tapping the screen when prompted to provide the answer to a question. Even in my dream, my leg jiggled impatiently just as it had back then.

Our classroom facilitator, Maro, stood like a statue in the corner. Sometimes he'd stand so still that with his crisp white shirt, waxen skin, and chalk-white hair, he'd appear to melt into the wall behind him. Maro had followed our group of twenty since we'd begun our formal education at the age of five, the age we moved into the dormitories.

Every thirty minutes or so he'd leave his alabaster camouflage corner, walk up behind each of us in turn, and pat our shoulders or provide other modest encouragement. He answered our questions respectfully, not in a way that made us feel like we were flies on his shoulder, as many adults did. We spent more waking hours with Maro than with any other adult in our lives. Even at ten, I knew we were lucky to have him as our facilitator. I'd heard others talk about their facilitators' short tempers. Heard stories of isolation longer than any in my class were forced to endure.

But on this day, the door to our classroom swung open abruptly and two Compos stormed in.

"Officers . . . ," Maro began with a slight tremor in his voice, obviously startled. "Is there something I can help you with? As you can see, I'm in the middle of a virtual session."

The Compos didn't answer Maro's question but instead roughly grabbed hold of him. Each with one hand on a shoulder and forearm, they pushed him up against the wall so hard,

I felt the pain in my own forehead. I stiffened in my seat as several young voices screamed out in surprise. Then they caught their tongues, knowing better.

I remained silent and terrified, and my leg ceased jiggling. The Compos leaned their faces in close to either side of Maro's, speaking into his ear. We couldn't hear the words, but the rough tone was enough for us to grasp the tenor of the conversation. Then, as if the Compo were saying the next words with the clear intention of us hearing them, the words *aim to subvert educational institution* went through the silent classroom. I didn't understand what they meant, but I knew they weren't good. Tears slid down the sides of my nose.

"I'm innocent. I swear. I have proof," Maro said in a pleading voice just loud enough for us to hear. Sitting there, in that small gray metal chair, my heart broke in two. "Please, please," he continued. "Not in front of the children."

Please, I mouthed along with him.

I knew what I was about to witness. Though I'd seen it play out in the distance and on the screen, probably hundreds of times by that point in my life, it was my first experience up close, with someone I knew and cared about. Someone who was now a traitor.

We watched the rest of the scene unfold in silence, as we were taught. My classmate Elliot's small shaking hand grasped mine underneath the table as the Compos pointed their pacifiers. I felt the tears continue to spill over as the body of the teacher I had spent hundreds of days with convulsed in front of me, emitting a noise so low and horrible, it caused me to flinch in my dream and in the present. My free hand crossed my lap and found Elliot's, encasing her hand in both of mine, offering the only comfort I could.

The scene in front of me blurred as my eyes lost focus. I was terrified to look at his face. Then one small detail grabbed my attention. Maro's shirt collar. Maro was always clean, always crisp. He clearly took pride in his appearance. He slicked his hair back in a way that said he went to great measures to perfect it before he left his home in the morning. The collar of his shirt rumpled in a way that would have ordinarily had him smoothing it out with both hands. I stared at the collar, followed it as they dragged him, unconscious yet still trembling, through the classroom doorway and out of our lives forever.

Back in the present, I woke up shaking. My sweaty T-shirt was stuck to my body. I clawed at its neck, willing the air to circulate. Maro hadn't crossed my mind in years, and I wondered why he'd appeared in my dream just now. Even after so much time, his memory elicited a feeling akin to having a fifty-pound weight dropped onto my chest. The realization that someone I thought I knew, someone I cared about, could willfully disobey the Board and put the rest of us in danger shook me to my core. I was crushed. That was the day I learned heartache, that those you trust could deceive you. Maro was replaced the next day, and we never found out why exactly he'd been taken into custody or what had happened to him. All we knew for sure was that he was a traitor.

My clammy hands pawed the nightstand for the glass of water I always kept at my bedside. I turned on a light to get my bearings and then drank slowly, absorbing the reassuringly familiar image of my bedroom. The large screen on the far wall reflected the light emanating from the small dome on my nightstand. My eyes wandered to the corner of the room, where the camera was mounted.

"Just had a nightmare," I said calmly and respectfully to the room at large before tapping off the light, lying back down, and pulling the scratchy green polyester blanket over my face.

I closed my eyes again and repeated one of the mantras we were taught as children. "You are safe. The Board will keep you safe. You are safe. The Board will keep you safe."

As I settled back into sleep, my consciousness ebbed and flowed. I found myself replaying the scene at the Wall. *Stay where you are.* The Compo's heavy words looped, stealing any hope of a deep slumber, until the rising sun illuminated the room.

With puffy, sleep-deprived eyes, I reached for my ID to check the time. A message was waiting from my supervisor.

REPORT TO THE DEPARTMENT TWENTY MINUTES EARLY TO DISCUSS THE RECENT MARK IN YOUR FILE.—G

CHAPTER 2

MY STOMACH SANK into the mattress below me. Suddenly my fractured night of sleep was the last thing on my mind. I reread the message and spun the tungsten ring that once belonged to my grandmother Lily around and around my index finger—a nervous habit. *Relax. Relax. You knew it would end up in your file as soon as that Compo asked to scan your chip. This isn't new information.* Well, it was new information that my supervisor had been alerted.

My mind searched for possible consequences like a bird probing for worms in the earth. Would it just be my supervisor, or would there be uniform-clad Compos there as well? I spun my ring faster. Would I even make it into the office, or would they be waiting outside? Would I see the pacifier before they shot me, or would it take me by surprise? Why hadn't I been more careful at the Wall? Why did I give them reason to think I, of all people, was suspect? It was something I'd never be able to erase.

No one is above the law, we were told. *Violation of the law is like a virus; it can start as nothing more than a simple tickle in one's throat, but before long it has taken over the whole body. To keep America functioning as a healthy body, we must eradicate the virus before it spreads.*

The Tier 3 apartment complex was five blocks from the Natural Resource Department office. Though we were sometimes called on to virtually consult on assignments in other areas and work with chapters across the country, physical tests were performed only within our territory. Our territory consisted of approximately seven thousand square miles, though it wasn't evenly dispersed. The map of our assigned territory reminded me of a hornet, its wings folded in and stinger poised to strike.

After getting dressed, I hustled to work with quick, nervous steps. Soon I reached the towering building where I spent my working mornings—the same building where I had returned my work vehicle the day before. The large streamlined structure sat smack in the middle of five identical buildings. The anti-reflective material that encased the towering forty-story building was as smooth as glass and warm to the touch, as it absorbed the heat from the sun and converted it into electricity. It got so hot in the afternoons, that when I first started working there, I burned myself a few times by accidentally leaning up against the glass. Now I knew to stand a good arm's length away from the surface.

Once I reached the front entrance, I swiped my chip to be let in. No officers were outside the building or immediately inside the doors. That was a good sign. Department offices were on the second floor and I took the stairs, wondering if those final steps would make up my last moments as an ordinary citizen. I tried to reassure myself—if they were going to take me, they would have done so already. They would have just let themselves inside my apartment. Hesitation wasn't an attribute of the Compliance Department.

I shook out my arms as I walked the final paces to Mrs. Gerardi's office, all the while tossing around various ways I could earn back the trust of those I'd let down. Knowing that someone—whether it was my supervisor, the Compliance Department, or even the Board—thought less of me gnawed at my insides. I knocked. Would she be in there smiling, scowling, or surrounded by reinforcements?

The door slid open and Mrs. Gerardi was seated behind her thick, kidney-shaped desk, her shoulders back and her chin high and pointed in my direction. I realized as I crossed the threshold that I'd never actually set foot in her office. She was the type of boss who made the rounds and called everyone by their first names. If we needed a question answered immediately, a virtual conversation was generally enough.

Mrs. G was in her mid-fifties, with pecan skin and eyes that let optimism shine through despite the stress lines that creased the edges. At that moment, though, her eyes were narrow and void of cheer. I crossed my hands defensively over my chest as she informed me in an exasperated tone that a new entry had appeared in my file.

Abuse of Privilege—that was all it said. *Abuse of Privilege,* I thought to myself. I had access to the buffer zone, and I'd abused it. It wasn't so bad, but my chin still dipped to my chest in shame as I formulated a response. After a moment I took a step forward and relayed to her—and those who may be watching through the surveillance camera in her office ceiling light—my account. It was completely my fault. I lingered too long at the site and got distracted paying homage to the Wall. I took off my ID and put it in my pocket. It was easy to see how my intentions could be misconstrued. The Compo was just playing it safe, and I should never have put myself in a position to waste his time.

As I spoke, Mrs. G cracked her knuckles and leaned back in her chair, leaving me to guess what she might be thinking. I waited for the blowback, but it did not come, and we stood there in silence for several awkward minutes. She pinched the skin at the bridge of her nose with her thumb and forefinger, and with an exasperated sigh she set the rectangular device she was holding down on her desk. I got the impression all she really wanted to know was whether the interaction was going to come back to bite her in the ass.

"Don't let it happen again, Patricia," she finally said, then waved me off toward the conference room.

"Yes, ma'am." As I was about to turn away, I spied the details on her screen. I lowered my head and left the office, the words I'd seen racing through my mind:

Abuse of Privilege
Level-Yellow Alert
Third-Generation Family History

I told myself not to read into something I didn't understand. The Board and the Compliance Department spoke in code for our protection. But still the questions came, cascading over one another like boulders in a landslide.

Third-generation family history? Family history of what? Slaps on the wrist? Abuse of privilege? Something more? Did Mrs. G put the device down so I could see it on purpose? Was she trying to warn me or was it purely accidental? If it was a warning, it didn't help me much.

My grandfather Patrick had died before I was born. My parents didn't talk about him. My grandmother Lily died when I was ten, and she didn't leave the house for the last several years of her life. As for my parents, they were model citizens. I had no siblings—everyone in my generation was an only child, by the Board's decree. The population needed to be kept static due to dwindling resources. Rising sea levels, air pollution, contaminated soil, and bacteria-ridden water all played a part.

I tried to shake off the tightening in my chest as I walked down the hallway and into my cubicle—one corner of a six-section rectangular workspace. Curved white walls divided each section.

"Morning," I said in greeting to the coworkers who currently occupied four of the other five cubicles.

I tossed my belongings onto my metal desk chair and then headed toward the conference room. I muttered a few comforting mantras, rubbed the base of my neck, and skirted through the door a few minutes early for the morning meeting.

Rexx, my coworker and best friend, sat alone at a long conference table prearranged for twenty. His thick jet-black curls bounced against his olive skin as he rapped his knuckles on the tabletop to the rhythm of the tinny electronic tune quietly playing overhead.

The bright lights cast shadows of Rexx's curls, giving the impression stretched-out springs were dancing across his face and his thick eyelashes. He flashed a goofy smile that dimpled his cheeks when he spotted me. I smiled back at the familiar sight of him. For the first time since the previous afternoon, I felt like everything was going to be all right.

Rexx and I had gone through our job training together, beginning at age sixteen, and we'd remained close friends ever since. We shared a passion for nature and a dedication to solving the whole overly-toxic-soil-and-water problem. We had both gained approval to become Tier 3 natural resource specialists, one of the few occupations in the country that allowed access to the unmonitored areas outside city limits. These areas included state parks, evacuated land, and research facilities located within our territory. For that, I was eternally grateful.

At the age of sixteen, all citizens selected multiple job categories they'd like to pursue as a career. A series of aptitude tests were administered to determine the best fit and the citizen's corresponding job tier. Tier 1 was the highest and Tier 5, the lowest. The chance of getting the job depended on the availability of vacancies and a variety of other factors. What those factors were, we didn't know. Some of us got lucky and were slotted into one of our chosen professions. Most didn't receive their first choice, or even their second or third. But we all did our duty for the country.

"What do you think's on the agenda today, Patch?" Rexx asked, inviting me to sit by way of kicking over the rolling chair next to him. Patch was the nickname Rexx had made up for me in training. I liked hearing it. Rexx wrapped both hands around his morning coffee, clutching it like a baby bird he was protecting from danger.

"I went to collect a sample near the Wall yesterday," I answered as I took a seat. Rexx nonchalantly brought the coffee to his lips. He had an ease about him that I wished I could emulate. Coworkers began to drift in and the seats on either side of us slowly filled. "Everything looked fine, same as always," I said. I wanted to tell him what had really happened as well as the words I'd just seen on Mrs. G's device. To unload some of the burden, to ask him what he thought, but I couldn't. Not in front of everyone. Not in front of the cameras. "The results should be in this afternoon."

I chose my words carefully—words have power, the Board reminded us, and they should never be settled on lightly. Words are voiced, recorded, and stored somewhere for all eternity. From a very young age, we had been taught to select our words well.

The primary objective of our branch was to determine how the landscape and soil health in the American Southwest was

changing over time by performing environmental-impact stud-
ies, biological assessments, and contaminant investigations.
Members of our department were called in to perform tests
following natural disasters such as floods or earthquakes, and
I'd taken part in these procedures a handful of times. However,
when it came to anything beyond the Wall, that well of information was dryer than a fallen leaf left in the sun. For instance,
when the 2088 tsunami hit the California coastline, we were
provided with the time that the earthquake occurred across the
ocean, its distance from the coast, and its magnitude, but no
other information. Not even a map. It could be frustrating,
but a little harder work on our end was worth the safety and
protection of the country. It was for the best.

We were educated, but like the rest of the citizens in our
country, we were only given the information needed to do our
jobs effectively, nothing more. Almost all our work knowledge
was considered classified to anyone outside of our department.
The devil lies in the details. The wrong detail shared with the
wrong person, and the virus of Un-America would spread.

"Listen up, everyone," Mrs. Gerardi said as she strode in,
reining in the various side conversations of the employees who
had filled the conference room. I waited for her to turn her gaze
to me, to do something that would let everyone know what a
massive failure and disappointment I was. But she didn't. She
just carried on as usual, and somehow that felt even worse.

A holographic image of a topographical map flickered to
life as Mrs. G pressed a button next to her seat. It extended
from the ceiling down to the table, like a translucent sideways
front door that balanced on a razor-thin edge. Stamped on the
top was the only portion of the image that never shifted—the
national emblem.

"We have a busy day ahead of us. Rexx and Patricia, you'll
be testing in the labs this morning before heading back out to

Zone 72 this afternoon. We're hoping to open a small portion of 72 as new crop areas because of the recent blight north of the city. The data you've collected is looking promising." The map zoomed in on Zone 72 as Mrs. Gerardi controlled it with her in-table panel. Several numbers hovered above the image—a compilation of data returned from our samplings. Higher than average levels of petroleum hydrocarbons but nothing too worrisome.

"Let's try to get this wrapped up by next week if possible." Rexx and I nodded, but I could feel Rexx's deflation. Zone 72 was one of the good ones. I knew he was going to miss going there. "Feel free to check out more supplies from the quartermaster if you need to, and I'll approve it." Mrs. G's voice had odd inflections as she tried to sound as if she weren't just paraphrasing the list in front of her.

"Lydia, you and I are wanted to consult on a conference call at twelve thirty, so please stay in the room after this meeting adjourns to discuss. The toxicity of Santa Cruz River is continuing to rise near the north edge of our territory, and ground seepage is becoming a considerable concern. The continuing restoration project might be impacted." A section of the barely flowing Santa Cruz River appeared in the air in front of me; a red outline radiated from a portion of the shore, highlighting the area of concern.

"Jordan." The techie perked up as Mrs. G addressed him. "We have two department vehicles in need of their biweekly inspections, and a diagnostic machine in Lab Three is malfunctioning. Please make these your priorities before moving on."

"Yes, ma'am, at your service," Jordan replied with a large grin.

My name was not mentioned again, and when the meeting ended, Rexx and I walked together down to Lab 3. We passed several familiar digital posters embedded in the walls of the hallway. One featured a group of five scientists smiling brightly and huddled together, as well as the phrase *The two goals of innovation work hand in hand—Enhance security, ensure safety.* Another, a picture of a triangle, with the national emblem resting at the top point. The numbers one to five, indicating tier levels, ran within the triangle from top to bottom. Underneath, the words: *Ask yourself every day how your work serves the Board, and therefore, the greater good.*

At the door to the lab, Rexx and I both scanned our chips then pressed a button that instructed us to accept on the touchscreen above the scanner. This indicated our renewed daily agreement that any information learned in the lab was confidential and not to be shared with the general populous.

When I entered, a few people were scattered around a long, central island countertop, already working. Others would follow shortly. The room had been sanitized overnight, and smelled of salt water with a hint of citrus, like a freshly cleaned restroom.

Seven of us worked in Lab 3, and that day there would be eight, as Jordan, our tech guy, was already sprawled out on the polished white floor, working on a malfunctioning diagnostic machine and talking to himself.

Every morning was more or less the same. We'd spend three or four hours performing lab work based on current assignments, then use our findings from the day before to readjust any management plans that needed readjusting. Next we headed out for field assignments. Or, if no field assignments were on the agenda, we retreated to our individual cubicles to input data, send necessary messages, and get a head start on management plans for upcoming assignments.

The lab was triangular, with full-length countertops lining two of the three walls. One held an array of lab equipment, some portable so they could be picked up and moved to the scientist's place of choice, and some fixed. A fluorescent imaging machine with several cubic sections took up most of the counter space on one side. One section was switched on, emitting a dim red glow as it analyzed three test subjects—algal colonies in petri dishes injected with three different bacterial strains.

A large interactive map covered the other wall from the countertop up. It displayed the geomorphology, topography, vegetation, and climate across the territory. Press a specific area, and more data pertaining to that region would appear. The map could be altered to view various metrics, such as the spread of a specific pollutant or natural disaster risk. We could also view predictive forecasts (of soil macronutrient, micronutrient, organic matter, and pH levels) based on current trajectories, and view the long-term results of hypothetical ecological models. The map was updated constantly based on the findings of our department. We used this information to come up with short-term and long-term management decisions for various locations.

Stu was in the corner talking loudly to someone on his ID, seemingly oblivious to the fact that there were others in the room. From the snippets I overheard, I guessed he was talking to his contact at a local vertical factory farm, going over the results of a recent crop sustainability assessment and relaying his fertilization advice and implementation plan.

I set myself up a few feet away from Jordan's legs, next to a SoilSkimmer diagnostic machine. Inputting samples that had been collected by various employees the day before was one of my favorite ways to start the morning. Once the first vial was placed into the machine, the label was scanned, the soil was analyzed, and the results were stored in the database and sent to the assigned scientist. A clean and sanitized vial emerged from the other end. Specific training had been required to operate the machine, though there wasn't much that could be done to mess up the process. It was about as easy to use as the vending machines scattered throughout the city.

I grabbed a second vial and turned it over in my hand, reading the code: TCSAZ624:5-15-2090. Location number 624 in the Tucson, Arizona, territory. May 15, 2090. It was the sample from the Wall. Almost a full ten minutes had passed without me thinking about the events from the day before. Suddenly I felt as if the word SUSPECT had been stamped onto the back of my neck and everyone in the room could read it.

"Everything all right, Patch?" Rexx was looking at me, his head cocked sideways. I snapped out of it, realizing I'd been sitting with the vial in my hand, my eyes unfocused and staring through those in my line of vision.

"Sorry, yeah, everything's fine. Just zoned out for a second there."

Rexx didn't look convinced.

"Did anyone catch *Goaltender* last night?" Stu asked nobody in particular as soon as he finished his call. I was relieved at the change in conversation. I looked over at Stu and smiled when I saw his large ears had turned a bright red, as they often did when he was worked up about something.

Lydia walked into the lab, returning from her preconference call meeting with Mrs. G, and set up shop on a barstool at the central counter.

"Yeah, yeah. I caught it for a few minutes," answered Jordan from the floor as he tinkered with the diagnostic machine. Jordan spent his days fixing any equipment used within our department that needed attention, ranging from a broken voice-activated door to a jammed printer. His knowledge regarding modern technology far exceeded that of anyone else in my life. One time I accidentally heard him receiving a rather stern lecture from Mrs. G because he'd rewired a centrifuge machine so it operated twice as fast. "Your job is to fix the equipment when it breaks," she had said, "and restore it to its original capacity. You do not have clearance to reprogram our machines. Do you understand?" I'd picked up my pace before I overheard any more.

Jordan was fun to have around, and I always enjoyed it when he wound up in our lab for a bit. Aside from me, Jordan was probably Rexx's closest friend, and the three of us would often find ourselves out to dinner, at the movies, or just hanging out at one of our apartments together.

For several minutes Jordan and Stu continued to discuss an interactive holographic show I'd never watched.

Lydia lasted about five minutes before moving her tablet device away from the commotion. She rolled her large eyes in Stu and Jordan's direction, and then smiled at me. "I got a new style drive; check it out." She pulled a small metallic item from her purse and pushed it into a minuscule pocket on the hemline of her dress. "It has five new patterns; this one is my favorite." A bright orange floral pattern suddenly covered the entire ensemble. "Too much for work?" she asked, and the dress rippled to reveal a more professional shade of solid dark purple.

"I like the purple a little better," I said as I weighed the color options against Lydia's dark-green eyes. She was naturally beautiful, with her bold eyebrows and edgy features, and seemed to pull off every outfit she tried on. The only permanent beauty enhancement she had received was a richer tinge to her lips. Lydia gave me a once-over as she whipped her jet-black hair up into a bun in one fluid motion. She was probably wondering why she would take fashion advice from someone who wore more or less the same clothes every day. I'll admit it; I was fashion incompetent and almost never took advantage of the settings outside of the default greens, browns, and grays provided by my wardrobe. I'd been told I was a fall. Lydia was a spring, I think.

"Yeah, maybe I'll wear the orange out tomorrow night. Do you think it would be too much? I have a date. She's Tier Two," she said with a wink.

"The lottery is up to a thousand credits this week," Jordan interrupted as he pulled himself up off the floor. His face was covered in some of the soil he had apparently unclogged from the machine, and he shot me a friendly *What are you looking at?* stare as I laughed.

A conversation about the lottery took place in the lab at least once a week. I never participated, choosing to save my extra monthly credits for my precious gardening expenses.

"They just released a new set of Undommable gamer gloves," put in Stu. "That's what I would get if I won. Has anyone else entered?" Undommable gloves were a virtual accessory you could purchase for a line of popular video games. Now, don't get me wrong. I played video games; everyone did. But I'd never been big on using my credits for incorporeal items. Some loved it, even skipping meals to fill their arsenal of game accessories.

Rexx was silent, and my lone "No" was lost in a sea of yeses.

My coworkers filtered out of the lab as the morning wore on. Eventually it was time for us to grab a quick lunch from the department cafeteria and then head out for the day's fieldwork.

Fieldwork was hot, sticky business, and I loved every single minute of it. When I told people as much, I was often looked at as if I'd just told them I hated the latest movie that everyone was raving about. They couldn't understand it. "But dirt is full of germs," my mom once told me as if I hadn't realized it. There were plenty of jobs in the science field, she'd continue, jobs that would allow me to keep my hands clean and allow me to bask in the comfortable air conditioning all day long. I likely could have landed one of them with my aptitude scores too, but I was grateful I hadn't.

For me, spending hours in the fresh air, even if it meant dripping with sweat and smelling like a wet dog, was restorative. I loved being away from people and exploring places that hadn't been seen by human eyes in decades. I loved the rush of discovering an overgrown trail, a cluster of cacti, or a trickling spring-fed stream and knowing I was one of the few Americans to witness it in person. It was an honor.

I relished the strength I felt when scrambling over rocks, pulling myself up a steep slope just to find an ideal place to collect a soil sample. The specifics of what we saw and discovered on our field assignments were classified, so it was impossible for me to articulate to others why I loved my job so much. No one understood. Except for Rexx.

It was a warmer-than-average spring day, and the heat had peaked when we rolled up to Zone 72 at about noon. Zone 72 measured roughly two square miles of rough desert terrain featuring occasional patches of trees, a small lake, and heat-tolerant bushes and cacti scattered around.

Mostly it was dusty and dry like the rest of southern Arizona, but occasionally we'd stumble upon a view that made us stop and stare in admiration. Eroded rock faces exposed swirling patterns of vibrant orange and deep red mineral strata. Cattails, sweep willow, and grass-like rushes grew near the water. They were so vibrant against their dry counterparts that it was hard to not be drawn in.

The central work spot was an airlifted mobile office with the ability to self-adjust its footers based on terrain, enabling it to set itself up on a mountainside or a field with similar ease. It was shaped like a capsule, similar to a SafePod but larger. With its self-adjusting legs, I always thought it looked a bit like an albino caterpillar.

A clear solar film capped the top to power the equipment inside. Two square exterior compartments stored gear best kept outside—a two-person drill for accessing soil in rocky areas, a couple pairs of waist-high wading overalls for water testing, and two large bins of hydrocarbon-digester—one for water applications and one for soil. They contained a blend of enzymes, microbes, and nutrients used for soil and water remediation in highly polluted areas.

The bins would sit largely unused for this particular assignment.

We were there to gather the info needed to make a harvesting plan. Healthy soil was a rare resource. Next, a harvesting team would be sent to the healthy regions we flagged, and they would take up to 50 percent of any healthy soil and fraction it off to America One factory farms. I hated to think what the zone would look like when they were done. So I didn't let myself.

Next to the compartments, a washing station was also built into the exterior. A door farther down from the washing station opened at the swipe of a registered chip, and a set of small steps cascaded downward. Inside the mobile lab, a booth with two benches and a table sat to the left of the entrance. To the right was an array of coolers and storage containers that could be released at the end of the day for transporting samples back to the department.

A map, similar to the one at the home office, displayed the region in great detail. Click on a section of the grid, and the section-specific assignments would be displayed—how many samples, how far apart, whether a sample contained water, that kind of thing. Once all assignments for a specific section were complete, it would turn green, and we would move on to the next section. After about two weeks at that specific location, the map was about 70 percent green.

That day, we were surveying and collecting soil samples about three-quarters of a mile from the car, a greater distance than usual. After about three hours, we headed back with our second round of samples, eager to collapse into the folding chairs we'd set up next to the car.

We spent a few minutes transferring vials from our portable cooler to refrigerated storage, inputting relevant metadata for future reference, and then we gulped down several glasses of water.

"So, what do you think, Patch?" Rexx grinned. "Should we do one more round? Maybe head to that spot we passed the other day but haven't surveyed yet?"

I smiled. The way he said it, I knew him well enough to know he wasn't talking about work. He wanted to do what we often did when our work wrapped up early. He wanted to explore. He wanted to go back to the lake we'd discovered a few days before. Generally I would have felt fine about it, as we frequently took time to enjoy whatever natural beauty a zone had to offer. But after the events of the day before and that morning, I found myself hesitating.

I still hadn't told Rexx about my encounter with the Compo, or the note about my family history I'd seen in Mrs. G's file. There had been plenty of opportunities, but each time I opened my mouth, I found myself unable to say the words. Embarrassment, I guess. Shame.

His brown eyes playfully searched mine and his hopeful tone made it clear how disappointed he'd be if I were to countervail his suggestion. Unlike collecting samples at the Wall, fieldwork put us out of the range of public surveillance. Our IDs had been stashed to keep them clean, so the tracker in our car was our only connection to the grid.

"All right," I said with a smile, imagining how physically and emotionally rejuvenating a dip in the lake would feel. Plus, I didn't smell too great. "But you're going to have to help me up. I think sweat has fused me to this chair." Rexx jumped up in one fluid motion and shook his head like a puppy. He seemed to have a bottomless supply of energy. He grabbed my sweaty palms and pulled me to my feet.

Rexx and I discovered the joys of unmonitored territory for the first time during our training, when we were taken by small group out of the city to receive hands-on experience. Not one member of our group of ten teenagers had ever spent a moment not being recorded. Once the instructors retired for the evening, we all stayed up late chatting. Even though our conversation covered the usual teenage topics—video games, dating, television shows, shopping—I realized our words were smoother, our laughter louder than it had ever been within city limits.

Then, when Rexx and I were sent out on assignment by ourselves, he began to act even bolder. He'd broach topics that would set me on edge, such as where our ancestors came from. My wavy amber hair and sharp blue eyes were clearly from a different gene pool than the one that had given him his prominent eyebrows and lashes, rich tea-colored skin, and curly, silky hair as dark as onyx. He wanted to pursue these topics, but I'd just smile and quickly change the subject. "We are all American now" was the answer we'd heard time and again from our parents, from newscasters, and from teachers whenever we asked about our ancestry. We were not supposed to talk about life before the Seclusion. Or about anything outside the Walls.

When we stuck to our shared love of nature and science, and to lighthearted topics, Rexx and I could talk for hours. There was a kinship there neither of us could deny. However, when it came to the Board, to surveillance, to patriotism, there was a rift between us. I was afraid to explore it, afraid that if I did, I'd be left with an impossible choice—patriotism or friendship. I knew where the rift originated—Amara.

Amara had been my best friend. We'd bunked next to each other in the dormitories. Her snoring had kept me up at night in the beginning, but I learned to live with it and even missed it when it was gone. I introduced her to Rexx after meeting him in training at the age of sixteen. They were perfect for each other. Both brilliant, charismatic, beautiful. They took to each other instantly and never let go. You'd think there'd be some resentment on my part, being the third wheel most of the time. But they were just so right together. They brought out the best in each other. There was no room for animosity. We'd double date occasionally, but none of my relationships stuck for more than a few weeks at a time.

For years the three of us were practically inseparable. Amara and Rexx were headed toward marriage; we all knew it. Two years ago, though, when we were all twenty, Amara disappeared. One day she was there, and the next she was gone. Apparently she'd been found guilty of defending a member of her family whom she thought was innocent—an aunt. The aunt was charged with treason, and Amara with obstruction. The only information was a message on a family member's device: *Amara Derrah is being held in federal custody on charges of obstruction. An investigation into the charges has begun. You will be informed of the results.*

We never saw her again.

After her arrest, Rexx sank into himself for a long time, doing his work in the lab and in the field without superfluous conversation. He ignored messages from his friends, heading straight home at the end of the day. There was a time when I thought the real Rexx might never come back. Naturally I missed her too. I was heartbroken. Amara, my best friend, whom I'd slept a foot away from since I was five, was a traitor. She'd broken the law—betrayed us and her country. I didn't understand how she could be so selfish, how she could defy the Board without sparing a thought for those of us she would leave behind.

I dared not share these thoughts with Rexx, but he sensed it. I knew he did. That just made me angrier—that she could do this to him, to the one person who would have done anything for her, who had plans for a life together, that she could leave him behind.

After some time had passed, Rexx started to build himself back up, but he didn't talk about her anymore. And I think it made our friendship stronger. We were both hurt, regardless of the form the emotions took. Occasionally, when we'd walk past a restaurant we all used to visit, or if Amara's favorite show came on television, his shoulders would sink and his eyes would moisten. But we never discussed it. To do so would be treasonous.

"You going to wade in past your shins this time?" Rexx teased.

I ignored him and sat in the shallows, savoring the coolness of the water and the warmth of the sun on my face. I had never been taught to swim as a child. Most kids weren't. Starting at age five, time with parents was restricted to three hours per day, so swimming wasn't a high priority. Besides, most natural bodies of water were too toxic. But Rexx didn't let that stop him. He taught himself to swim at the first chance.

"Oh, go on then," I replied, splashing water at him. "Do your tricks. I'm perfectly happy sitting here in a pool of fresh water instead of my own sweat for a change." I tipped my head back into the water and closed my eyes. I could feel Rexx watching me, amused.

When I heard him splash off, I opened my eyes to watch Rexx swim. His well-defined muscles reflected the comfort and ease of his strokes. His wet hair wrapped his skull like a cap and was so long that it touched his bare shoulders. I was asked repeatedly by friends, my parents, his parents, and our coworkers if there was anything deeper going on between Rexx and me. We spent nearly every day together and had a bond that was clear to anyone. Of course, the thought of being with him had crossed my mind, and there was no denying he was a catch, but any attraction I felt was always accompanied by guilt. Amara's arrest had left a permanent crack in our relationship.

I watched from the shore as Rexx swam in large strokes. After he'd worn himself out, I let him help me up. Rexx smiled as he brushed the long, wet hair out of my eyes. It was a sad smile, as if he were reading my thoughts. As if we both understood how important and essential this friendship was to us, and how swiftly the crack could become a canyon.

We followed an alternate trail back to the camper, hoping to stumble upon a glimpse of unwary wildlife, as we had in the past. I knew it was selfish, but being one of the only Americans to see true wildlife (insects, lizards, and the occasional squirrel didn't count) was a rush. On one assignment, we happened upon a baby bobcat playing near the base of a tree. We'd slowly backed away until a safe distance was between us, in case Mom was nearby, then sat down on a rock and watched. The little guy played for several minutes, practicing balancing on protruding roots. His paws seemed too big for the small fluffball. Eventually he bounced out of view.

As I walked, my mind wandered. I hypothesized about what used to take place here. There were loops of primitive roadway by the lake, rusted-through grills, and rotten picnic table frames slumped into the earth. The skeletal remains of several docks marred the shoreline. I thought back to the first time Rexx and I had been sent out on assignment without a trainer. I remembered our conversation as if it had taken place yesterday. Our first real conversation, just the two of us, with no one watching or listening.

We had been sent to test a spring-fed stream outside a local hydroponic farm. A dense canopy of trees hung overhead, and we'd just completed the hike in.

"Well, here we are," Rexx had said, his eyes wide and unblinking. "IDs stashed safely out of range." He'd said the words slowly, slyly, as he smiled.

"Yeah. Here we are. So, what did you have for dinner last night?"

"Are you kidding, Patch? Really, that's what you want to talk about?" Rexx rolled his eyes and laughed slightly under his breath. "We're out here in the middle of the forest, with no one looking over our shoulders. And you want to talk about what I ate last night?"

He was right. I knew it was a silly thing to ask, and I would replay the stupidity of that moment for years to come. But, at the time, I hadn't been able to come up with anything better to say, and we'd been taught that, when you didn't have anything better to say, you asked about dinner, or the weather. "I've been dreaming about this moment for months. Haven't you?"

I inadvertently shuffled back a step or two and turned my head away. Had I? I'd been looking forward to getting to work, certainly, to wrapping up our training, to moving on to the next stage of life, to exploring the outdoors. But had I been aching for unsupervised time to talk about what was on my mind? Not really.

I didn't know what to say next. What was it exactly Rexx had been itching to talk about? At that point, Amara was in training to become a biomedical engineer, a field that did not provide opportunities to avoid surveillance. Part of me felt guilty he had the chance with me and not her.

"I guess . . . I guess I just don't trust it yet," I said dully. The truth was, I only said it because I imagined it was what he was waiting for me to say.

"That's fine," he said. "If you aren't ready to talk yet, then . . ." His voice trailed off as he looked around. His gaze settled on something in the distance, and then he was off and running. He began scaling a tree about ten yards away.

"What are you doing?" I said, laughing. I had to hand it to Rexx. He always knew how to break the tension. It was one of my favorite traits about him.

"I'm climbing a tree!" he yelled back. "I am climbing this rare resource that since we were children we were told not to touch. And it feels good, Patch. It feels so incredibly good."

At the time I'd scowled and then returned my attention to the job at hand, but now I smiled at the memory. Over time, I'd accepted the realities of constant surveillance. We couldn't disparage our leaders or talk about anything that made me too uncomfortable, but we could hike and go swimming. But still, I left the tree climbing to Rexx.

Now I looked around for a climbing tree to point Rexx toward when, suddenly, I spotted something large and out of place up ahead.

"What is that?" I asked. I quickened my step and my vision narrowed in on the large metallic object nestled in the foliage. Was it an old picnic table, or maybe a broken toolshed?

Rexx caught up to me and followed my line of sight. I watched his face for some sign of recognition. His eyes widened.

"I think it's a vehicle," he said excitedly.

"So far from the road?" I said dubiously. "That doesn't make any sense." Any path wide enough for a vehicle to make it out this far would have become overgrown long ago. Nothing with wheels would be able to make it through.

"We have to check it out!" Rexx exclaimed. He dashed toward it, abandoning the trail and hopping between downed trees and branches as if they were mere wrinkles in the earth below his feet. I inched closer, not really believing it, until it became clear that a vehicle was exactly what it was. I halted immediately.

"Rexx, come back! We have to call this in!" I yelled. But he kept going, pulling off branches to reveal the shape of the vehicle. It was a van.

CHAPTER 3

AT LEAST, I thought it was a van. It didn't look like any vehicle on the road today. But I'd seen older vehicles in videos, and *van* was the word that came to mind. It was maroon in color and boxy, that much I could tell from a distance.

Alarm bells went off in my head and I felt the color seep out of my face. The only way a van could have wound up out there was if it had arrived when the paths were still functional. Long before our time. It was exactly the sort of thing we should not be approaching. The sort of thing the Board would expect model patriots to report. The sort of thing those of us who spent time outside the city limits were specifically trained to report.

"Rexx!" I yelled in sheer panic. I yelled the way you shout at someone when they're about to step on a light-rail track when a train is in view. A *freeze before you get run over* kind of shout. But he didn't even pause.

"Rexx! We'll be expected to report this! You don't know what's in there!" I yelled louder.

He either didn't hear me, so preoccupied was he with his mission, or he heard me perfectly but chose to ignore me. I scanned the perimeter for any sign of drone cameras or

Compos, but the horizon was empty. It was up to me. The panic bubbled up again, and I stood there, incapacitated.

"Well, it's been here a long time, that's for sure!" Rexx shouted. "Look here—the tires are rotted down to the rims." Rexx's excitement came across in his inflection as he continued to near the vehicle.

I did the only thing I could think of: I started to walk toward him, intent on grabbing his arm and dragging him away if I had to. I feared what he might do, scared I might lose him like we'd lost Amara if he were found out.

Rexx reached the vehicle and gave the right rear wheel a kick. Then his hand reached out to touch the back window, swiping it with his finger to try to clear away some of the dirt. But it was caked on, and it quickly became apparent that no amount of rubbing would remove it.

"You should really get over here and see this!" He hadn't noticed me approaching, and he continued to yell. "Several decades old if I had to guess! Never seen a model like it before. There's rust in the crevices, but really not so bad, as old as it looks. Probably be worse if Arizona weren't so damn dry." There was no sign of nervousness in his voice. My cheeks turned bright red in anger in response to his nonchalantness. Was he insane? How could this not be raising red flags for him?

I caught up and put my hand on his shoulder.

"We need to go, Rexx. It's an old van. Can we go now?"

"You aren't even the least bit curious what's inside?" he snapped back.

No, I'm not curious; I'm responsible, I thought to myself. *Why should I care what's inside?* Just because it had likely been there for decades didn't mean it contained anything other than dust and rotting upholstery. We'd been taught what to do in such a situation. *Leave it be; call the CD.* A rhyme we learned in childhood, in which CD referred to the Compliance Department.

"Come on, Patch! There's no one around. It's just me. And I'm going inside." He ripped his arm away and I stood frozen, unsure of what to do. He was taller than I was, larger. I should have turned around, left. But I couldn't.

"We should be reporting this," I said as I stood with my feet planted, declaring for the universal record that I was on the right side of the scenario. I swallowed the air I'd been holding in my cheeks and bit my lip. Now that I was up close, I couldn't help but take in the details of the vehicle.

Rexx was right—there was virtually nothing left of the tires, and the rims looked as if they would crumble if you stared too hard. I was surprised Rexx's kick hadn't caused one to give way. The rear bumper dangled from one side. I noted the absence of a solar array and a charging port and wondered how the vehicle used to run, if it was old enough to be one of those responsible for a large portion of our environmental restoration work.

Don't get distracted, I told myself. But something pulled me forward as I eyed the dusty windows. There was something in there; I could feel it. Whatever it was, I was not supposed to see it. *Details.*

Rexx maneuvered around the van and toward the left passenger side, which was tucked out of view. I told myself to turn back, repeatedly, but my feet followed Rexx anyway. Several vines had intricately curled around the door, blocking access.

"I don't know—" I began, but then suddenly switched directions. "Be careful." I swallowed hard, feeling a knot rise in my throat.

Rexx smiled then cleared his way through most of the scrub with a large stick and sturdy kicks, but he had to wrestle with a few tough vines. He whistled while he worked as if he didn't have a care in the world. As if he'd been waiting for something like this to happen his whole life.

After a moment he managed to pry open the rusty door.

"After you," he offered.

This was where I needed to turn around, before it went any further. My legs, tuning out my conscience, approached the opening. My senses were bombarded with the pungent odor of mildew.

"Board save us," I whispered. *Today of all days.* I couldn't bring myself to move forward, so Rexx pushed past me, climbing deep inside the van.

"Patch! You've got to get in here and check this out." I stood there for several moments. Not going in but not backing away, either. The words displayed next to the mark on my file—*Level-Yellow Alert. Third-Generation Family History*—taunted me. I reluctantly hoisted myself inside the vehicle, ignoring the voice in my head that reminded me that what I was doing was a crime. That I was already on thin ice, and Amara had been arrested for much less. But I pushed through the voice and then I was inside the van.

It was like stepping into a cave of the past. As my eyes adjusted, I noticed Rexx leaning over a tattered seat that looked nothing like the seats in regular vehicles. He was tugging desperately and unsuccessfully at something on the floor in the back. From my angle, I could not tell what it was. I became distracted by a crystal hanging from the rearview mirror that refracted just a small amount of light around the interior, creating a speckled effect that undulated as our weight caused the van to shift and the crystal to sway.

My eyes continued to adjust, and I followed the crystal's soft light as it illuminated several unfamiliar items. I picked up a trinket within reach. It appeared to be some kind of decoration, heavy and faded to a beige color, square on the bottom with triangles on each side that met at the top to form a point. On each side were odd little symbols—one resembled a man, another a sun, and another a horse. I carefully set it on the dashboard, making a note to examine it more closely later if I had time.

A faded baseball cap sat upside down on the front seat. I picked it up, careful to not spill the contents as I inspected the outside. I didn't recognize the logo, a snake curled into the shape of a D. Inside the cap were several small, round pieces of metal, bronze, and silver in color, of various sizes. I picked up a bronze piece and examined the man's head and the words IN GOD WE TRUST embossed on the surface. On the other side there was a building and the words UNITED STATES OF AMERICA, E PLURIBUS UNUM, and ONE CENT. I tossed the disc back into the baseball cap.

"What are these things, Rexx? Have you ever seen anything like this before?" I held one of the pieces up for Rexx to examine, but he was still fixated on the object I could not see. His tendency to get distracted and ignore all other stimulus around him could be both endearing and incredibly annoying.

The entire middle row of seating was covered with what I assumed were personal belongings, though most were too decomposed to classify. I grasped a reusable coffee mug, not dissimilar to the ones I used, featuring an image of what looked to be a green-and-white mermaid sporting a crown on her head and two tails. It was all so bizarre. None of it made any sense.

Random articles of what looked like men's sun-bleached clothing were scattered about on the floor and draped over the backseat, as if someone had spent an extended time in the vehicle, possibly even lived out of it. I spotted the edge of an empty soda can peeking out from underneath the front passenger seat. I picked it up and saw that though most of it was covered with a green-dominated rainbow tarnish, the top revealed a splash of its presumably original bright red.

Three white cursive letters were still distinct—*COK*. I searched the can until I located the dull, barely visible expiration date stamped onto its base—05APR30. April of 2030? That was just over sixty years ago, thirty-eight years before I was even born. The year our country seceded from the rest of humanity.

It then became clear. This van was a time capsule, a relic that had somehow managed to escape the Board's purges of the past. What had I done? If the authorities knew we'd seen this, it would spell the end of both of our lives.

I searched the van for further signs of who the owner might have been. *This is wrong,* I told myself. *Get out of there right this minute. Go grab your device and report the van to the Compliance Department before you make this worse.* But here was another feeling creeping in, not necessarily pushing caution and fear out of the way, but still demanding acknowledgment . . . excitement. It was like a door had been flung open, clearing out years of musty cobwebs, and I couldn't bear to shut it just yet.

My hand grazed the dusty dashboard. I prodded around until a loud noise behind me froze me in place. For a moment I envisioned being dragged out of the van, shot with a pacifier, and left seizing on the ground. I closed my eyes tight, my senses heightened, and I listened.

"It's okay. Just the door falling the rest of the way off the hinges," Rexx said, leaning back to look out the new exit.

"Oh, thank the Board," I muttered through a shaky breath, then realized the hypocrisy of that statement. If the Board knew what we were doing, they would not be lenient on us.

I pushed my worries aside, like you would a pair of shoes blocking the front door, and dug through the various compartments for anything with a name on it.

I unearthed some kind of folded map. I opened it carefully, afraid that if I was too rough, it would break on the folds. It held up okay, as it was covered in some kind of protective laminated coating. I decided that even if the seams ripped, the sections themselves should remain intact. The unfolded image was of America, that much was obvious, though the coastlines were farther out and there was an extra state on the East Coast I'd never heard of before. Florida. It was no secret that the borders of our country had shifted. The oceans kept rising, and coastal cities were always considered one large storm away from decimation.

On the map, there were several dark black circles, obviously drawn by hand, and inside the circles, the names of cities. The circles appeared all over the map, several in every state, too many to count without a concerted effort. *What in Board's name is this?*

I looked down to Arizona and squinted to read the names within the circles. *Phoenix, Tucson, Gilbert, Sierra Vista, Scottsdale, Tempe, Peoria, Surprise.* Those were the urban centers in Arizona, the same as I knew them, though they were larger than depicted on the map. I lived in Tucson, but the town center was considerably south from the area described as Tucson on this map. What was not the same were the other, smaller names that surrounded the circled ones. Cities that did not exist. I didn't know how to make sense of what I was holding, and the unease I felt escalated rapidly.

The only thing drawn on the map other than circles and names was a strange symbol in the upper left corner. In Oregon. It looked like a sideways eight and was drawn larger than the circles, so it covered the top half of the state:

∞

I wanted Rexx to look. But he was still trying to free that object from the floor of the backseat, talking incoherently under his breath as he struggled. I removed my backpack and carefully slid the map between two reference guides. *What the hell are you doing?* my conscience screamed, but I pushed the invading thoughts aside. I didn't recognize myself. It was as if I were still standing in the clearing, yelling. Telling the young girl rummaging through an old van that she was going to get herself killed. She didn't listen.

Rexx had gone outside to look around some more, and I climbed out of the cramped vehicle. I was starting to feel light-headed, and I needed to stand up straight and breathe fresh air for a moment.

Behind me, Rexx spoke up, startling me: "He must have been running to the border. I think people could still get out at that point." I instinctively grabbed his arm to steady myself. He placed his hand between my shoulder blades, a swift, passing comfort, then stepped away again.

"He must have been a criminal, then. Otherwise, why would he want to leave?" I asked.

Rexx rolled his eyes, leaving me thoroughly confused and a bit hurt.

Why would the owner have left so many valuable things behind? None of it made any sense. If he hadn't been a traitor, then why had he been trying to escape, anyway? What kind of person runs straight toward danger, away from the promise of protection?

"Maybe the van broke down on the way and he had to hide it," Rexx continued. "It certainly didn't hide itself in these bushes."

"Sure seems like he left a lot of his possessions behind if he did run," I said.

"Well, he might not have had a choice. Come back in for a minute and give me a hand with this suitcase—maybe there are some answers in there. We've got to be quick, though—we're due back at the office with the soil samples in an hour and a half, and we still have a bit of a hike ahead of us."

I followed Rexx. Maybe if we found a clear sign that the owner of the van was a traitor or a terrorist, I'd feel better about his disappearance. I'd understand why he was running. It would make more sense.

Rexx took my hand and together we navigated our way through downed branches and briars (he more gracefully than I) until we reached the passenger side. Rexx pried open the back door. "It's stuck under the seat. I think it's catching on something, but I can't get a good look. Maybe if you sit in the very back and push with your legs, we can get it out."

I spotted the suitcase to which he was referring, wedged underneath the third row of seats. Clumsily, I climbed over the seats until my body was crammed next to the back window, between a spare tire and a gas can. Beside me a small metal sign poked me in the ribs. *Ouch.* I maneuvered it into my lap and used my sleeve to wipe away the collected dust.

JOIN THE RANKS OF NEW AMERICA
PROVIDING YOU WITH A <u>SAFE</u>, <u>SECURE</u> NATION
YOU WILL BE <u>PROUD</u> TO CALL HOME!
NEW CREDIT SYSTEM ENSURES
EVERYONE CAN AFFORD BASIC NECESSITIES
EVERY CITIZEN RECEIVES COMFORTABLE
HOUSING HEALTH CARE FOR ALL
A COUNTRY FULL OF LEGAL, PARTICIPATORY PATRIOTS
JOBS FOR EVERY AMERICAN
INFORMATION YOU CAN TRUST
A STREAMLINED AND MORAL EDUCATION
FOR EVERY CHILD
NEVER WORRY WHERE YOUR
NEXT PAYCHECK IS COMING FROM
YOUR SAFETY IS OUR PRIMARY CONCERN

I read it again. Words that had a hint of familiarity.

"Hey, Rexx, check this out." I handed the sign up to him and waited. I spun the ring on my finger while he read the text.

"These aren't that different from the billboards that appear around town every once in a while, touting the achievements of the Board. Same old government bullshit."

I flinched at his use of the word *bullshit*, becoming increasingly aware that my day—well, possibly my life—had taken an extreme turn. My instinct was to be angry with him for disparaging the Board, but questions of my own crowded out the anger.

"But this can't be right. All these things were happening before the Seclusion. The building of the Walls, the protection from terror . . . that was all that really changed," I continued rambling, not giving Rexx a chance to interject. "America's always been America: a country of patriots. The Board just increased our security."

I tried to think back to everything I knew about the Seclusion. The borders were built to protect us from the rapidly increasing global threats taking place in the twenties and thirties. The Board had always presided over the nation, and they chose us, our safety, over everything else. They carried the burden of toxic historical information so that we didn't have to.

The devil lies in the details. Leave the devil to us. The words played on a loop in my brain. *The devil lies in the details. Leave the devil to us.* I was not supposed to question the decisions of the Board. They protected us. They took care of everything. Our only task was to be grateful. I shook my head rapidly, cracking my skull against the back window. *Board help me, what should I do?* But they wouldn't help me, not after the treason I had committed with this van. The treason I was committing. *Traitor, I'm a traitor. Just like Amara.*

"The question is, what was there before and why did it have to change?" Rexx's eyes grabbed mine as the words flowed out of his mouth. He reached over the seat and put a steadying hand on my shoulder. "We'll be okay, Patch. Let's see what other information we can learn today." None of it made any sense, and the knot in my throat returned. I had the overwhelming suspicion there was something Rexx was not telling me. I shifted my body into position so I could push at the suitcase with my feet.

"Ready?" I asked.

Rexx nodded, his brow furrowed in concentration. "Go ahead; push as hard as you can."

I pushed and he pulled until we heard a ripping sound and the suitcase was liberated from its dark resting place.

"No wonder it was so hard to get out," Rexx said. "It feels like it's loaded with bricks."

I climbed into the seat in front of me so I could give Rexx a hand with the suitcase. "It's too crowded in here," he said. "Let's drag it outside."

He bent his body to look out the windows. I did the same. It was instinctive and ingrained, checking to see whether anyone was watching.

Working together, we wrestled with the heavy suitcase until we could maneuver it to the floor near the door and push it out. And in another round of emotional ping-pong, excitement pulled out its chair and sat back down at the table.

"The zipper is stuck. I guess that explains what the ripping was," I said as I pointed to the fabric caught in the teeth, misaligned and unable to perform their basic function without significant force. I bit my lip and tugged at the zipper until the rusted teeth started to separate and slowly release their grip. Rexx reached over and lifted the cover. What the hell?

Books.

Printed, bound, ink-and-paper books. The entire suit-case was packed from top to bottom with them. My whole life, I'd only seen pictures of books like this on vintage news-reels. Usually they were being thrown into fires for inspiring dissidents. Printed books not only contained toxic history and knowledge according to the Board, there were other reasons they were banned as well. They couldn't be tracked, margins could be written in, they could be changed. Digital books were better; they were immutable and contained only cleansed information.

A memory suddenly struck me, vivid and nightmarish. A memory I'd long since repressed. There was one other time I'd seen a book like this. I was a child and he was our neighbor. Claude. He had always been kind to me. He used to have long conversations with my parents and he had a contagious laugh. That was what I remembered most, his laugh. One evening I was watching birds from my bedroom window before being sent back to the dormitories. I was enchanted with the birds and they served as a regular form of entertainment for me. I envied their freedom in a way that I could not put into words at that age. Claude was strolling down the sidewalk with his wife, an arm around her waist and a broad smile on his face. A compliance officer approached him. To this day, I don't know what the officer said, but what happened next happened fast.

In an instant, Claude was convulsing on the ground, and his wife was yanked away from him. Another officer grabbed an item that had fallen, then rummaged through his pock-ets, finding nothing else as far as I could see. The first officer did the same to Claude's wife, running his hands first up and down her spread legs and then putting his gloved hand under-neath her shirt. She stood frozen, her arms above her head, while her husband writhed in semiconscious pain. The officer then started to look at the item he had grabbed off the ground.

It became clear to me that it was a book. He leafed through the pages, then, after apparently concluding that it was an unapproved text, turned and gave Claude a sturdy kick to the face. I heard the crack of his nose break from across the street. At this I dropped below my window and put my back up against the wall, gasping, tears running down my cheeks. When I got the nerve to look again, Claude was gone, and all that was left was a pool of his blood on the sidewalk.

After what felt like an eternity, Claude's wife managed to stand up. Alone, she hobbled back into her home and shut the curtains. The trail of blood her husband (now traitor) had left behind remained for days before the rain washed it away. I did not sleep that night or for many afterward.

I picked up book after book without recognizing even one of the titles. "Have you heard of any of these authors?" I asked Rexx. "Tolstoy, Homer, Nei . . . ummm . . . Neet chezee," I stumbled as I looked at the spelling . . . Nietzsche. "Austen, Shakespeare, Kafka?" I turned each book over in my hands, stroking my palms against the covers, my skin thrilling at the texture. For some reason I could not explain, I held one up to my nose and inhaled. Grassy, with a hint of vanilla.

Rexx gave me a look I was familiar with, one that he saved for those times when we were discussing one of the gaping holes in our knowledge. Holes that we had been told countless times were there to avoid unnecessary burdens in our lives, to protect us. That day, for the first time in my entire life, I started to question the purpose of those holes.

"We have built a new nation, one free from fear of terror and war, in which we leave behind our past and focus on building our bright future."

I'd heard that saying more times than I could possibly count—it, and others like it, had been recited to me since birth. It preceded many television broadcasts, was woven into my virtual education, and was periodically delivered as an alert to my ID just for good measure.

I reached for a random book that caught my eye: *A Tale of Two Cities* by Charles Dickens. I flipped it open and began to read:

> *It was the best of times,*
> *it was the worst of times,*
> *it was the age of wisdom,*
> *it was the age of foolishness,*
> *it was the epoch of belief,*
> *it was the epoch of incredulity,*
> *it was the season of Light,*
> *it was the season of Darkness,*
> *it was the spring of hope,*
> *it was the winter of despair. . . .*

I wondered what age the author could be referring to. I scanned the front pages until I saw the original publishing date was 1859. Over 230 years ago. I carefully set the book down, as if handling a delicate, dried flower that may crumble on contact, and grabbed another: *Siddhartha* by Hermann Hesse:

> *In the shade of the house, in the sunshine of the river-*
> *bank near the boats, in the shade of the Sal-wood for-*
> *est, in the shade of the fig tree is where Siddhartha grew*
> *up, the handsome son of the Brahman, the young falcon,*
> *together with his friend Govinda, son of a Brahman. The*
> *sun tanned his light shoulders by the banks of the river*
> *when bathing, performing the sacred ablutions, the sacred*
> *offerings.*

Fig tree? Sacred offerings? Brahman? Half of the words were nonsense, and yet I was completely enthralled and wanted more. The cadence was beautiful, even if the true meaning was lost. Next to me, Rexx was in a world of his own, talking under his breath as he quietly repeated passages from the text before him. I knew the clock was ticking; our samples needed to be locked up in the lab before closing. I reached for one last book: *The War of the Worlds* by H. G. Wells:

> *No one would have believed in the last years of the nineteenth century that this world was being watched keenly and closely by intelligences greater than man's and yet as mortal as his own; that as men busied themselves about their various concerns they were scrutinized and studied, perhaps almost as narrowly as a man with a microscope might scrutinize the transient creatures that swarm and multiply in a drop of water. With infinite complacency men went to and fro over this globe about their little affairs, serene in their assurance of their empire over matter.*

A rustling sound emerged from the trees behind me. A muffled scream escaped my lips before I could stop it. I shut my eyes and braced for what I knew was coming.

"Patch. It's okay. It was just an animal. A mouse, I think."

I opened my eyes again and looked at Rexx. He was sitting on the other side of the suitcase, his face pinched with worry. He reached out and rubbed my arm, and I released the breath I'd been holding. I picked up the book I'd dropped and placed it back in the suitcase as if it were red-hot. In a way, it was—the contents of the suitcase could burn down everything we knew, take away everyone we loved.

We carefully packed up the books, having to take them out and try again when they didn't fit as before. A sense of longing welled up inside me, as if I were saying good-bye to a loved one.

My head spun. Countless feelings and images flooded my brain, and I couldn't separate them long enough to form a coherent thought. Then, when Rexx was turned away, my hand acted of its own accord. I picked up a book, just one. Before my head could catch up, my hand had slipped the book inside my backpack. As it did so, I caught the title—*Les Misérables*. I'd just strapped a live grenade to my chest.

"What do we do? What the hell did we just do, Rexx?" I finally blurted out after several minutes of silently following Rexx's footsteps on the walk back.

"I don't know. Everything in that suitcase, *everything*—it's outlawed, Patch. What's in there hasn't been seen by an American in decades. Except maybe the Board, but who knows, maybe even not them, not the current generation of members anyway."

I didn't know exactly what he was getting at, but he was right about one thing—the books were outlawed. Taking one made me an outlaw. But I loved my country. I respected the Board. I was just confused; that was it. It would all work itself out. It would all make sense soon. I just needed more time to think, to understand.

That evening, my entire belief system upended itself as question after question popped into my brain, piling on top of one another like dishes in an overly crowded sink. With each outside noise, I was sure they were coming to get me. Maybe they should; my judgment could obviously not be trusted. The ache in the back of my throat grew with each minute that passed. I thought again about the mark in my file, about the words *Third-Generation Family History*. Then, suddenly, I knew what I had to do.

I quickly changed out of the dirty work gear I'd been wallowing in and sprinted the three blocks to my parents' house. I had questions, and though I realized I was about to alter the course of our relationship forever, the people I was going to possibly had answers.

CHAPTER 4

THE EARLIEST SWEEP I'd remembered took place when I was four. Seemingly inconsequential details crept back every so often. But that day, specifics I'd repressed for years flooded in. I was a trench, the memories a relentless rain.

Sweeps were never prearranged. Apartments were swept periodically in search of prohibited items. An item once considered benign may not be permitted five years down the road. *We must always move forward.*

I was playing in the entryway of our apartment with some of my mother's knickknacks when the front door swung open unannounced. They looked so large, so towering, from my place on the floor: the Compos. There had to have been four or five of them. I stared, not knowing what to do, as they spoke to me. I couldn't understand their words or their questions; I felt only an overwhelming sense of confusion and fear.

As their voices rose, I began to tremble. They started to yell, words I was not digesting. In retrospect, they were probably just telling me to move out of the way.

Suddenly my father was there, and he scooped me up, his large arms wrapping around me, securing me to him. He whispered in my ear, "You're safe, Patricia. This sort of thing happens once in a while, and it will be over soon. They are just trying to keep us safe, my dear. It's for the best."

I looked around, still trying to make sense of what was happening, but scary uniformed people barging into my house to keep me safe made about as much sense at the time as my parents convincing me I needed painful shots to keep me healthy.

The Compos I'd seen so many times looked colossal inside my home. They ushered my mother and then my father into the hallway. One barked orders at my sullen grandmother Lily, who was slowly making her way to the front door. On the way out, my father tripped, and I gasped. I remembered that gasp. My small hands clutched at his shoulders, holding on as tightly as I could, squeezing my eyes shut as I felt us fall together. He landed on his knees but didn't loosen his hold on me in the slightest. I could feel his ragged breath as he rose to his feet again, the warmth of his hands on my back. At that moment I realized my father was scared, that he was holding on to me as desperately as I to him.

We sat in the long hallway of the apartment complex, and my father cradled me in his lap. With a shaky yet placating voice, he began telling me a favorite bedtime story. His rapid heartbeat echoed in my ear. My mother leaned against my father's shoulder and robotically stroked my hair, her wide eyes darting from place to place. As my father's voice recited the familiar words, I stared at the energy weapon pointed in my direction by the officer left to watch us. I squeezed my eyes shut and buried my head in my father's chest until it was over.

As I got older, I saw how it could go if something turned up. An incinerator truck would be brought—a large, glossy black beast of a vehicle with COMPLIANCE DEPARTMENT written on the side in boxy letters. When this truck drove down the street, everyone turned to see where it was going. Wondered who had deceived us this time. Which friend or neighbor was a malefactor with unlawful tendencies that we'd failed to notice. We held our collective breath until the truck passed us by.

When it reached its destination, other residents of the complex would peek out their windows as the owner was brought close, forced to watch, pacifier pointed at the head. The prohibited items would be thrown in the incinerator, the door would close, leaving a two-foot-wide heat-proof window as the only proof of what was taking place inside. A bright orange would fill the window, just for a moment, and then it would fade back to black. About ten minutes later, a metal-bristled broom scraped out the ashes, which remained on the road long after the owners were taken away. Until the rain came. A mark of shame. A warning.

The event was often replayed for all to see. A close look at the items was never given; the Compliance Department didn't want to give traitors any ideas. No details. But you could guess what was being thrown in the truck: stolen signs and posters, anything deemed disparaging to the Board, hidden items from before the Seclusion. And, likely, books.

The vividness of the memory stopped me in my tracks one block from the Tier 4 complex. My mouth was dry and I rubbed my clammy hands up and down my pant legs as I willed my thoughts to stop skipping from place to place. Just get through this. Watch what you say and how you say it.

I wound my way up to the third story of my parents' apartment building and pressed the button next to the door placard:

GEOFFREY COLLINS
TIER 4
NURSE

LOUISE COLLINS
TIER 4
PHARMACIST

Their familiar voices rang through the door in muffled, chirping tones. The door swung open, and they greeted me almost in perfect unison: "Patricia!"

My father reached out and grabbed the back of my head and eagerly pulled me toward him. I lost my balance and fell into his chest. "I've missed you, sweetie," he said as my nose was pressed up against his shoulder. The feel of his hand on the back of my head. Safe. Familiar. I almost broke down right then, but I blinked away the moisture in my eyes before they noticed.

I'd always suspected my parents longed for a larger family more closely resembling the ones in which they were raised and would have had more children if it were legal.

"It's good to see you too; I'm sorry it's been so long. Really. Do you mind if we head in and sit down? It's been a long day."

"Are you okay, sweetie? Did something happen?" my dad asked as I straightened myself back up. He cocked his head to the side and studied my face.

"No. No. Nothing like that. Just tired from work; that's all."

My appearance was reflected in both of them, but mostly my father. He had the same amber hair, though his was shorter, speckled with gray and thinned out considerably. His eyelashes, like mine, were so light, you could barely make them out. A bit of mascara was the only makeup I wore on a regular basis. My mother had passed on her glassy blue eyes. Her hair, once a light brown, had lightened so much with age that it was now the color of a white opal. She painted her lips bright red, and kept her hair curled as tightly as young desert ferns. It had always been the same, as far back as I could remember. Age had worn on both of their faces like striations in a crystal.

"Well, come on. Come on in—I'll start some tea," said my mother as she led us to the sitting area before continuing over to the hot-water dispenser.

I seated myself on the couch, the same beige couch that had been there since I was born. My parents' apartment wasn't that different from mine. All apartments were more or less the same. Sectional furniture, a few shelves for personal belongings, and fixed screens and cameras that could not be moved. Because my parents were married and in Tier 4, they were issued a unit only a bit bigger than my single Tier 3. It had enough room for one small child, to sleep in the bedroom as well, until age five. I hadn't slept in this apartment for seventeen years.

I spun the ring around my finger. *Relax. Just relax.* I crossed then uncrossed my legs a few times as I waited for my mother to return, and mentally rehearsed what I was going to say.

My dad had meandered back into the den to watch television—a routine I was used to but found unusually aggravating considering I'd only just arrived and I needed to talk to them.

"Dad, can you please just come out here for a minute?" I said in an annoyed, regressive teenage tone. Nothing like being around your parents to set you back a few years. "I just got here."

"I'll be out in a minute; the game's almost over. Just be a minute, sweetie. Don't wait for me. Enjoy your tea. Just a . . ." His voice trailed off.

Maybe it'll be easier if he's not in the room, I thought. I remembered a time when he was different. When the three hours I spent with Mom and Dad after school were filled with smiles, hugs, and focused attention. We'd go on walks, play games in the living room, sometimes go to dinner together. Even though Dad was often tired from a long shift at the hospital, he was a good father.

Over the years, he'd whittled down his personality, scraped away at his passion and his fire, until not much was left. Just an old man distracting himself with mindless entertainment. I never understood what had changed.

Sitting on the sofa in the living room where Amara and I had spent so much time, I thought about what my father had said to me when she disappeared.

I'd been avoiding him and Mom for weeks. Dodging their calls, ignoring their persistent messages. Dad showed up unannounced one evening. I opened the door and he looked at my frayed, despondent face. I wasn't in the mood, and I didn't say anything, just glared back in annoyance at his presence. He was trying to make me confront something I didn't want to process with him. Something I didn't actually know how to process. I thought wallowing in anger had worked perfectly well so far, thank you.

"I'm not going to stay long," he said. "I just wanted to let you know, we're sad too. We miss her." She'd disappointed everyone, even my parents. *Great,* I thought at the time. "Just do me a favor, sweetie. Try to remember five things. Just five. Remember five things you loved about her. Five things that made her a person." Then he turned and walked back toward his house, and we never talked about her again.

Sitting there, spinning my grandmother's ring, I did something I hadn't done at the time. I thought of five things. Amara snored. She only washed her hair once a week, said it got too dry if she washed it more. She kicked my ass, and Rexx's, at video games, but was good-natured about it. Her apartment was always a mess; she hated when they made her make her bed in the dormitories, and she wasn't about to do it once she lived on her own. She held my hand in the space between our beds when I was scared. Five things. Five details.

I hadn't realized what he'd done for me at the time, but those details kept her alive for me. They kept her a person, not just another nameless traitor.

Back in the present, my mother hummed in the kitchen. Soon a warm cup of tea was set in front of me. Tea of an unknown origin, ordered through a Board-run shopping website, having gone through mysterious channels that enabled it to be sent from its country of origin and end up on my mother's coffee table. Where did tea plants grow? The thought had never occurred to me. I realized that no matter how hard I searched the depths of my brain, no answer would be forthcoming. This wouldn't have bothered me before, but that particular day, after everything, it did. *Where in Board's name does tea come from?* My mind fixated on the question, and I felt my heart rate rise. Surely someone must know the answer to such a simple question.

"So, Patricia, the weather, it's been so dry lately. . . . It hasn't rained in months. Has that affected work?" my mother asked, snapping me out of it.

"No, not really. I mean, sometimes it takes a bit longer to get a sample when the ground is hard, but otherwise, no. Maybe we'll get rain soon. What do you think?" There was only so much I was allowed to share about work. A short, unclassified insight, then a question to turn the conversation. A skill we'd all mastered.

I studied my mother as she talked about the forecast for the next two weeks and how there was no rain anywhere on the horizon.

My brain swirled; I started to feel ill. *Focus. You're letting your mind wander too much. Focus.* I needed to figure out what my parents knew, but anyone caught speaking of the past or passing on confidential information was tried for treason. I was treading dangerous territory. At once both disgusted with myself and thirsty for information. Shoving away my nausea, I pressed my palms down on my twitching legs to steady them.

"Anyway, hopefully it's not a sign of the type of summer we'll have," she continued. "So, what else is new with you? What shows are you into these days?"

"A few different ones. But, Mom, is it okay if we talk about something else?" I said without making eye contact, though I could feel her staring at me curiously.

"Let's see," she continued, "I like the new soda flavors they have at the restaurant on the corner. Have you tried them?"

My mother smiled as she added a bit of syrup to each of our cups of tea. I searched for the right phrasing, something that would arouse the least amount of suspicion to the camera mounted in the corner. Something that seemed like an every-day family affair.

"Actually, I came over because I wanted to see if you or Dad had plans for the day after tomorrow, it being your day off. Rexx and I found a beautiful"—I paused, catching myself before I gave too much away—"a beautiful spot, and I thought you might like to join us for an afternoon picnic, if you're both off work at the hospital. I have something I want to share with you," I said in my best *I have good news you don't want to miss* voice.

It was obvious she was skeptical. I understood why. Though I loved both of them dearly, aside from the occasional visit, my parents and I didn't exactly hang out. Dad shouted at the television in the next room, offended in some personal way by the actions of the virtual baseball players on the screen. I took my mother's hand, fully aware of the peril in which I was putting us both. Knowing deep down that I shouldn't have been doing this; it was wrong. I did it anyway.

"Please?" I swallowed hard and ignored the rolling feeling in my stomach.

"Well, where are we going?" she asked as she removed her hand from mine, placed her tea down on the table, and repetitively smoothed out her skirt like she often did when she was anxious.

"Well, that part's a surprise. Rexx and I . . . we have some news to share." I punched the word *news*. Her face brightened, and she shot me a hopeful look and poured more tea. My words technically weren't a lie, but I felt terrible playing on my mother's long-held hopes that Rexx and I would get married.

She loved Rexx, and I knew she missed the days when we were teenagers undergoing our training. When the two of us and Amara would lounge around the living room of that very same one-bedroom apartment, passing the time in the early evenings by playing video games and raiding the cabinets before heading back to the dormitories.

"I suppose we could do that," she finally said.

"Great! Can you guys meet me at home the day after tomorrow, around noon?"

It was a risky move, getting the four of us into the state park undetected. But law enforcement had been absent from the entrances to that particular site, undoubtedly due to budgetary restraints, and my dorsal chip was all I'd need to open the gates. Assuming I could somehow convince my parents to leave their IDs at my house so their whereabouts were not tracked, and they were capable of remaining absolutely silent during the entire drive. One thing at a time.

When I arrived back home, Rexx was slumped in the chair next to my garden bed, looking as frazzled as I felt.

"So, were they available?" he asked. I'd sent him a message an hour earlier letting him know I was going to pay my parents a visit. I nodded. He eyed me contemplatively for a moment while he tapped his foot on the concrete slab. The camera above my door swiveled, increasing its arc now that two people were within range. Sweat beaded on Rexx's forehead, and I wondered how long he'd been sitting there.

"Want to grab some dinner?" Rexx asked.

I chuckled under my breath. The thought sounded comfortingly simple. "Let me check my credit balance." I sat down on the concrete slab so my back was to his knees, and fiddled with the screen on my ID until the allowance page projected in the air. Rexx graciously averted his eyes.

It was polite but unnecessary, as I was sure our accounts looked more or less the same. Tier 3s were allocated ninety meal credits per month—enough for an average of three meals per day at one credit each. However, restaurant meals cost two or three credits compared to the dehydrated and delivered options like the one I'd eaten the night before, which cost one credit each. If you ran out of meal credits, you could use your miscellaneous credits. I had twenty per month, but those were precious. If you ran out of both, you were out of luck. There was no savings, no safety net—your credits reset at the end of the month whether you had any left or not. It was common for folks to skip breakfast or lunch so they could enjoy a dinner out. It was also common for people to reach the end of the month and feast on nothing but protein and nutrient bars (a steal at five for one credit) until everything reset on the first.

"I have enough. Just, if I end up with leftovers, don't let me forget them on the table," I said. Rexx laughed slightly. It was commonplace for me to forget things, and it had become an inside joke. I laughed lightly in response.

It felt strange to be laughing after everything that had happened that day. My smile wavered, and I rubbed the middle of my forehead with my thumb. Rexx reached his arm down and placed a hand on my shoulder, prompting me to look up into his eyes.

"Do you want me to call Lydia or Jordan to meet us?" I asked. We could both use a distraction, and Jordan and Lydia would have no trouble filling the air with conversation if we didn't feel like talking.

"No. I don't really feel like being around anyone else tonight," Rexx said solemnly as the camera above my archway silently scanned us, its unlit eye shifting from me to Rexx and back again.

I nodded. I didn't really feel like being around anyone else either. We walked wordlessly to one of our regular hangouts, America One Pasta and Pizza. Every single establishment, whether in the food industry or otherwise, existed under the umbrella of America One.

Rexx and I wound our way between crowded booths and tables until we reached a two-top with a green light in the middle, indicating it was open and available. We sat down and tapped the screens, flush with the tabletops, claiming the space so our light shifted from emerald green to a dreamy red. I scrolled through the menu options, made my selection, and then looked around.

There were about thirty tables in the room, and all but five were red-lit. Several lights made to look like candles and create ambiance floated down from the ceiling.

A group of teenage girls were gathered around a large circular table in the corner. Underneath their headphones, they all sported the same short hairstyle and had on matching cerulean-blue outfits. Some type of sports team, perhaps, celebrating after a victory, though I heard no cheerful conversation. The entire restaurant was eerily quiet, considering the number of bodies in the room.

The girls kept their faces pointed down. Periodically, one or more of them discreetly laughed at the in-table entertainment holding their attention. Maybe that was all I needed. To drown everything out with entertainment for a few days.

Two women who looked to be in their mid-thirties sat at a table next to us. They held hands across the table and stroked each other's fingers in a way that told anyone who looked that they were in love. They poked at the screens in front of them with their free hands, likely playing a linked game of some sort.

Rexx also scoped out the scene, not being discreet in the slightest, tapping his fingers on the tabletop and humming as he surveyed. After a moment, he caught my glance and rolled his eyes in the direction of a table next to us.

A mother and a father were sitting at a four-top with their toddler, who looked to be about two years old. The little guy was trying desperately to climb out of his high chair, though the various straps thwarted his efforts. With a strained smile on her face, his mother held his shoulder with one hand and tapped the in-table screen before him with the other, trying to rein in his attention.

When that failed to work, she reached up and adjusted the headphones on his tiny head, which he immediately ripped off in protest. Without ever looking him in the eyes, she pressed a few buttons on the tabletop until the toddler seemed pleased, his focus drawn in at last. She gingerly placed the headphones back on his head. Then, as if backing away from a snake ready to strike, she inched her hands away slowly, turned her attention back to her husband, and let out a long sigh of relief.

A tune started to play, indicating the start of a news special. *America One: Portrait of a Redeemed Patriot.* All tabletop entertainment paused, and screens were replaced with the national emblem. A large screen covering a wall of the restaurant also blinked to life.

These played often in public places, and it was common to catch the same special multiple times. I generally enjoyed watching them. They filled me with hope for those I'd lost, and admiration for our beloved leaders, who risked everything to keep war out of our backyards.

Rexx's eyes shot to the screen the way they did every time the familiar tune played, though with less urgency than two and three years prior. I knew he was hoping for a glimpse of Amara. A chance to see her alive, whole, and well. As usual, he was let down. The photo that began to materialize on the screen was not of Amara, but of a young man, about twenty-five if I had to guess.

"This is Billy," Aelia declared. His skin was bright red, and his left cheek was raw with road rash as he thrashed around, trying to get away from the Compos who had roughly pinned him to the ground. His eyes appeared unfocused, his movements jolted, and it was obvious to everyone watching that the footage was captured after suffering the effects of the pacifier, which disrupted his body on a cellular level.

"This footage shows Billy being arrested five years ago for treason. His selfish and ungrateful actions put his family, friends, and country at risk. Fortunately, his blasphemous language against the Board was caught by our surveillance system before he was able to cause real harm." Aelia paused as applause erupted from the screen, its source veiled.

I looked around the restaurant to see that every single person, customers and employees, had stopped what they were doing to focus on their individual screens. It was the first time in my life I found the practice unnerving. I could feel the color spilling out of my face as my heart hammered inside my chest. My eyes narrowed in the direction of the screen. *What is happening to me?*

"A true patriot never puts their country at risk." The footage of a struggling Billy still played behind Aelia. Then, after a drawn-out moment, it morphed to show a clean-cut man standing upright in front of the national emblem, wearing a military uniform, his blond hair slicked back and a stoic expression on his face.

"This is Billy today." Canned oohs and ahhs resonated from the unseen audience, echoed by the oohs and ahhs from diners surrounding me. "The Board does not leave the unfit to rot the way that the rest of the world does, on sidewalks ignored by their society, starving in their own homes, or behind the bars of a prison. Instead the Board sees the promise in these people who are not able to see the importance of patriotism, and invests in their rehabilitation. Now Billy plays a vital role as an esteemed member of our military, protecting you and me from those who wish us harm." I looked at Billy as she talked. Tried to look in his eyes. *Is what she is saying true, Billy? I want to believe it's true. It has to be true.*

"In fact, just last week, Billy earned a medal of honor for his role in ensuring dangers remain outside of our borders. He even lost a hand fighting for our causes," Aelia continued, and the camera zoomed in to show a bandage wrapped around the end of one of Billy's arms, crossed respectfully in front of his abdomen. "While you may feel betrayed, or even angry with those you once knew who selfishly put themselves above their patriotic duty, know that the Board will not forget about them. The Board will work to ensure their life is full of valor and honor and, ultimately, redemption."

Just the day before, I'd have felt a sense of pride after watching the familiar story play out, imagining everyone who had disappeared from my life over the years in the face of the redeemed soldier, standing there looking safe and strong. I'd have pictured those I had known, proudly making amends and serving their country. That day I did not feel peace. I felt paralyzing confusion, and something else under the surface. Something that was heating from a simmer, on its way to a boil. I think it was anger.

"Don't forget to sign in to watch today's episode of *America One: Helping Our Nation Succeed* by the end of the day," continued Aelia.

Then, in unison with Aelia as the program ended, every person in the room, including my disassociated self, chanted, "They have hurt our nation. This is how they redeem themselves. This is how they prove their allegiance to the Board."

The program ended. The screen lit up with user-selected distractions and the message:

Bask in uninterrupted gratification with tonight's selection of featured entertainment until your food is delivered.

Below this, a counter dropped an integer with each passing second:

3 minutes 45 seconds
3 minutes 44 seconds
3 minutes 43 seconds

I unwrapped the cloth napkin from the utensil set and carefully laid it over the screen—a practice my father employed occasionally over the years. It used to annoy and embarrass me, and that night was the first time I'd done it myself.

Rexx swiveled from side to side in his chair and the click, click, click of his nails on the armrest filled the space. "So, how about that weather, eh?" he said in a sarcastic voice.

I didn't answer. Instead I sat with my head pointed down and my hands combing through my hair. After two more minutes, the waiter returned bearing full plates of food and set them in front of us, pushing my napkin to the side. He then shot me a baffled glance and walked away.

I pushed my food around on my plate. I knew I should eat, but the tangles of noodles in front of me failed to pique my appetite. I'd ordered pasta with red sauce and cheese—the "cheese" being a bright orange substitute. Rexx had ordered a different dish, one with wide, flat noodles, strips of flavored protein, and a bright green sauce. I leaned over and took a bite of his. How could two dishes of such different colors and varying ingredients taste almost identical?

Rexx suddenly stopped swiveling, reached across the table, and took both of my hands in his, causing me to drop my fork on my plate. He stared intently, concern spreading across his face like a rash.

"Whatever is going on, Patch, we'll figure it out. We'll get through it together. I know how you feel. I feel it too. But we have to keep ourselves safe in the meantime. We need to tread lightly."

He was right. We didn't need to bring any more attention on ourselves. I felt the weight on my shoulders lighten. I nodded and gave his hands a small squeeze, picked up my fork, and tried to enjoy my meal.

Full from our carbohydrate-heavy meals, we decided to take a long walk. The sun was setting as we wound through the city. I couldn't help but view it with fresh eyes. The national emblem was everywhere—on the lumicomms, on signs high above us, on coffee shop and restaurant windows, on small storefronts, and even on the vehicle-charging meters.

A scream cut through the evening air. A scream so shrill that my whole body tensed in response. *What in Board's name is happening now?* Rexx reflexively put his arm around me in a protective fashion. I quickly identified the source of the scream. A middle-aged woman was pointing upward at a building, and before I could shift my vision up, a large mass dropped from the sky. It smacked into the ground right in front of me, wet and final. Rexx tried to direct my head onto his chest, but I pushed his hand away, confused.

"It's a suicide, Patch. We've seen it before; let's just keep walking," he said.

I stared at the lumpy shape on the ground, and the world around me slowed to a trickle.

In a blur, I pulled away from Rexx and sprinted in the direction of the shape. *He might not be dead,* I told myself as I ran. *Please don't die. Not today.* I knelt next to the man, placing my palms on either side of his face. His body was slightly contorted, yet at first glance he looked relatively undamaged, peaceful even, as if he were merely taking a nap on the sidewalk. He wore a fitted black shirt and his dark hair was powdered with bits of ashen gray. He appeared to be in his late forties.

"Someone call an ambulance!" I shouted as the immensity of what had just happened filled my body like lead.

I looked around. Rexx was standing behind me, his ID positioned in front of his mouth. Onlookers had gathered, drawn by the screams. They stood yards away, backed as close to the nearby buildings as one could get without fusing with the siding. They whispered and gawked, yet no one approached.

I laid an unsteady hand on his chest, and my heart sank at the stillness I felt. Not today. I lowered my head and rested it above his heart. Nothing. Though I knew in my core that it was hopeless, I refused to admit it. I brushed the hair out of his face.

"Sir, sir, can you hear me? Can you hear me?" My words were in vain. His eyes were vacant. Certain visuals stayed with you forever, and you knew, even as your brain processed the image for the first time, that it would return to haunt you. His eyes would stay with me for the rest of my life.

Within seconds blood started to trickle, like water on a windowpane, from the side of his mouth. Blood so red, it appeared fake, as if it were nothing more than an elaborate staged scene, replete with costume makeup. A warm drip hit the back of my hand, and the warmth quickly spread through the crevice between my index finger and thumb, and I knew, instantly, blood was oozing from his ear.

I checked his pulse; though I knew what I would find. Gone. As my fingers left his wrist, I discerned the tiniest sliver of black protruding from under his sleeve. A tattoo, I assumed. I slid his sleeve up a few inches. Scrawled in ink, a message—not tattooed, but written in haste:

I WILL NOT GO WITH THEM. I WILL GO ON MY TERMS.

I quickly pulled his sleeve back down.

"I reported it. I got a message," Rexx said from behind me. "It says—*Message received; a department member will handle it shortly.*"

What? What did that mean? I glanced around, but my surroundings did not seem real. People were dispersing, continuing about their regular activities. I wanted to scream at all of them. *A man just died in front of you! A man, probably with a family. A man not so different from you and me. How can you be so complacent?* I wanted to scream at myself. I wanted to scream with the entire force of the day from hell that just wouldn't end.

I looked up. There, at the roofline of the five-story building, where this man had chosen to take the final step of his life, two uniformed silhouettes stood against the sunset.

A drone approached and hovered right above me. Habitually, I raised my hands behind my head and rose to my feet. Rexx had already assumed a similar position. Two compliance officers marched up to the scene.

"We were walking down the sidewalk when it happened," I said meekly. "I tried to help, but he was already gone." The words faltered as they spilled out.

Neither officer replied, but instead one removed four small devices from his uniform and then placed them on the ground around the body. He pressed a button on three of them, and flame-orange holographic caution tape connected three of the points. He held out his arm, motioning for us to leave the area. As soon as we did, he ignited the fourth.

We turned and walked away, and Rexx placed a shaky arm around my shoulders.

He walked me home, and we said good night with a sad, lingering hug. I held back the tears that threatened the entire walk back. As Rexx had said, we'd seen suicides before. Why had I felt the need to insert myself into the situation? What had I been expecting to happen? I didn't know. I didn't feel like I knew anything anymore.

"Do you want me to come inside and keep you company?" Rexx asked.

"No, I just need to be alone. I need this day to end."

Inside my house, I headed into the bathroom and turned the hot water dial on the bathtub. After plugging the drain, I slowly poured in a packet of bright pink crystals, watching them swirl and dissolve, turning the water a light rosé. As the tub filled, I glanced at the camera in the corner; the national emblem appeared as a tiny image next to the lens. Even in the most private of rooms.

I determined from the angle the camera was mounted that my plan just might work.

The hot water steamed the room. The words *I will not go with them. I will go on my own terms* replayed repeatedly in my mind, interrupted only momentarily by other words—*Level-Yellow Alert; Third-Generation Family History; Join the Ranks of New America; Providing You with a Safe, Secure Nation You Will Be Proud to Call Home!*

I left the tub filling while I walked to the living room to grab my work backpack. As naturally as possible, I headed back to the bathroom and set my binder, with the forbidden book inside, on the counter. I often wondered what it would be like to undress in total privacy, and whether it would affect my behavior in any way. Well, at least I wouldn't be imagining a team of gawking Board-appointed goons staring at a screen somewhere every time I used the bathroom, slipped into the shower, changed for bed, or had a romantic encounter. That day, I didn't care. As the steam rose, I undressed, letting my clothes fall to the bathroom floor.

I sat on the edge of the bath and swung my legs over the edge. I lowered myself into the steaming abyss, the intense heat of the scalding water enveloping my body and instantly turning my skin pink. I glanced at the camera, but it was hard to see through the vapor. I could only hope the same was true from the opposite end as well. With a smile on my face, my heart beating wildly in my chest, and sweat pouring down my brow, I opened the binder that contained the first non-American, non-digital book I'd ever owned—*Les Misérables* by Victor Hugo. I began with the preface:

> *So long as there shall exist, by reason of law and custom, a social condemnation, which, in the face of civilization, artificially creates hells on earth, and complicates a destiny that is divine, with human fatality; so long as the three problems of the age—the degradation of man by poverty, the ruin of women by starvation, and the dwarfing of childhood by physical and spiritual night—are not solved; so long as, in certain regions, social asphyxia shall be possible; in other words, and from a yet more extended point of view, so long as ignorance and misery remain on earth, books like this cannot be useless.*

Books like this cannot be useless, I repeated in my mind. I raised the binder to cover my face, and I silently cried until there were no more tears left.

CHAPTER 5

I HAD SEEN my parents exchange frequent glances throughout my childhood. Glances that puzzled me. I began to notice the exchanges occurring at certain times, during a television broadcast, whenever compliance officers drove by, or anytime I asked them questions about their past. As we rode in silence out of city limits, fully aware of the voice-recognition software installed in the department's vehicle, I saw them exchange one of those same glances.

My father held my mother's hand and gently stroked her fingertips, calming and reassuring her. She rested her head on his shoulder and her eyes were closed. Guilt flooded over me, but I knew I couldn't say anything yet. When we approached the gate, I was relieved to see that, as usual, there was no guard on duty, just a chip reader mounted next to the automated entrance. Rexx rolled down the driver's-side window and waved his hand under the reader. A green light flashed, and the metal gate began to grind open.

Rexx and I had rushed through enough work to buy us a couple of hours, then led my parents on a hike toward the van. Rexx and I left our IDs in the car before heading out, and my parents had left theirs at my apartment. Since ideation devices served as trackers, for all official purposes that was where my parents were for the day. I'd already convinced them to break the law, something I'd never known them to do, and I still wasn't sure exactly why I'd asked them to do it.

I didn't know if the van was as important as it felt. But the words *Third-Generation Family History* pulled me along, telling me there was more I needed to know. I needed to know if there was truth in everything I had always believed. I hoped there was.

The day before, Rexx and I tossed around several ideas regarding how to proceed, and decided the best course of action would be to just show them what we found, read their reactions, and go from there. I was basing my entire future on the hope that their love for me would keep them from reporting us, as good citizens would be expected to do. That I could hear what they had to say, take them home, and all would be well. As we walked, I could tell my parents were concerned with my rushed, anxious demeanor.

"Patricia, what are we doing out here?" my mom finally asked, her voice unsteady. There was a hint of something else behind her words—the emotion children dread hearing in their parents' voice above all others—disappointment. "You're starting to worry me. I don't like this place. It's so dirty, and the ground is so uneven, I'm finding it hard to walk. Can you just tell us, please?"

"Mom, it's too difficult to explain, but you'll understand in a few minutes, I promise. Try to enjoy the hike! When was the last time you were out in nature like this?" As the words came out of my mouth, it hit me. I took for granted my slice of freedom. Neither of them had ever been outside the city limits in their entire lives. They were understandably overwhelmed.

"You're putting us in danger by bringing us out here. We're supposed to stay in city limits; it keeps us safe," my mom said, her voice breaking. "You knew we couldn't argue with you in the car." Her voice grew increasingly shaky, and the anger started to slice through her words. "Please, just tell us." She started mumbling to herself under her breath, "The Board keeps us safe, the Board keeps us safe, the Board keeps us safe."

I glanced at her face, puffy and bright red from the heat. She wasn't used to the brisk pace, or our elevated emotions. I questioned all of my decision-making capabilities. *What have I done?* I'd crossed a threshold, and there was no going back. I wasn't invincible, and neither were they. Suddenly I was filled with self-loathing as I stopped and took a deep, pained breath, my eyes closed.

I'd never doubted the Board's decision to keep sensitive information from us before. They must have deemed it harmful for a reason—look what a couple of books and a baseball cap full of metal had done to me after just two days. I had never questioned my leaders' motives before. Why start now?

Then I had an epiphany as I opened my eyes again and watched my mom huff and puff ahead of me, sweat dampening her back enough to show through her canary-yellow shirt. I didn't know what went on inside my mother's head and she certainly didn't know what went on inside mine. Superficial conversations about sports, television, and weather—was that all we were to each other? Between the ages of five and eighteen I saw my parents for three hours a day, if I wasn't with my friends, then returned to sleep in the dormitories. None of us knew one another. Not in the true sense of the word. *Perhaps, by the end of today, that will be different,* I hoped. *Justify all you want,* I then thought. *They have no idea what you are dragging them into.*

I glanced at Rexx and saw he looked as nervous as I felt. Just as I was contemplating abandoning the entire idea and returning my parents to their home, hoping they'd forgive my irrational behavior with enough time, my father interrupted my train of thought.

"What's that up there in the bushes?" he asked, pointing to the spot where the van was hidden. His tone was curious, and I noted he had barely broken a sweat. I'd been concentrating all of my energy on reading my mother, and had barely glanced at my father. He seemed like he'd been enjoying the break in his routine, despite my mother's growing anxiety.

"That's kind of the reason we invited you out here. Rexx and I, we stumbled upon this van the other day and, well, let's just take a look."

My mother and father halted and immediately exchanged worried glances, like deer transfixed by the headlights of oncoming traffic. I handed my mother a cloth from my pocket for her to wipe her forehead.

"You'll want to see this, believe me," Rexx said.

Rexx's mood turned as swiftly as a wind turbine in a thunderstorm, and he ran ahead eagerly to clear the weeds back from the door. It only took a few minutes to dismantle our meager camouflage. Apparently reassured by his enthusiasm, my parents cautiously followed him. My father went first, followed by my mother a few steps behind. They kept glancing over their shoulders—a motion as habitual to American citizens as blinking and breathing.

By the time the three of us reached the van, Rexx had already hauled the suitcase back out onto the forest floor and was working on the jammed zipper. Then he lifted the lid. My father let out a gasp behind me. It wasn't a gasp of fear, but rather one of wonder, and when I heard it, my heart fluttered excitedly. He knew what we were showing them. I could feel it. Without even glancing at the titles, he knew.

"What, what is it? What is it? What is it, Geoffrey?" my mother exclaimed, wearing a look of worry and extreme confusion. One arm was crossed over her chest, the other raised to her mouth as she chewed on her fingernails.

My father squatted in front of the suitcase. "Are you absolutely sure we're alone out here?" he asked me in a hushed tone.

"Why? Why do we need to be alone?" my mother asked rapidly, her voice getting higher as she spoke. "Patricia? Rexx?"

"I'm absolutely sure," I said, nodding. "One of the only untouched places left in the country. Purely research land now. Only accessible by Tier 3 or higher in the Natural Resource Department, and even then, only with prior approval. I'm absolutely sure." I placed my hand on my father's shoulder. He reached up and covered mine with his.

"Plus," Rexx added, "if this area were under surveillance—heck, if it were even patrolled occasionally, you can be sure this van would no longer be here."

It was a good point. Though we'd spotted the occasional patrolman outside the park entrance, I had never seen another living soul inside. In fact, it was rare to see anyone else inside any of the zones. Abandoned land only warranted so many resources from the budget.

My father took a moment to process.

"Well, unless it's a trap . . ." he finally said. His words knocked the breath out of me and I mentally repeated them a few times.

I'd never even considered it could be a trap. It seemed like a lot of information for the Board to reveal to set a trap. Either way, my illusion of invincibility was instantly knocked down a few pegs. My mother looked pale. The confusion on her face had not diminished. She crept up beside my father and intertwined her hand with his. I stepped back to give all of us some space, and took a big gulp of water before steadying myself against a nearby rock.

"I brought you up here to show you this, for one." My voice was shaking, and I suddenly felt as if I were fifteen years younger, standing at my parents' feet with my head hanging, sheepishly admitting to breaking my father's prized model train. "And also, because, well, I think that it's about time we had an honest conversation." The words felt stilted as they escaped my mouth. "About what you know about the past. Now, I know this is dangerous. All of us are breaking the law right now." I looked at my mom. She tapped the heel of her left foot nervously, then let go of my father's hand and crossed her arms across her chest. I continued with the memorized speech I'd prepared. "Rexx and I already discussed it, and we are willing to take the risk. If you want to leave, if you don't want to be involved, we will go right now. We will drop you off at home and never talk about it again."

My father sighed, shifted on his feet, and then led my mother back into the clearing without a word. At first I thought that he was signaling a retreat, but he stopped just a few yards away and started talking to his wife. She started to cry. He placed his hands on her shoulders, and the two of them talked quietly. I watched them, trying to decipher what they might be saying. Rexx gently nudged me, and I snapped out of it, reminding myself not to stare. They would decide what they would decide.

Rexx and I shared looks of concern as we passed my water bottle back and forth. Not so much because we were thirsty, but because it gave us something to do while we waited. So far, it was going exactly the way we'd anticipated, but that didn't diminish the tension.

We then busied ourselves by examining the books again. I shuffled through the titles without opening them. I had a sinking feeling I'd have more than enough new information to digest by the end of the day if my father's reaction to the suit-case was any indication.

My parents returned after about fifteen minutes. My father looked eager, and my mother looked resigned. They sat on a downed tree, and my father's story began.

"Did you know your mother and I are the same age? We were both born in 2035." His gold-and-gray eyebrows fur-rowed as he chose his words. "This was only five years after the Northern Wall was built, you know." I nodded, but he avoided my gaze.

"The Board had only been in control for a short while. It was all timed to happen at once, the moment the Northern Wall was complete in 2030. That wasn't a coincidence." He rubbed his hands through his short, thinning hair, and looked as if he were struggling with something. *How does he know all of this*, I thought, *and where is he going with it?*

"My mom—your grandmother Lily—she, uh, she had a lot of anxiety. It was so common then. It got worse once Dad disappeared, but even when we were kids, she had a hard time. But, once he was gone, well—"

"What do you mean 'disappeared'?" I interrupted. "I thought he died before I was born? I thought he was sick."

"I know, sweetie. I know we told you that," he said, then his glance shifted to my mother. "I know I told you that too, Louise. Truth is, we never really learned what happened. One day he just didn't come home from work. There were too many to send notices back then. It's slowed down since, but mostly because people stopped testing the limits. Back then the weap-ons were lethal." My father looked intensely at me and Rexx.

I nodded, signaling for him to continue. *Third-Generation Family History*, I thought.

"Anyway, Mom, she became afraid all the time. I mean, who wouldn't be? It was terrible. People stayed in their homes, afraid to walk down the street. Her generation, they remembered when it was different. You two, well, you two don't know anything else. You're so young. I've thought about that a lot. . . ." He paused here for quite a while. I leaned toward him, my heart swelling with anticipation, eager for him to go on.

"So, it didn't always used to be like this, Dad? Before the Wall? Did the laws change? What's different?" But he didn't acknowledge my questions, just kept on with his story as if I'd never spoken.

"She managed to pull herself together most of the time. We were always fed, at least. But she worked at home, and didn't leave the house much. She was afraid. She thought that they were coming for her, too. Every time someone knocked on the door, she jumped, and her eyes became cloudy. The truth is, we were left to fend for ourselves a good bit." I knew as he spoke that the "we" he was referring to was himself and his two older brothers. He was born before the Board made sterilization mandatory after the birth of one child.

"We wandered a lot, mostly in the evenings. When I was fourteen, well, my brothers let me in on a little secret pastime of theirs. Now, you have to understand, Patricia, back then the speech auditors and cameras had only been installed in homes and outside important buildings. They weren't everywhere yet. Drones didn't follow us down the street like they do now. There were times, times when people were still free. We didn't think so then, but now, looking back, well, we didn't see how much freedom we had. I didn't want to be the odd one out, being the youngest, so I joined them. I was terrified every step of the way."

"What do you mean 'joined them'? What were they doing?" I asked. I put my hand on my father's knee and his leg stopped jiggling. The corner of his mouth cracked a smile and his eyes widened. Rexx leaned in toward us also.

"They were informants."

As my father spoke the word, his voice changed slightly, as if he had been transported back to that time. He no longer met my eyes, but focused his gaze on his shoes. *Third-Generation Family History.*

"Talking in alleys and green spaces was common, but people ran and hid at the slightest commotion. They talked about ways to get out of the mess the country was in, about whether or not what they were hearing on the news could be trusted. A lot of them didn't think so. Without widespread surveillance, the government used watchdogs. Traitors were shot on sight. I saw . . . terrible things, Patricia." He paused for a moment before adding, "I know you have too, but, well, back then it was on another level. They were still making their point. And they made it loudly."

I listened to my father, glued to his every word, mentally filling in some of the lost pieces of the jigsaw puzzle in my mind. I tried to imagine conversations like the ones he described taking place today, and I couldn't. But it still didn't answer why. Why things had changed.

"Despite the risks," my father continued, "many groups would meet discreetly to vent; memories of the way it used to be were still fresh. They didn't all believe the atrocities we were shown on television. They thought the Board might have been behind the bombing in 2029—the one that was labeled a terror attack and left thousands of people dead in Nevada. It was used frequently as justification for the Board's policies in the beginning, the threat that it would happen again if we continued the way we were. The Board made it clear that, from then on, there were only two types of people—patriots, who lined up to follow their leaders, and non-patriots. The latter were no longer welcome in America." I looked at Rexx. His eyes were wide, and his fingers gripped his knees tightly. My father was still looking down.

My mother had turned her body away from his and her arms were crossed again. I considered moving next to her, but my attention was reined back in as my father continued to speak.

"Apparently, before the first wall was completed in 2022, political divisiveness had reached an all-time high. The country was deeply split on almost every major issue." He started naming issues and counting on his fingers until six fingers were in the air. "Immigration, religious freedom, gun control, health care, environmental protections, women's rights—you get the point, I guess." He put his hand back down.

I didn't get the point, actually. I didn't know what political divisiveness meant, or how anyone could have a say in any of the issues he mentioned.

"Anyway. People didn't believe their leaders anymore, and they didn't believe each other. They started to not believe anything, even if it was presented to them with evidence. There was too much conflicting information.

"By the time I was born, all references to people on the outside, all connections to the rest of humanity was coined *unpatriotic history*. We saw only what the Board deemed appropriate for us to see. *For our protection,* they told us."

My father continued his tale and I listened, hanging on every word. It was a tale far beyond what I could have ever imagined. It was a tale of mass deportations, of uprisings squelched by force. Of the downfall of what was once known as "democracy," and the replacement of old institutions by what we now know as the Board. A tale that was long and heart wrenching, that left as many questions as it provided answers. A tale with a lot of holes, but that concluded with the blood of tens of thousands of protesters, and citizens resorting to living their lives in the only way they had left—in fear.

"There was a lot of confusion, a lot of anger still. By the time I was old enough to hear the stories, there were rumors of a revolution simmering in the northwest, mostly those in the generation before me, preparing for an uprising, preparing to oppose with everything they had. They called themselves the Veritas Ring."

A strange name, I thought. I wondered what it meant. Glancing at my mother, there was no recognition in her face. Either she didn't know what my father was talking about, or she was very good at hiding it.

"They signed their communications with an insignia," my father continued, "an insignia that represented all there was to lose, but also the undeniable nature of history, of the pursuit of knowledge, and, most important, of the truth."

My father picked up a stick, and in the dirt in front of him he drew the symbol: a sideways eight. The same odd symbol we'd seen over the state of Oregon on the map from the van. My eyes widened.

$$\infty$$

My father continued. "My brothers and I, we joined Veritas. We helped pass on messages when we could, but they became fewer and farther between. Then, one day, when I was sixteen, my brothers did not come home from school. They'd been found out. I never saw them again. That was the day I stopped. Someone had to take care of Mom."

My father fell silent. I wanted to say something, but no words seemed sufficient. Was I to believe everything he had just said to me? He was my father. My father, who had never spoken like that a single day in his life. My father, who sat idly by as I watched ideology videos from the age of two. My father, who every night walked me to the dormitories run by the same government that had taken his brothers. I started to open my mouth to speak but promptly closed it again and then hung my head.

"I knew it," Rexx muttered under his breath, then got up and stormed away.

I said the only thing I could think of. "Dad, what do you think is out there now, beyond the borders? Do you think there are still members of the Veritas Ring? Somewhere in the northwest?" As the words left my body, I suppose it meant I believed him.

"I don't know the answer to either question," he replied.

My mother still hadn't spoken. Rexx was now several yards off, pacing, holding his head in his hands.

"Mom? Is there anything you want to say?" She didn't answer me. Was all of what my father had revealed news to her as well? Her body language suggested an element of betrayal, and if I had to guess based on what I knew about my mom, she looked angry and confused more than anything.

The man sitting in front of me suddenly seemed a separate entity from the father I'd grown up with my whole life. The man who had driven me to soccer practice, who had taught me to ride my bike on the sidewalks near our complex, who had kissed my palm every evening before I left to go sleep in the dormitories, so that when I missed him, I could simply place my hand on my cheek. He was another person entirely, burdened with a secret past hidden even from those he held dear. I'd never known the darkness that plagued his thoughts, never even suspected it, and from the look on my mother's face, neither had she.

I realized his situation may have been unique for his age group, but not for the generation before. An entire generation, forced to lie to their children or never see them again. A generation forced to pretend that they didn't know the truth or be labeled a traitor.

It hit me like the jolt of a pacifier. I believed my father. Everything we'd been told was a lie.

I was no longer a believer.

And that made me a traitor.

CHAPTER 6

MY FATHER HELPED us pack away the books, return the suitcase, and rearrange the brush. We then began the trek back to the mobile office without a word. My steps were heavy as we trudged up the trail. I honestly didn't know what would come next. What did someone do with this kind of information? It was so much input, I felt like the Earth was flipping on its axis. I also had a feeling there was much more my father didn't know. There would always be more. How was I supposed to go back to my old life and pretend everything was normal? My insides had been fractured into thousands of tiny shards, unable to be pieced back together again even if I wanted them to be.

My mother trailed the rest of us by a good ten paces. I kept looking back. Her eyes followed my father's shoes. I considered dropping back to walk with her, but I sensed she wanted to be alone. When we arrived at the mobile office, I dug my ID out of an interior compartment. An alarm was beeping, and the screen was flashing. I saw Rexx's was doing the same as I handed it to him.

AIR QUALITY RED. REPORT INDOORS OR WEAR MASK FOR NEXT EIGHTEEN MINUTES.

Damn. I looked at the time stamp on the alert and saw it was sent fifteen minutes prior. Fifteen minutes breathing hazardous chemicals. It'd happened before, and it would happen again. Leaving our IDs in the car while doing work that was often very dirty and labor intensive was commonplace for us. But I could suddenly add "put parents' health at risk" to the list of selfish acts I'd committed that day.

Face masks were portable, about four inches in length, just enough to cover the nose and mouth and filter incoming air. They telescoped out when in use, and folded flat to fit in a pocket. Citizens were required to have them on their person at all times, and clothing was designed with this in mind.

We all dug our masks out of our built-in pockets and put them on.

Once we were safely inside the car with the windows sealed and filtered oxygen circulating, we drove back to town in the same silence that had chaperoned us on our walk. Rexx sat next to me, his head bobbing forward and his shoulders sunken as if gravity were deforming his spine. I wondered if he might find a way to approach his parents next, to uncover the mysteries of his past, his ancestry, his parents' inner thoughts. I thought about Rexx's reaction to my father's story before he walked off: *I knew it.* Was it just a panicked reaction, or something more? The answer would have to wait.

My mother sat in the backseat, her head leaning against the window, her body guarded, angled away from the rest of us. She appeared to me a hollow shell. My father stared out the window. There was a slight satisfied smile in his reflection. Their hands were now miles apart.

Guilt and anger fought for primacy inside me. Guilt over placing my parents in danger, anger at the realization that I truly didn't know either of them. Anger at all the lies fed to me my entire life. Guilt at being so willfully ignorant, and simply accepting what I was told as fact.

I thought about the books again, both the ones in the suitcase and the one at home. I thought about how our assignment would be wrapping up soon. I wondered how I was going to part with the magnificent portal into the past that had changed everything in just a few short days. The thought of never reading from any of those pages again scared me more than the consequences. *Where would I even hide more books?* I wondered, knowing full well the danger of the thought.

After swinging by my apartment to fetch my parents' devices and drop my parents off within walking distance of home, I drove me and Rexx back to the office to turn in our samples and return the car. Rexx tapped his leg anxiously and I placed my hand on his shoulder. He released the breath he'd apparently been holding, but his mood stayed in the trenches. He was sitting right next to me, but he felt far away.

About one block from the hangar, my ID beeped and vibrated. "Can you check that?" I said as I held my arm out in front of Rexx's face so he could read the alert.

"Patch, pull over."

"Why, what's wrong? What does it say?"

"Just pull over and get out of the car, okay? Let me drive." His voice was weighed down with a palpable, grievous tone.

"Why?" I asked again. "We're almost there. Just read it to me."

"As soon as you pull over and step out of the car, I'll give it to you." His somber voice did little to quell my misdirected confusion and anger.

But I pulled over on a side street and out of the main line of traffic, near a grassy patch outside a movie theater. Rexx got out of the car and I did as well. We met in the middle behind the vehicle and he handed me my device and put a hand on my back as I read.

Geoffrey Collins is being held in federal custody on charges of treason. An investigation into the charges has begun. You will be informed of the results.

I stared at my device. We *just* dropped him off. The words didn't seem real. And then, all of a sudden, they did. My vision blurred, like someone had just placed a glass bowl over my head. My breath came in short, ragged gasps. I lost my footing and fell to the ground. I tried grabbing the grass in front of me, but the dizziness only escalated. I resisted the urge to vomit. *What have I done?*

"Patch, we need to get back in the car." Rexx's words were distant, like an echo in a tunnel. "We have to go. Patch! We have to go. We have to get out of here." Suddenly he was half carrying and half leading me to the car and pushing me into the passenger seat. "We have to go back to the work site," he said forcefully, ignoring in his panic the fact that his voice was being recorded, and that the car was repeatedly prompting us to return our vehicle to the Natural Resource Department. "We need to get there before they do." The world spun, and his words wobbled.

This isn't real. This isn't happening.

"Patch, I think you're having a panic attack. Try to sit up, try to breathe." His hand found the spot between my shoulder blades and rubbed in small circles. My mind rooted for the mantras that usually helped in stressful times, but I spit them back out again as quickly as they came. "Try to breathe," Rexx continued, sounding as though there were a wall of water between us. The world started to stabilize, slowly, as I took deep breaths through my nose. Rexx came into view.

My mind reeled as I rubbed my still-tight chest, trying to figure out what had happened. I didn't receive a message about my mother—only my father. There was no message for either Rexx or me, no demand to report to the Compliance Department. What happened? What were they doing to him?

The guard was the first thing I noticed as we approached the gate. At the sight of him, Rexx instinctively slammed on the brakes. Then he pressed the accelerator again, realizing he couldn't react as if anything were wrong. We couldn't give ourselves away. I wiped the sweat off my puffy face as he approached the gate, then rolled down my window and put my arm out to scan my chip. Nothing amiss.

Each government-issued vehicle had a tracker in it. During work hours, employees were expected to go to their assigned location, and nowhere else. Tracking logs were randomly reviewed, scrutinized, and compared to the data on one's ID. Users were expected to keep their IDs on their person at all times. If the vehicle was tracked to an authorized location, no red flags were raised, as far as we knew.

The guard walked toward us slowly, bringing into focus a sweaty face riddled with exasperation. Rexx introduced himself confidently, told him we forgot something inside, then showed his ID to confirm his identity. My stomach flopped over as the guard eyed me. I could feel the tearstains still on my face but forced a weak smile as I passed my device to him as well. We had to hold it together. He, like all citizens, was trained to recognize suspicious behavior.

I wondered briefly if he would insist on accompanying us, but instead he simply said, "Hurry on up, will ya? I've got to wait until everyone is out before I can submit the entry and exit logs." That explained why I'd never encountered him before. He only came at the end of each day. He looked annoyed as he walked away.

We continued through the gate and Rexx parked as close to the trailhead as he could manage. He threw his device in the backseat and then came around and opened my door. I took off my device as well and stepped out of the car.

"Why are we here?" I asked. "We need to go check on my mom, make sure she's okay."

"It can't be a coincidence, Patch. This has something to do with us. I think your father might have tried to come back here. Maybe they caught him leaving the city without clearance. We aren't in custody, so they don't know everything yet. We need to find out what's up and we need to stash it or destroy it all before someone finds it. Our fingerprints are all over that van. Who knows what they are doing to him, Patch." At this I choked. "He might tell them everything," Rexx continued, then he stopped and turned to look me in the eye. "Patch, this backfired, and we need to figure out a plan."

His words snapped me out of it, and I felt my head start to clear. He was right. We could be, we probably would be, next. My grief would have to wait.

Rexx grabbed my hand and began sprinting toward the rugged trail that wound its way to the van. I felt like I was falling down a well, grasping at handholds that diminished with each foot until the edge was as smooth as glass and no hope remained of returning to ground level. Three times I had to stop and steady myself against the crutch of a nearby tree to catch my breath.

We were almost there, ready to dash in and grab as many books as we could carry, when Rexx's arm shot out and grabbed me around my waist so swiftly that I doubled over.

There were voices up ahead. We ducked behind a tree and dropped to our knees. *What is going on?* I tried to quiet my rapid breathing and listen. Listen for clues as to whether they'd heard our late-afternoon run through the forest. I could distinguish multiple voices, but we weren't close enough to hear what they were saying. We should have turned around and left right then, but curiosity got the best of me and I slowly inched forward on all fours until the scene came into view and the voices started to make sense. Rexx followed behind me.

Board help us.

There were six of them, all in uniform, surrounding the van, digging around and carelessly tossing things out into a large pile. They were making enough noise that they likely couldn't hear us. As I watched, I felt as if a stranger were rifling through my underwear drawer.

"DNA scan is complete," one of the Compos declared above the sound of the commotion. "Forensics will shoot back with a report. We can't carry all of this out of here. The incinerator's never going to make it through the brush or up the trail."

"Hang on, let me get the commander on the line," said a female voice. The owner of the voice then walked a good distance away, her ID held up to her ear. My hand clasped over my mouth, an extra precaution as we watched in horror. Rexx grasped my forearm. *No. Please don't do this.* I wanted more than anything to run up and grab everything I could before it was gone, because I knew what was coming next.

"He said to burn everything but the vehicle. They'll send someone to do away with it later. Just into a pile there, probably farther away than that. We need to clear away these leaves first. See, this is why I avoid nature. It's so damn dirty out here."

The Compos started moving all the contraband items to a new, more organized pile several yards away, where the trees didn't crowd and the flames would have room to breathe. From a distance we watched as they tossed in the rare antiques we'd found—the baseball cap, the empty soda can, the clothes that had been strewn over the backseat. Then, without even opening it, two of them hurled the entire suitcase full of books out of the van, lugged it over, and dumped it onto the pile. As they did, I caught the slightest hint of the musty, aged paper—that grassy, vanilla smell. Sadness and panic were replaced by one primal emotion—anger. Those books that had continued to exist all this time, despite the odds against them, were now about to be reduced to ash.

Several minutes later the contraband coming out of the van started to diminish. *How can they just throw it all on there without even looking at it?* I thought. *They aren't even curious.* I squinted to get a clearer look at each one of their faces. They were loving this. Who knows how long it had been since any of them had gotten to take part in a proper burning. Treasonous paraphernalia was rare, as far as I knew.

One pulled what looked like a stylus out of his pocket, and with a satisfied smirk on his face, he pointed at the pile, now about half as tall as he was. Out came a flame about ten inches long. He pressed the tool right into the clothes until their partially decayed remains smoldered and then burst into a bright orange. The old suitcase caught shortly afterward, igniting those beautiful words. Words I would never get to see again.

As I watched everything go up in flames, I thought of what my father had told me about Amara. I needed to remember five things about the man in the van. What had I learned? What did possessions really say about a person? He'd lived until at least the year 2030. He sometimes drank out of a reusable mug. He enjoyed soda. He liked baseball, or at least he'd had a baseball cap. He collected trinkets such as crystals and decorative three-dimensional triangles. He loved to read; he safeguarded an entire suitcase full of books for at least sixty years. He knew a lot of things I would never know, things I wanted to find out.

As the fire coughed up black smoke, we crawled backward until we were a good distance away and felt safe to stand up and start to run.

A DNA scan had already been conducted. A DNA scan that would return the names of the two people who had extensively crawled through the van and touched the contents. Rexx Moreno and Patricia Collins. It was only a matter of time before Rexx and I were charged with treason. We had to leave. But how?

CHAPTER 7

WE HAD TO survive the next several hours. That was goal one. To remain alive and out of the custody of the Compliance Department. We thought about the map in the van and my father's story as we walked back to the car. A rough plan started to piece itself together. Whether the pieces would form a well-connected whole was yet to be seen.

Arriving back in city limits, I pulled the vehicle to a stop in front of Rexx's apartment building, despite the beeping and the flashing text on the dash repeatedly reminding us to return the vehicle.

"Well," Rexx said in a steady voice as he turned to look at me. His dark curls clung to his forehead with sweat. "I'll meet you back here in an hour, okay?" He shot me a small, lopsided smile. I searched his eyes for something. Hope, confidence, reassurance maybe? A sign he honestly believed he'd see me in an hour.

I nodded, then broke eye contact. "See you in an hour." Rexx squeezed my shoulder then climbed out of the car. It felt as if he'd taken my guts with him. As I drove away, I watched Rexx in the rearview mirror, hoping that it wouldn't be the last time I saw him. I couldn't do this alone.

Once the car was parked under the lumicomm in front of my apartment building, I immediately walked the few blocks to my parents' house. I walked quickly, painfully aware of the eyes of both pedestrians and surveillance technology around me. Cameras that just days before had made me feel safe and secure were now invasive and threatening. With each step, I expected to be knocked to the ground by Compos or jolted with a pacifier.

I was walking to check on my mom, make sure that she was all right. See if I could get her to come with us. I didn't know what I was going to say. She wouldn't listen, not after reeling from the loss of her husband. She would have received the same alert I did, if he hadn't been taken in her presence. I knew that, but my feet propelled me nonetheless. The knot in my chest grew a centimeter with each step. Something didn't line up; the Compos had to have been tipped off for everything to have happened so quickly. It hadn't been more than twenty minutes after dropping them off that I received the message of my father's arrest. I needed to confirm a suspicion.

As I approached the front of the building, I saw her through the window three stories up. Pacing back and forth, still wearing the same yellow shirt she'd worn to the park. I stopped walking. Just stood there, observing her, and my heart sunk like a stone dropped into a pond. She alternated between wiping her face and wringing her hands together behind her head as she patrolled the window, back and forth, back and forth. She'd been crying. The knot in my gut tightened, and that was when she spotted me. Our eyes locked and I knew I'd never forget that moment. The way she looked at me. A mix of soul-crushing disappointment, guilt, and anger. No words were necessary. In that moment I knew.

My own mom had turned in my dad.

Our eyes remained locked and then the world started to blur once again. I shook my head to clear it, straightened my sinking shoulders, and took a deep breath. She came back into view. Time was up.

Good-bye, Mom. I turned and walked away.

I had to set aside the feelings of betrayal that threatened to overwhelm me—those I'd have to add to the pile of unprocessed emotions to deal with later. I quickly ran through the possible scenarios Rexx and I were facing. Mom likely reported the van using one of the anonymous tip kiosks on the sidewalk—freestanding rectangular boxes roughly the size of a coat closet that were scattered throughout the city. Every citizen was encouraged to use them to report suspicious activity, as an alternative to calling something in on one's ID, under the guise of anonymity. But how anonymous could they be with multiple cameras a stone's throw away?

Did she report only my father out of resentment and hurt? Did she believe what he'd confessed at the park? Or did she think he had fabricated all of it? Did she, in some convoluted way, think she was protecting us? What else had she said about the events of the day? I had to assume the worst. I had to assume that, at that exact moment, the Compliance Department was using whatever method necessary to get the full truth out of my father. Part of me knew that if he gave us up, it wouldn't be his fault. I swallowed down the lump forming in my throat.

It was pretty damn easy to draw a line from the van to Rexx and me. The Board, as I was painfully realizing, had managed to brainwash an entire nation, myself included, so I was sure they could figure it out. If they didn't, the DNA sweep results would be back soon enough.

We had to stay alive. Stay alive, and out of the Compliance Department's custody. I ducked into my apartment and promptly filled my backpack with protein bars and several dehydrated meal pouches. I added the book I'd swiped from the van, then quickly completed a mental checklist. There were a few other field-related things in the car still, which would be of use. I took one last look around the home I'd lived in for four years and then walked out the door.

I turned to look at my garden bed. Something so simple that brought so much joy and peace. I bent down and quickly grabbed a few of the hardier items ready for harvest, shoved them into my backpack, and continued to my car.

This is the only choice. It's this or military redemption. It's this or military redemption. It's this or military redemption, I repeated this to myself on a loop as I drove back to Rexx's apartment. The car continued to beep and flash at me the whole way. Rexx was waiting on the corner, and he climbed in as soon as I pulled to a stop next to the curb.

Rexx's eyes met mine briefly. *At least we're in this together,* I thought.

We drove out of town limits, through an automated checkpoint that formed an arch over the roadway, and away from everything and everyone I'd ever known.

I pulled over to the side of the road, about two miles after the city checkpoint.

We took off our IDs and set them on our seats. I grabbed my backpack from the rear seat and we walked away from the vehicle.

"It's this or a military redemption camp," Rexx muttered under his breath, and I could tell he was talking to himself and not to me.

I thought about the message again. My father was imprisoned. My mother had turned him in. My father was in custody and it was my fault. For the first time in years I found myself aching to talk to Amara. Once we were a comfortable distance from the car, I knelt on the ground and started beating the dirt in front of me with my fists. Rexx knelt beside me. When I looked at him, his eyes were glazed with tears. I leaned back on my heels and looked at my hands, my knuckles caked with dirt, a feeling I usually loved. I took a deep breath.

I thought about the plan that Rexx and I had discussed while leaving the scene at the park. The car, checked out to Rexx and me, would be reported missing soon enough. They would then track our IDs and send out search drones.

We needed to get somewhere safe, somewhere far away, quickly. Somewhere where we could think clearly and form a plan. Somewhere where there might be others who could help us. Help us develop a plan to find my father.

There were two types of zones that the Natural Resource Department frequented. Quarantined residential zones tended to exist on the border of a populated city and had been in use at some point, and the goal was to reopen them for either integration into the local city or as factory land. Non-residential zones, such as the state park in Arizona, were quarantined because of the exact opposite, ironically. They were healthy ecosystems that contained some of the last strains of beneficial soil for food and medicine production.

The quarantined residential zones were polluted to the point that they posed a significant public health risk and were deemed unsafe for habitation. We were sent to perform a series of tests on groundwater and soil to determine current levels of chemical contamination, and the rate at which they were stabilizing.

After years and years of citizens developing cancer and other maladies by living in proximity to these sites, entire regions were evacuated, their occupants reassigned. Our job was to determine whether these polluted zones had become habitable once again—though the definition of *habitable* was a hotly debated topic in my field.

There were over 150 closed-off zones in total within the borders of the United States. I thought about my father, about the map, about the Veritas Ring and the symbols. I knew exactly where we needed to go. There may be nothing there, but we needed to try. We needed to go to the northwest.

One of the largest zones happened to be in northern Oregon, where the infinity sign had been drawn on the map. The zone had been shut down for at least twenty years, if I remembered correctly. We'd learned about it in our training. If we could get there unseen, we might be able to find something that could help us. Something that could possibly lead us to answers. If nothing else, it was large, and it was empty. It would give us time to think.

"My mom turned us in," I said to Rexx after he sat down next to me. "At least, she turned my dad in and reported the van. I'm fairly certain."

"What were we thinking? Huh? Why on earth did we think we could get away with any of it? No one gets away with any-thing!" His voice rose as he talked. He was yelling at himself just as much as at me. "So, that's it? We just leave? Never see our families again? Disappear forever? Can we even disappear? I mean, has anyone ever done that before? There could be drones out looking for us now for all we know. Compos could turn that corner at any second."

"Unless you have a better plan," I snapped back. I felt guilty but also fairly sure that we would have been hustled into the back of a Compo vehicle by now if we hadn't done what we just did.

Rexx unzipped the backpack and flipped it upside down.

Sprawled between us were the following: the food I had grabbed from home, *Les Misérables*, one department-issued topographic map of the United States, a geology reference book, a water bottle with built-in filter, the map found in the van, the first aid kit, and a multi-tool we often used in the field for soil sampling (it opened to reveal various attachments, including a knife, rock pick, laser level, a sighting compass, an inclinometer, a flashlight, and a manual soil-sampling probe).

Rexx sighed as he looked at the pile.

"The food should last us about five days if we don't overdo it. I think we're about right here," I said after opening the map I'd swiped from the van.

"Wait. Why does it look so different?" Rexx perked up and leaned in to have a closer look.

"I've been trying to figure that out. Look at these sections the driver circled; these are the major residential areas in the US. I don't know if it used to always be that way. Look at all of these towns in between."

"Wait. So, you think people used to live all the way out here?" he asked as his finger circled the areas surrounding major cities in Arizona. We'd passed a few run-down buildings in our work, but nothing to justify the hypothesis. "Why would they force everyone to move?" Rexx continued.

"Surveillance." The word came out naturally. Like trying a piece of a puzzle you'd overlooked repeatedly, obvious when it fit that it had belonged there all along. "They needed everyone close so they could monitor them; otherwise, it would never work." The lump in my throat returned.

"I wonder if that's why he was trying to leave—the man in the van," Rexx said as I placed the topographical map next to the other and folded it so the corresponding segment was showing—easier said than done since the topo map was three-dimensional to designate elevation variations. I considered his words. Was the owner of the van running to the border simply because he was told to move? There had to be more to the story. I looked at the map again.

"Well, first things first," Rexx said. He hustled away and came back with our IDs, waving them in the air. He tossed me mine. He set his on the ground and dramatically stomped on it. We both leaned down to look when he removed his foot. It didn't do anything.

Rexx held up a finger, indicating that he wanted to try one more thing. He motioned for me to hand him the multi-tool. Then he set the device on a nearby rock and aligned the metal pick on top. I got the hint.

I searched until I found the closest large rock I could find that I thought would accomplish the job—small enough to hold but large enough to provide the force needed. I handed it to him. He raised it above his head and then brought it down. The ID splintered into five pieces. Rexx handed it to me, and I started to pluck it apart. He did the same to mine. Once he was finished, he came and knelt next to me.

The biggest thing we had going for us was that law enforcement operated under the assumption that every single person was tracked and accounted for in real time. With our IDs out of the picture, it was almost as if we didn't exist.

I thought if anyone could get to the northwest, we could. After all, we knew more about the landscape than the majority of citizens and possibly some members of the Board. But the journey there wouldn't be easy.

"Hand me the knife," I said.

Rexx closed the rock pick attachment on the multi-tool and pried open the knife.

"I'll go first," he said. "Will you do the honors?"

I ran my finger across the tip. It was sharp, but not sharp enough to cut skin without a decent amount of pressure. After digging the sanitizer from the first aid kit, I cleaned the blade and took a deep breath. I could feel myself disassociating, similar to how I'd felt when in the van for the first time—as if

I were watching the situation unfold in front of me and not personally taking part in the events.

Rexx probed around the back of his hand until he felt the small lump between the intersection of his thumb and index finger—the location of his dorsal chip. "It's right here; watch the veins," he said, then lifted his shirttail, stuffed the bottom of it into his mouth, and bit down.

"Sorry," I said gently. And then, as quickly as I could, I brought the metal down.

Rexx's blood trickled onto my knee. He flinched only slightly, looking up at the sky and gritting his teeth into the fabric. The cut was executed, but I still had to get the chip out. With adrenaline pumping through my veins, I squeezed on either side of the incision, and the chip exposed itself. *Huh. It's even smaller than I thought.* I flicked it into the grass.

"Okay, it's done," I said.

His usually dark skin was pallid. He closed his eyes and dug his head into the palm of his other hand for just a moment, then released the tension and turned to me.

"It wasn't so bad," he said. I gave him a small smile at the reassuring, yet utterly unconvincing, gesture.

"Guess it's my turn," I said, wiping the glistening metal off as best I could with the hem of my shirt. After placing my hand on his knee, I turned away and closed my eyes to avoid seeing the metal pierce my skin. There was a spike of pain, but then it was over.

Rexx placed the chip in the palm of my hand. With the index finger of my unmaimed hand, I rolled the chip around and around, enthralled. It was strange to see it on the outside, this thing that had tagged me since birth.

Rexx sat down next to me.

"What? You're just going to let it bleed everywhere?" he said with a stifled laugh. He took my bloody hand and started wiping it off with his shirt, which he'd just soaked with water.

Between wipes of the still dripping blood, I saw the cut only measured about an inch in length. Rexx apparently had a raw talent for skin carving that I did not possess.

"Just keep pressure on it," Rexx said gently. "Now, what do we do next?"

"I say we start by getting the hell out of here."

CHAPTER 8

I'D ONLY EVER seen cargo transports when I was returning from a field assignment. The Tucson charge port and unloading station was settled just outside the city, on the north side.

A large robotic arm the size of a three-story building loaded and unloaded cubes the size of bedrooms on and off transport flats. Each flat held four shipping containers end to end, leaving only a gap large enough for the arm to maneuver in between. The flats were just wide enough for their cargo, with several wheels underneath that hugged the tracks.

Once each flat was emptied of the cargo needed in Arizona and reloaded with cubes headed elsewhere, it was then recharged and sent on its way. The removed cargo cubes were put on a conveyor belt and routed to a distribution center within city limits. It was from these cargo boxes that many everyday items arrived.

Arizona was the end of the southbound line. The flats shuffled essential goods to where people were not permitted to travel, between state lines. I knew which direction they came from, and which direction they headed when they pulled out of the port. There were three tracks. Due East, Northeast, and

Northwest. Though I had no idea how long they continued in each direction. Details.

We left the vehicle on the side of the road, hoping when someone found it that they would check the last programmed destination and assume we were headed toward Zone 72 to hide. Then, ignoring common sense, we left the road and quickly walked through the thickening darkness the two miles back toward the city.

Our hands were swathed with bandages from the pocket first aid kit in my backpack. We'd been careful not to exhaust its meager contents. I could feel the crimson blood soaking through the white gauze, but it was too dark to see.

And though we had a light on the multi-tool, it was too dangerous to turn it on.

My mind sifted through what had happened that day. It seemed that with each step, a different thought popped into my head. Step. My father had been a rebel when he was a child. Step. He'd been arrested. Step. My mother had turned him in. Step. I was a criminal on the run. Step. I'd probably never see my family or friends again.

Rexx trudged along beside me. Neither of us had much to say. It wasn't time yet. He was mourning too.

My adrenaline waxed and waned as we continued on. I juggled the feelings of guilt, of rage, and of self-loathing that accompanied the realization I'd done something life-altering, potentially life-ending. Though I was listening intently for any sign of pursuit, I couldn't help but feel like I did when I tackled a particularly difficult problem at work. I was on a mission, and I would see it through to the end.

After about thirty minutes, we spotted the cargo port. Our destination grew brighter with each step. Rexx and I kept pace with each other, quickening our steps if we fell behind. It felt odd to hurry toward our own potential death.

When we arrived on the outskirts of the cargo port, we sat in the shadows and waited. I peered in all directions, taking in our surroundings. Right in front of us was the loading/unloading station. A football field's distance away was the distribution center, inside the city limits. In the light of the distribution center I could see two dark figures patrolling next to the conveyor belt that entered and left the center with the cargo cubes. Guards. There to ensure nothing and no one exited the city without permission. We waited some more.

What felt like several hours passed, though I had no way to tell the exact time. Then there it was. The front of a flat pulling out of the port on the Northwest-bound track. We both saw it, and together we jumped to our feet and started to run. The light overhead illuminated us like we were in the center of a stadium. We just had to hope that no one was looking. That the Compos at the distribution center were only focused on what was coming and going on their side of the conveyor belt. We had to hope that the loading/unloading port outside the city limits—run fully on autopilot—contained no Compos or cameras. And if it did, that we would at least get a head start.

We ran as fast as we could, having planned out the exact steps we would take during the hours we'd waited. We had to catch the flat before it picked up speed—as it was still emerging, if possible. We had to move fast, to aim for the small sliver of space between the towering cargo containers, and hope it was as wide as it appeared from a distance, since we'd have to fit inside it.

My chest tightened as I ran. There had never been seconds in my life that mattered as much as what happened right then. If we succeeded, we would catch the flat and escape. If we failed, we would be spotted—or worse, fall under the wheels of the train.

I could hear Rexx running behind me, right at my heels, but I didn't look back. I concentrated all my attention on one spot, one sliver, one crack, behind the first cube, and I timed myself as I ran. *You can do this,* I repeated. *Faster.* My backpack banged against my lower back with each step. Why hadn't Rexx passed me? He was faster. He wasn't carrying anything extra. He should have passed me. If he hadn't, it was on purpose.

We approached the flat, the top of which was waist high. I put my hand on the edge of one of the cubes, hoping for a grip, but it slipped right off like I had grabbed ice. *Looks like I have to lunge, then.* So I did. I jumped straight in between the containers. Then, as quickly as I could, I steadied myself and shimmied to the far side to make room for Rexx to do the same. He didn't wait, and he landed on the back of my leg. I felt his hand wrap around my knee. I started to panic, thinking he was about to fall off and take me with him, but then he pulled himself up. We were both on the flat. We did it.

I pulled my leg out from under Rexx's chest, and we helped each other maneuver in the tight space. I steadied myself against the slick surface of the cube behind me and tried to slow my rapid breathing. There was just enough room on the flat to sit with both legs crossed, knees against the other cube. It was about ten feet wide if I had to guess, so we would be able to take turns lying down and sleeping, at least.

"How is your chest? Is it okay?" I asked through pants.

"Yeah, yeah, it's fine. Your foot? I didn't twist it, did I?"

"No." Though, with all the adrenaline, I doubted I would know if my foot were injured.

I leaned over Rexx to glance back in the direction we had come from. Miles in the distance, near the road where we'd abandoned the car, lights danced like fireflies in the night sky. Search drones.

They've realized we're gone, I thought. *But, for now, they are searching in the wrong place. Hopefully, by the time they notice their mistake, we will be far away.*

I felt like I could finally breathe fully for the first time in hours. I leaned my head back against the cargo cube and took a deep breath.

"Hey," I said to Rexx as we both sat in the darkness.

"Hey," he replied.

"We made it this far."

"Yeah, we made it this far." Rexx reached out and squeezed my hand. "We made it this far," he repeated.

After a few more moments of silence, Rexx asked the question I'd been dreading. "Hey, Patch? What's the end game here if there is no one left to find? What if this Veritas Ring has been reduced to the ash pile like everything else? Are we just going to live our days in an abandoned zone? Hunting radioactive squirrels?" At least his sense of humor hadn't disappeared completely.

"I don't know. I haven't gotten that far yet." I didn't intend for the words to come out as rash as they did, especially after Rexx's attempt to lighten the mood. "Everything I thought I knew up until this point has turned out to be wrong, so I don't know." I heard Rexx move next to me. I knew, even though it was dark, that he had turned his head toward me. I continued. "Everything I was, everything I prided myself on, it's gone, Rexx."

Rexx didn't say anything, just stretched his arm out behind my head and pulled me into his shoulder. I didn't really want comfort. I was afraid that if I let my guard down, I would fall apart. But after about two minutes, the tension released like the unwinding of a string. We stayed there like that for several minutes. My eyes started to tingle, and I lifted my head.

"We did what we had to do," he said.

"Yeah." But that didn't alter the intense events and life changes that had taken place. We were surviving minute by minute and had no disillusions about how it could end. How it would likely end.

I wondered as I sat there if others before me had taken the same journey. Would I ever know? Would there be answers where we were headed, or just more unanswered questions?

We used the light on the multi-tool to illuminate the compass attachment every few minutes, to make sure we continued to head northwest.

About two hours into the journey, the flat started to slow down. We looked past the edge of the cargo box in front of us, but there was nothing to suggest an approaching city or lights of any kind. All signs pointed to us still being in the middle of nowhere, on a track in the desert.

I put the backpack on and got up into a crouching position, ready to jump off the flat if needed. And run where, I didn't know.

"There's nothing here. Why are we stopping?" I whispered. The answer came when a robotic arm came into view up ahead on the right side. It looked like a smaller version of the arm that loaded and unloaded the cargo cubes at the port, but there was no clawlike hand at the end. It stood mounted next to the track like a snake raised and ready to strike. A large solar panel and a wind turbine were mounted on top.

"I think it's some kind of charging station," Rexx whispered back.

The flat slid to a complete stop, and Rexx and I readied ourselves to jump off if anything should happen. We heard a subtle swooshing sound and the flat jostled slightly. Rexx crawled to the other end and peeked over the edge.

"It's plugged in," he whispered. "I think it's just charging."

It made sense. It was nighttime. Even if there were solar panels on top of the cargo cubes, the battery top-off in Tucson would send the flat only so far. I realized with relief that these charging stops could be the key. They would provide a chance to get off if needed.

After about five anxious minutes, the snake released its jaws and the flat started to move once more.

"Why don't I take the first shift and you try to get some sleep?" Rexx said as we rode on in the absolute darkness. After the hours of waiting outside Tucson, and the travel so far, it was likely two in the morning or so. The stars and the small sliver of moon provided the only light overhead. But away from the city, the stars were brighter than I had ever seen them.

"All right. But keep an eye on the compass, to make sure we are still heading northwest. If we change direction, we need to get off. Somehow."

Rexx held the light so I could rearrange myself. The beam illuminated some words on the side of the crate.

"Wait, hold that a little higher. What does that say?" I said.

Rexx guided the light up so that the words printed on the side of the cube were visible.

PROTEIN POWDER. CONTAINS BLEND OF MEALWORM, CRICKET, AND BLACK FLY LARVAE.

"Oh my Board, did you know that's what the protein powder is made out of?" I asked, trying for what seemed like the fifth time that day to keep the bile from rising in my throat.

"Umm. No. No, I didn't," Rexx said. "I guess I thought it was probably dried beans or something. But it makes sense. They reproduce quickly."

"Yeah, I don't think I can think too much about that right now," I replied. I saw Rexx crack a smile.

I set the backpack right next to Rexx's legs and maneuvered myself so that I was parallel to the cargo cubes, then laid my head on the pack. I didn't know how I was going to fall asleep. But after only a few minutes, the rocking of the flat, the warmth of Rexx's hand on my arm, and the darkness of the night won out, and my eyes closed.

Rexx, Amara, and I were standing in front of the couch in my parents' apartment. We were eighteen and each strapped with gold sensor rings around our wrists, waist, and ankles. Holographic avatars stood opposite each of us as we beat, struck, and pulled the semitranslucent globalist soldiers to the ground. I swiped at one with a holographic laser, and her head disintegrated into a red mist. Once one was down, another popped up, ready to be defeated.

Amara took out an average of two for every one Rexx and I each defeated. She had an innate talent. Once we trimmed down twenty, we advanced to the next level.

Duty, Honor, Country—one of our favorite amusements. We'd play it for hours after being let out of training for the day, determined to work together to protect our nation from globalist combatants. My mom peeked in the room several times to check to see if there was anything we needed. It was a physically exhausting match, and after about an hour we collapsed on the couch, laughing.

Rexx put his arm around Amara, pulled her close, and kissed the top of her head. I skipped out of the room and came back with snacks, and we chatted until the alarms on our IDs alerted us in unison that it was time to return to the dormitories.

"Patch. Patch, get up. The flat is slowing down again."

Rexx jiggled my shoulder and there was fear in his voice. I shot straight up and clutched my backpack to my chest as I tried to get my bearings. Amara's laugh echoed in my memory. *I'm so sorry I ever doubted you.*

The flat was indeed slowing down, but there was no sign of another charging station or city anywhere in sight. Why would it slow down for no reason? Had someone found us? I looked up and searched the sky. It was starting to lighten, but it was still too dark to see much. There were no telltale lights of search drones. Why were we slowing down?

Then the answer became apparent as I heard a click and the train started to veer to the right.

"Oh shit," Rexx said. "It's changing directions. We have to get off. We have to get off now. Come on, come on. Get up."

Rexx stood, balancing against a cargo cube as I flung the backpack over my shoulder and secured the clip in front of my chest.

"We have to jump. Before it picks up speed again," Rexx said. I tried to shake the tiredness from my still-sleeping brain. The flat had slowed to what I guessed was fifteen or twenty miles per hour to make the turn. Not exactly a speed I was comfortable landing at. Especially since I couldn't really see what we'd be landing in. We'd anticipated this moment could come, but now that it was here, I was silently panicking.

Rexx took my hand and we both inched to the edge.

"Can you do this?" I asked as we looked at the blur of passing ground. "Yes. We can do this," I answered myself before Rexx had a chance.

Rexx flattened himself against the cube, creating space for me to go in front of him. He wanted me to go first. He knew jumping would be more natural for him. He was the type of person who jumped.

I squeezed in front of him and looked out over the edge. Rexx still held the multi-tool in his hand and he turned the light on quickly, illuminating our surroundings slightly. Silhouettes of a tall brush to the edge of the tracks. A field maybe? It didn't look so bad. I bent my legs slightly, but they buckled. I prepared to jump against every instinct telling me there was nothing but pain on the other side of the decision. The train was picking up speed.

"Just push me," I said quietly.

"What?" Rexx yelled as his hand found my shoulder.

"Just push me!"

Part of me didn't believe he would do it. But then I was tumbling on the ground, over and over like a log cascading down a hill. Flashes of metal, flashes of wild grain, elbows, knees. I closed my eyes, unsure whether I'd cleared the tracks at all, whether my body was simply tumbling or being ripped apart. When I stopped, faceup at the night sky, I couldn't find my breath. I opened my mouth to inhale, my lips reaching for something, but my lungs wouldn't respond. I started to panic, wondering if perhaps I had a collapsed lung. Then, after about twenty seconds, the spasm ended, and air seeped into my lungs slowly, like water filling a bathtub.

I tried to focus, to listen to my body to see if it demanded acknowledgment of a serious injury. There was an aching in my hand where my chip had been, and my arms felt bruised and scraped from the brush, but there was nothing drastic. I moved one arm across my chest, then the other. I bent my legs to make sure they still worked, then raised my head from the ground. A slice of sun had begun to rise over the horizon.

"Rexx?"

No answer. Had he jumped? Was he still on the flat? He'd pushed me; he'd actually pushed me like I'd asked. But had he been able to make the jump himself? Then, in the distance, I heard my name.

"Patch, Patch, are you okay? Where are you?" We were both alive. Alive, and off the flat that was about to head in the wrong direction. My surroundings became more visible. I was lying in a dusty field. Then I realized it wasn't dust—it was ash.

A field covered in ash. I turned my head. Behind me was a large expanse that had fallen victim to a wildfire sometime in recent years. A few small saplings measuring a foot or less were the only signs of renewal.

I got to my feet and looked around for the backpack, which had come off during my tumble. It was several yards from where I'd landed. I put it back on and then headed in the direction of Rexx's voice. Pain radiated through my aching body with each step. Who knew how many more jumps like this we'd have to take before our journey was over? I rubbed the ash off my arms and felt moisture. Blood. My bandage was no longer on my hand, and the cut had reopened. From what I could tell, all other injuries were just surface wounds.

Rexx drew near me. He had a slight limp but didn't look too worse for wear.

"Are you all right?" he said as he wrapped me in a big hug. Then he stepped back and scanned me up and down.

"Just bumped and bruised. You?"

"Same."

I took a closer look at his face. A large bruise on his upper cheek was darkening by the second. I dug out the first aid kit and began to dress our wounds.

"Where do you think we are?" I asked.

"I don't know. Can't be sure how fast the flat was going, but I'd think we would at least be in northern Arizona or southern Nevada by now. You were asleep for about four hours. You even slept through another charge."

Four hours? I felt terrible; Rexx had been awake all night. We would have to find a place out of sight for him to get a few hours of rest.

I dug in the backpack for a handful of protein bars (they weren't large but boasted enough protein and nutrients to sustain someone for five hours), and one of my cucumbers.

"What flavor do you want? Looks like a few blueberries, a couple lemon, and some vanilla."

"I'll take a lemon," Rexx replied. "Well, lemon, cricket, mealworm, and fly," he added with a smirk.

I broke the cucumber in half and handed one end to Rexx. I wolfed down my blueberry-flavored protein bar, but savored every bite of cucumber. Who knew when, or if, we'd ever taste fresh vegetables again once our supply was gone.

We walked alongside the track until we reached the place where the ties split. One path continued northwest and one veered off east. I was instantly relieved. There was a track still heading northwest; the flat we'd been on was simply not traveling in that direction.

"We should probably just follow the track until we come across one of those robot arm things," Rexx said. I looked around at the fire damage that surrounded us. The air tasted clean enough, but you could never be sure.

"Do you have your mask with you?" I asked Rexx, trying to keep the alarm from my voice.

"Yeah, it's in my side pocket."

"Maybe we should put them on for a bit." Death by pollution still wasn't a threat as immediate as the others we faced, but it gave me an ounce of control. I put my mask on, securing the band around my head so my hands were free, then dug out the compass again. The tracks likely continued northwest, but I wasn't about to take any chances. I felt incredibly exposed. We were out in the middle of nowhere, which was good, but also dangerous. Likely no one would find us unless they already knew where to look, but if a search drone showed up, there was nowhere for us to go.

As we walked, I thought about my father's story. Tried to remember every single part I could, but it all had felt so abstract at the time, and the details, the pesky details, mixed and molded until I wasn't sure which bits belonged where. But I tried to sift through the dust and pick out any stones I could.

There had been uprisings during the time of the Seclusion, in the late twenties and early thirties. People who fought back were removed, imprisoned, killed even? The survivors formed the Veritas Ring. The bombing of 2029, always blamed on North Korea, may have been the design of our government to persuade citizens to fall in line in the name of safety. That was what some thought. Things used to be different—very different, it seemed. How exactly? People used to have a say in the way the government operated. In the beginning, many didn't believe what the Board showed us was the truth. Which raised the question: *What is the truth?*

Rexx and I finished the last of the water. We wouldn't make it long without more.

I thought of my dad, not his story, but him. I replayed memories and conversations. What was he going through? Was he talking about his daughter? Would he ever know it was his wife who had turned him in? I wondered what he was thinking of me at that very minute. Was he angry? Was there a chance he was proud? I imagined him as an adventurous teenager, hiding behind fences and recycling bins with his brothers. I struggled to recall every feature of his face, painfully aware that without my ID, there were no photos. *I'll see his face again,* I told myself. *I'll see his face again.*

A couple hours later the sun was high in the sky and our thirst had become hard to ignore. The fire damage started to peter out, and up ahead we saw a thicket of towering bushes. We picked up our pace. But as we neared the bushes, getting close enough so that what was beyond them came into view, we immediately halted and dropped to the ground.

Beyond the bushes was a city.

CHAPTER 9

I RECOGNIZED THE contours of buildings. My eyes darted around and my senses spiked.

"Patch, I think it's abandoned. Look—there aren't any streetlights or signs for ports of entry. This could be one of those towns people used to live in before the Seclusion. Like on the map."

I squinted to try to get a better look. When I was convinced we weren't in imminent danger, I slowly inched around the bushes. He was right: there were no signs of habitation, but we were still a bit too far away to be sure.

"Well, we should get a little closer," I said after several minutes of squinting into the distance. "Where there's a city, there's usually a water source." From my current vantage point, I searched for valleys and foliage that appeared greener than that around it, a tactic often employed at work when looking for water to test. Water runs downhill, and surrounding plants are typically well nourished. I spotted a valley in the distance.

Rexx was peering around as well, likely scouting for the same thing. He looked nervous, as if he would startle if I touched him, but there was a hint of something in his eyes that had been missing for the past two days—excitement. Danger be damned—he was eager to explore. It was good to know that part of him was there to stay.

Rexx and I trudged through the brush to scope out the area. The grass was so thick, it felt a bit like walking through waist-deep water. We had to lift our knees high in the air, and when we emerged, our pants were sporting a few hitchhikers, grass strands and burrs, from the trek.

The goal was to find some water and perhaps a place to rest. Somewhere indoors, or beneath a natural overhang, anywhere that would help us avoid detection if a search drone passed overhead.

We approached the city. It was large and sprawling. The first thing I noticed was how short the buildings were compared to those at home. The tallest I saw was three stories, but most were a single level. The misuse of space would never pass in a modern city, and it instantly became clear—my first interpretation of the map was plausible. The city was uninhabited, and not registered as a zone considered for future development with the Natural Resources Department. My heart rate started to climb—a bit from fear, but primarily from the impatient eagerness I felt. There was something important in the town. Something we needed to see. I could feel it.

The abandoned streets were deeply saturated with echoes of a former life. We stepped gently. An eerie cloud hung over us, casting a darkness as we walked.

There were no apparent signs of surveillance, only visuals that confirmed it'd been decades since anyone had set foot there. I clutched my arms to my chest.

Vehicles lined the road, wearing coats of rust. Large buildings and shopping centers with hollow window frames showed off their empty shelves as we passed. A sign lay on the ground, clearly separated from its support rods, which stood a few feet away. I crossed to get a closer look.

CHEAPEST IN WILDCLIFF—ONLY $7.49 REGULAR $8.75
DIESEL

Wildcliff, I thought. The word appeared on numerous weathered signs. Rexx and I continued walking in silence, but our hands hovered an inch apart, one ready to grab the other at the slightest sign of danger.

The artwork on signs was different than anything I'd seen before, and storefronts were void of the national emblem. The words *America One* were nowhere in sight.

I thought for a moment that some of the buildings might contain food, but then realized anything remaining on a shelf after roughly sixty years should probably not be ingested.

"What do you think?" I asked.

"Well, we can probably pull out the topo map and see if we can get a better idea of where we are. Maybe Wildcliff is on the map from the van and we can compare the two. Then try to find some water," he said. He was like me in that way; giving himself a job helped him catch his bearings. "Now that we know where we are," Rexx continued.

"Good point." We wandered a bit farther until we found steps to sit on, in front of a large brick building. I spread open the maps, located Wildcliff on the old one, and tried to deduce where it would be on the new. We were near the border between Arizona and Nevada. There were numerous lakes nearby, but with the scale, it was difficult to tell where exactly they were. Our best bet was to continue downhill and into the valley.

"What is that about?" Rexx's voice suspended my chain of thought. I looked to where his eyes were directed behind me. The doors to an expansive building were shackled shut with a thick chain coiled several times around the handles. The facade of the chained building was mainly brick, two stories with a third jutting up from the middle. The steps I was sitting on led up to the chained doors. To my left, aligned with the foot of the steps, was a wide brick wall with the word LI__ARY in rusty metal letters decorating the front. The word had a hint of familiarity to it, but I couldn't put my finger on a definition.

The windows were boarded up. It was odd, chiefly because all of the other buildings that we passed had seemed wide open, their doors ajar or missing, the windows broken. I didn't like it.

"Should we check it out?" I asked. "We're looking for any clues that could lead us to information about the Veritas Ring. Anything suggesting they were still around when this town was shut down would be helpful. Maybe there's something in there."

Rexx smiled a half-convincing smile, scratched the back of his neck, and then said, "Well, we did want some answers, didn't we?"

We stared at the chained door. There was something in there. Something people either wanted to keep in, or keep others from finding.

"Well, here we go." Rexx kicked hard at the wood. The rotting pieces broke more easily than he anticipated as his leg became stuck in the splintered opening. I jumped forward to balance him as he pried it out. Together the two of us tore away at the remaining sections of withered lumber until there was a substantial hole in the door.

"You sure about this?" I asked.

"Look, Patch . . . ," Rexx started gently. "I know you want to make things right. I don't see how we're realistically going to help your father, but what I do know is it's not going to happen unless we start finding some answers." He gestured toward the hole in the door.

We locked eyes for a moment and then both ducked inside. It was dark, and it took time for our eyes to adjust. The first thing I noticed were the bookshelves, from floor to ceiling, stripped bare and covered in a thin layer of ash. We walked farther inside, with slow, cautious steps, and something crunched in the dark underneath our feet.

"It's a library," Rexx said. "A place that used to be filled with books, printed books from all over the world. My grandfather told me about them."

We spotted a large dark pyramid of objects in the back of the library. I couldn't tell what they were. As I walked, my limbs became shaky and a sour taste filled my mouth. I inched closer. Burned, curled shapes. There had been a fire here, and we were standing in its ashes. With each step, gray particles swirled into the air. The shapes, what were they?

Then, all at once, I realized what they were, and I stopped in my tracks. I realized what I was breathing. The entire horrific reality shifted into focus.

The decaying remains were as forgotten as the victims' names. My stomach rolled, and I placed my hand on it instinctively and turned my torso away from the scene. I was overwhelmed with competing urges—to run and to vomit. Rexx's clammy hand reached out and grabbed mine and I grabbed his right back, tightly. I couldn't look again, not just yet. I stood there, hunched over, catching my breath. Slowly, I felt my blood pressure stabilize and I straightened myself up. Together, we walked forward.

The dead were lined up against empty shelves. In other places, skeletons were heaped in a crisscross pattern five feet high.

The grisly remains served as silent witnesses as we looked around: an echo of our country's dark past. Rexx dropped my hand, causing a chill to run up my spine, and walked closer. I watched. He wanted to see the details, but most of the details were gone, rotted away with the passage of time. A few scraps remained—bright blue fabric with a floral pattern, a clump of hair that had somehow escaped the flames, charred jewelry on a detached hand. Rexx was careful not to disturb them. He mumbled to himself, and I watched his lips; he was counting.

I imagined the bodies in their full forms, wondering what they looked like. How many men and how many women? There were smaller frames too—children. I thought about the chain on the door. Someone must have come in and stacked them afterward, perhaps even added more bodies to the pile, then rechained the entrance to keep them hidden away. I couldn't contain it anymore. I turned and vomited behind a shelf. Tears of anger welled in my eyes when I stood again. My mind unbidden, played the scene—the atrocity as it took place, what the room would smell like days and weeks later, the feast that the wiggly maggots must have had, and imagining it happening again and again in other towns, in other buildings.

Who were these people? How was this ever justified? Why didn't someone stop this?

"Seventy-five," Rexx said matter-of-factly. "There are seventy-five bodies in this room alone. Seventy-five." He stormed out of the building, punching through what remained of the door as he left. Whether he was going to search for other buildings occupied by the dead, wanted to be alone, or just wanted to scream outdoors, I didn't know.

I stood in the deafening silence, not ready to leave yet, ignoring the musty smell that surrounded me. This was no accident; it was a calculated slaughter. But why? Were these the remains of those who would not submit, would not move to the dense urban centers, or who would not part with their possessions? The sheer thought of it tore at my insides.

At that moment, even though I still didn't know the full picture, I hated our government. I hated the Board's lies and all they stood for; hatred overtook the fear. There was something else alongside the grotesque hate—shame. Shame at being so willfully ignorant for the first twenty-two years of my life. My eyes grew hot, and I memorized the room, letting the despair wash over me as I tried to absorb the courage of the departed and silently let them know that someone was here, that some-one had seen what happened. I knew right then that Rexx and I had a part to play. I just wasn't sure what it was yet.

CHAPTER 10

AFTER LEAVING THE library, I caught up with Rexx as he walked swiftly out of the city. We wandered, haunted, for nearly two hours until we found a creek. I pulled out the water bottle and held it under a small cascade so that fresh water ran through the built-in filter. Any lightening of the mood we'd felt on our exploration was gone.

We found an inlet with a rock overhang that would shield us from overhead surveillance, and I decided to give Rexx a few hours to sleep before navigating back to the tracks. While he dozed, I spread out the maps and tried to focus on what lay ahead.

My thoughts kept getting interrupted by the scene I'd just witnessed. The little details, like the scraps of fabric that survived their owners' demise, imprinted themselves in my brain. I would never forget how the charred bones appeared—stacked as heedlessly as the pile of the contents from the van before it was set ablaze. Would I ever have the chance to know the full story of what had happened to those people? I thought about my father's history, and wondered if the generation before his knew the scale of what had happened to those who'd disappeared.

I tried to reconcile the map from 2030 with the world I knew. Cities like the one we were in had been shut down. Everyone lived in dense urban centers such as our former home in Tucson. However, the area of these large cities had expanded greatly since 2030. Other circled cities on the old map were underwater. I read some of the names—Miami, Jacksonville, New Orleans, Houston, Boston, New York City, Los Angeles, San Francisco. Oceanic rise happened slowly, inch by inch, or all at once after a tropical storm, when the waters simply did not recede again. I wondered if people were still living in these cities at the time they were wiped off the map, or if the residents had already been moved.

There were multiple states with no red circles in them—Montana, North Dakota, South Dakota, and Wyoming. I didn't know why I'd never wondered about these before. The sight of the empty states bothered me, but I couldn't pin down why.

Seeing how many smaller cities had been wiped out and picturing all of the people who had once lived there, who had made a life in cities just like the one we were in, threw me. I compared their location to my topographic map. I racked my brain for zone activity in the apparently empty states. I came up blank. What was taking place there now? Could they be the sites of the elusive redemption camps?

As I sat, all my senses on alert, I played through various scenarios of our current situation. Then, when an hour or so had passed, I dug through my backpack and pulled out my book. I started to read. I didn't understand most of the references; I didn't know what was fact and what was fiction. I didn't know whether the places and dates mentioned were real. But I read anyway. Sometimes I reached a passage and read it several times over.

I did this on page fourteen.

If the soul is left in darkness, sins will be committed. The guilty one is not he who commits the sin, but the one who causes the darkness.

And on page twenty-seven:

Have no fear of robbers or murderers. They are external dangers, petty dangers. We should fear ourselves. Prejudices are the real robbers; vices the real murderers.

And again on page fifty-one:

In passing, we might say that success is a hideous thing. Its false similarity to merit deceives men. . . . They confuse heaven's radiant stars with a duck's footprint left in the mud.

I wondered as I read, if it was a book that I would ever finish. It was so long. Longer than any other in the suitcase that day. Was that why I had reached for it? I didn't really know what had compelled me to grab that book over the others. But, as I looked around at my current predicament, I realized that the chances of reaching the final pages were slim.

"Do you really think they can help us, Patch?" Rexx said from the ground next to me, apparently now awake from his rest. "If the Veritas Ring is real? I mean, you saw the same thing I did back there," he continued. "They weren't able to help them; why would they be able to help us?"

"I don't know. But hope is all we have."

"Hope," he said bitterly. "We can't believe anything we were taught. Maybe there aren't redemption camps at all."

I knew he was thinking about Amara. I had never doubted that she ended up in the military, that there was a chance she was still out there somewhere, healthy and happy. That flame of hope had been reduced to a fading ember, and now even that was dying.

Something popped into my mind. "Hey, Rexx? When my father was talking yesterday, you said something, before you got up and walked away. You said, 'I knew it.' When we were in the van, you didn't seem surprised by anything we found; is there something I should know?"

Rexx dug his hands into the loose earth and stretched his bare feet into the stream. He didn't answer, and I could tell he was carefully formulating his words. Rexx was not the sort of person who felt the need to say all his thoughts out loud immediately. It was one of the qualities I most admired about him. He always meant what he said and never used words lightly.

"There are a lot of things I never told you, Patch." What could he mean? We shared everything, or so I'd thought. I tried to prepare myself for what might come next. He reached his hand out to the side and wrapped it around mine. "I don't know why—we've had so many opportunities by now, and I wasn't trying to hide things from you. I guess I just didn't think there was any use dredging it up. I mean, what's the point?"

Where is he going with this? I wondered.

"But now it's different; it's just the two of us." He looked at me with sad eyes.

I knew what he meant about things being different; I could feel myself changing. Like a snake shedding skin that had become too constricting, I was ready for my new self to emerge.

"I found a letter once," Rexx said.

"A letter?"

"A paper one. It was hidden in an old cabinet, taped to the underside of a drawer. It must have survived so many searches. How they never found it, I don't know. It was from my grandpa Victor. He died before I was born. I think I told you that, at least. He wrote about his parents and how they were from Mexico."

Mexico. We weren't taught much about it, one of the many countries listed as dangerous on newscasts. Countries outside our borders were always presented as abstract locations that seemed to exist on a different plane than America.

"In his letter, he explained what happened to several members of my family before I ever came into the picture. It just, it started to make more sense after your dad's story. I read the letter curled underneath my blanket with a flashlight," Rexx said. He picked up a stick and started swirling it in the water in front of him. "Then I burned it. I knew it was risky, and I still play the scene over and over. I think about how it could have gone."

"What else was in it, Rexx? What did it say?" I put my hand on his upper arm.

"It was about three pages," he continued. "My grandfather talked about how people were getting kicked out of our country left and right. Good people. People who'd been here for most of their lives. People just like us. I didn't know what to make of it. He said the requirements kept changing for who could stay and who had to go. That his family would try to meet the requirements, only to have them change again. He said one day his family reported for a mandatory English language and patriotism test. They reported in good spirits, with high hopes after months of studying. They never returned. He never heard from them again, Patch. My grandfather said they must have failed the test, or there was never really a test to begin with. He lived the rest of his life wondering what had happened to them."

I didn't know what to say. To do absolutely nothing wrong, to spend months bending over backward trying to make yourself fit in, and still be discarded . . .

"The letter, I didn't understand it all up until this point. I just knew it used to be different, that there was more to the story than what we've been told. For the last few days I've been trying to remember every word. At the end, he talked about how the Board said everyone would be treated equally under the new laws. He talked about how equal did not equate to just, and under the new system, with 'so-called' equality came a loss of history, a loss of tradition, a loss of heritage, a loss of plain and simple facts and the ability to use discriminate judgment. It came with a total loss of identity. It came with the loss of everything. Patch, I've known all this time where my ancestors are from. I've known about this one, blurry piece of history. And I never told you. But now you know."

Rexx's ancestors were from a place not far from where we grew up, yet they couldn't be part of his life. I wondered if my future held any days without a constant barrage of new information.

When dusk was imminent, we walked back in the directions of the tracks. It took longer in the dark, but it was better than being exposed in the daylight.

We had drunk all the water we could and topped off our bottle. We had enough food to last roughly four more days if we scrimped and conserved energy. After that, well, we didn't know yet.

When we finally reached a charging station several hours later, we found a spot to sit and wait. We took turns sleeping and keeping watch. In the early morning, a flat finally arrived. Climbing on a stopped, charging flat was a breeze compared to jumping off and jumping on a moving one. We settled in for the ride.

It became clearer with each passing hour how much of the country was either abandoned or zoned off. In the span of just a few hours, we passed half a dozen other ghost towns. We passed entire landscapes that had been clear-cut of all trees and strip-mined for resources. We passed areas that had clearly been lashed by storms. But we also passed serene, open land. All this space, I thought. What a damn waste.

As a Tier 3, I had been fortunate to have my own apartment. But Tier 4s and 5s, their buildings were stuffed to capacity. Knowing there was plenty of space for everyone to live comfortably was appalling. Seeing it on a map was one thing, but riding through abandoned tracts of land hour after hour was another.

I fell asleep for a few hours and woke to Rexx insistently jiggling my shoulder. I looked at his face. His eyes were burning with anger, and he looked harried.

"What? What's going on? What happened?" I asked, confused and disoriented.

He didn't answer me, just pointed out the side of the flat. I rubbed my tired face and leaned over so I could see. At first I didn't notice anything, but then I saw the lights up ahead. Still far away, and not in the direction the tracks were headed. We sat frozen for a moment, unsure of what to do. If the tracks stayed on course, we wouldn't pass through whatever was taking place over there.

"Are we still headed northwest?" I asked Rexx somewhat rhetorically. He would have told me if we'd changed directions. "Where are we?" As the words came out they sounded accusatory, as if Rexx had led us there on purpose.

"Somewhere in northern Nevada. There shouldn't be anything here," he hissed back. "It's a whole lot of nothing on the map."

"Maybe it's just a factory, or some farmland," I suggested.

"We're so far away from a city; why would they put a farm out here?" He was right. Farming and food production mostly took place indoors, and farms were usually right on the edges of urban areas so workers didn't have to venture far. "Also, I don't see any buildings," he said.

The flat pulled us closer to the site. Within minutes, we would be passing within a quarter mile of the lights. I reached over and grabbed Rexx's hand. We had no choice. We had to keep going and hope we weren't seen.

We rolled closer, until soon we were almost directly across from the lights. We could make out several silhouettes of people. Guards maybe. Then, as the flat ascended slightly, the view changed.

"No. It can't be," Rexx blurted out. But he wasn't talking in a scared tone—rather one of astonishment.

When I realized what we were looking at, I couldn't contain the gasp that escaped. Out in the distance was something I'd seen images of since my childhood.

The site of the 2029 Bombing.

CHAPTER 11

IT WAS MAGNIFICENT. An enormous bowl-shaped depression with a raised rim. The steep, lifeless edges revealed striations in the earth—a mix of bright reds, browns, and oranges. Images on a screen did not do it justice and I stared in awe. Not even the sprinkling of Compos around the rim, like ants crawling on a left-out bowl of milk, diluted my fascination.

We had both memorized the specs of the nuclear bombing and had been given tests on the details throughout our training. *It left a crater with a diameter measuring approximately two miles wide and 450 feet deep. The radiation in the vicinity remained at lethal levels for twenty-six years, and the area still isn't free of radiation,* I recited to myself. *Due to America's swift retaliation, we have remained free of further nuclear threat to this day.*

I remembered what my father had said—that some suspected the bombing was not the work of foreign terrorists at all, but rather staged by the Board to get people to fear the outside and submit to the new laws of the land. It sounded crazy when I first heard it, but after what we had seen in Wildcliff, it now seemed par for the course.

The Compos did not move around a lot, mostly stayed two at each post, spaced at equal distances around the rim. Compo vehicles were parked along the road near the site. I spotted three drones hovering above the crater. Rexx and I stayed still. One drone started to wander closer, and we flattened ourselves against the cube behind us. Did it realize we were here, or did the drones always check the passing cargo flats? There was no way to know as it continued toward us. The drone was about the size of a crow.

I tried to think of what on earth we could do, if there was anything we could use if it approached. I quickly thought through the contents of the backpack. Was there something we could throw that we were willing to part with? We could go without a meal or two, but if our protein bars didn't knock the drone down, then all we'd have done was waste food. It continued straight for us, and I felt every muscle in my body tense as it approached. The drone dropped as it approached the back of the cargo flat, maintaining the same speed. Neither Rexx nor I dared speak, just in case it had an audio sensor. Then it disappeared. I could no longer see it. *Where is it?* I mouthed to Rexx. It must have been behind us, out of view. I considered peeking around the cube behind me, to see if I could spot it, but I froze. It had appeared right next to Rexx. Hovering right by the opening, staring at us. Then Rexx did something that I would never have expected. In a flash, he reached out and grabbed it. Grabbed one of its quadcopter legs, pulled it down, and chucked it underneath the cargo flat. Instinctively, I grabbed the back of his shirt, afraid he would fall. The flat didn't even bump as the drone was crushed under its wheels.

Rexx and I sank to the floor in relief. The cargo flat curved around a mountain pass, and the sight of the 2029 bombing disappeared from view.

"I can't believe you just did that!" I said in astonishment after several minutes of sitting in shock. "That was incredible."

"That was insane," Rexx replied. "It could have pulled me off the flat. I don't know what I was thinking."

"Well, you just saved us," I replied. "Thank you."

"It probably saw us, Patch. Once they notice it's gone, they'll review the footage if they haven't already." He didn't say more. No more needed to be said.

Night fell again, and we stayed on the flat without incident. I jumped off only once (to empty my bladder) while the train was charging.

Zone 36 was our target, an eleven-mile-wide zone southwest of Portland that had been shut down for at least twenty years due to fracking-induced pollution that had seeped into the soil and groundwater. The last known location of the Veritas Ring.

I felt good about our plan, but when we got within a hundred miles, my blood pressure started to rise, and the hair on the back of my neck stood on alert. Zone perimeters implemented different security protocols, dependent on size, landscape, the reason for the original quarantine.

Zone 36 shared a significant border with the city of Portland, now more than double the size it allegedly was in 2030, according to the maps. We would need to get off the flat and enter the zone from the southern side if we stood a chance of not being caught. Problem was, we could only make a slightly educated guess as to when we'd be close. If we started walking too soon, the distance might be too far to cover on foot. If we started walking too late, there was a higher risk of being noticed by Compos, farmers, factory workers, energy workers, or others given clearance to work outside city limits.

Based on our maps, we would pass over a decent-sized river before nearing the city of Portland. We decided to use that as our landmark. We just had to figure out how to get off the flat, which was cruising along at top speed.

I had an idea. The night before, the flat had slowed down when there was a large boulder in the middle of the tracks. A mechanical arm moved the obstruction out of the way; then, with the route clear, the flat recommenced its journey.

If we could somehow convince the flat that there was an obstruction in the tracks, we might be able to get it to slow down.

Throwing something in the tracks in front of us wouldn't work. We were moving too fast for the object to hit the ground before it would already be behind us. But, if we could somehow trick the sensor . . . It was worth a try. All we had to do was get to the front of the flat.

We were riding behind the first cube from the front. The cubes were approximately ten feet high. It wouldn't be easy. I told Rexx what I was thinking. We decided we needed to go up and over for it to work.

Rexx squatted down as best he could in the cramped space, and I climbed to a sitting position on top of his shoulders. I balanced myself by digging my hands into the two cubes on either side while he stood up. Rexx was about six feet tall, so, when sitting on his shoulders, I could grab the edge of the top of the head cube.

I was relieved to find that unlike the smooth sides, there was a lip skirting the edge of the top. *The cubes must open from the top,* I thought. I raised myself up into a standing position, with one foot on each of Rexx's shoulders, painfully aware of the speed we were traveling. Even in the dark, I could feel the trees whipping past. I took a deep breath and lunged forward. We were moving so quickly, I had to stay in a kneeling position for a moment to get my bearings.

I crawled to the front and looked down. There was a small ledge, only about six inches, between the cube and the front of the flat. I wasn't confident I could land on it without support.

Rexx needed to come up as well. I crawled back over to the other side.

"You have to jump up. There's a lip. I think you can grab it if you jump," I said.

Rexx tried, but his fingers landed a few inches short.

"I have an idea," he said. Then he removed his shoes and began climbing up, one foot on the first cube, and one on the next. I had no idea he could do that. He shinnied with ease up to the top and clutched the lip. I gripped his elbow and helped him hoist himself the rest of the way.

Once we were both on top and at the front, it was time to lower me down safely. I swung my legs over, painfully aware that if I slipped, I would be crushed underneath the train.

Rexx lay down, his arms hanging over the side, and together we managed to get me down to the ledge. Clutching one of Rexx's hands, I used my other hand to unclip my backpack.

Then we stayed like that, listening intently in the darkness for rushing water. Rexx turned on our multi-tool light every few minutes to see if there were any signs of a bridge ahead. After about thirty minutes, we heard it: rushing water, right below us.

Rexx shined the light briefly just to make sure, but there it was, the river. The city wouldn't be far. All signs indicated that this flat was headed to a cargo port outside of Portland.

I gently lowered my backpack with my free hand and swung it back and forth in front of the ledge, where I was hoping there was a sensor beam of some sort used to detect obstructions.

Nothing happened.

No, I thought. *This has to work. This has to. If it doesn't work, we'll be carted right into the Portland cargo facility.*

I tried again, stretching my arm, ignoring the tears of frustration filling my windburned eyes. The knuckles of my other hand whitened as I tried to keep my grip on Rexx's hand.

Then the flat quickly slowed down. I had managed to trick the sensor. Rexx's hand tightened on mine, keeping me from losing my balance with the abrupt change of speed.

As the flat's arm rotated around to clear the tracks, we hopped down into the low-lying brambles and started walking west. We needed to put some space between us and the destination of our ride. After a few hours and several miles of walking in the dark, I started to worry we hadn't ended up where I thought we would. What if that hadn't been the right river? What if we were nowhere near the zone at all? We shifted our direction slightly, turning northwest, and after another hour we stumbled upon an old dirt road and a rusted sign.

ROAD CLOSED—AUTHORIZED PERSONNEL ONLY

About twenty yards later, another sign:

UNAUTHORIZED TRESPASSERS WILL BE DETAINED

Then another:

TURN AROUND—YOU ARE ENTERING A RESTRICTED AREA

"I think we might have found it," Rexx whispered. The well of hope that had been draining slightly with each step now started to refill. We kept on alert for any lights, cameras, or sounds of people. "Do you think we are in the zone already? Or do you think it's farther up?" he asked nervously.

Sometimes zones were clearly marked, but other times they weren't. It was entirely possible that we were already inside. We decided to wait until dawn before continuing. There could be cameras we weren't seeing, and we couldn't take the risk. We had made it so far. We had actually made it.

We waited until the first ray of light shone over the horizon, and then we started to walk parallel to the road.

"Wow, it looks like someone really pulled out all the stops on this one," I whispered as a pit settled in my gut. The barrier we were approaching looked as if it protected some kind of unstable explosive threat. A metal fence stretched north and south, with warning signs adorning it every few yards. This was the first zone I had ever been to that appeared to be entirely surrounded by fencing. Usually, a combination of caution wire, signs, and a single approved point of entry was sufficient. The fencing before us stretched farther than my field of vision.

We had been assigned to previous hydraulic-fracturing sites before, but the borders here indicated another level entirely. Then it dawned on me. The barrier wasn't simply to keep people from poisoning themselves. *There must be something in there that they don't want anyone to see,* I thought. Something that would soon involve us. And maybe some answers.

I noticed cameras and solar panels suspended on metal posts every few yards. Electric fencing. *Shit.* I grabbed Rexx's arm and pulled him behind a large tree with me as my heart leapt up into my throat. After a moment, Rexx pivoted so that he could peek out from behind our hiding place, his mind calculating something I was missing. I watched with hopefulness.

My heart thumped with the anticipation of getting inside the most secure location we had ever seen and discovering what necessitated such measures.

"I don't think it's on," Rexx finally said.

"The fence? Why wouldn't it be on?"

"Look at the panels; they are over two feet wide, larger than any manufactured in at least twenty years. Also, the fence—if you look closely, you can see where the wires used to be taut and they now sag. This hasn't been maintained in years." My thoughts scrambled to understand. I hoped he was right, but I didn't trust it.

"Are you sure? What about the cameras?"

"Those could very well work still. The question is whether anyone is actively monitoring the footage or if it's just being stockpiled somewhere." This wasn't the first time Rexx had said something like this. He had mentioned his theory before when it was just the two of us during fieldwork.

The manpower needed to watch every camera in every room, in every home and building in America, would require, by his estimates, three spies for every two citizens and that was if the monitors did nothing but work and sleep.

It was much more likely, of course, that all the footage was set on some sort of motion detector, and was simply recorded, saved for later, and only reviewed after a red flag was raised. If that was the case, citizens were free to do as they pleased unless suspicion fell on them. If it did, there would be unlimited hours of evidence to sift through for the slightest sign of disloyalty. Maybe the cameras didn't even work, and people were condemned on nothing more than a hunch. It was a nice theory, but not enough to make me walk up to the fence.

". . . however, I think if we keep going . . ." Rexx was still talking, and I realized I hadn't been following.

"Sorry, I missed that last part."

Rexx turned around and slid his back down the tree until he was squatting underneath. He gestured for me to join him.

"Okay. So, from what I can tell, the fence is aging. We know this zone has been here for at least twenty years, possibly more. My guess is the fencing hasn't been updated in that time. The solar panels look worn and the fence is sagging. The main concern is the cameras. I think we need to skirt around the fence and check out each individual camera. There might be one missing, or one obviously broken."

"That sounds like a start, but how do we get over the fence?"

"Yeah, that might be a bit trickier, but I have a plan." He picked up a small stick and a small rock. "Put your hand down on the ground like this." He showed me how he wanted me to place my hand, open and perpendicular to the ground, standing on the outside edge. "Pretend this is the fence." He then placed the rock a few inches from my hand and laid the stick on top, with one side wedged underneath my hand. He pressed on the other end of the stick, and it raised my hand off the ground. "We don't go over. We go under. We just need to find something to wedge underneath long enough to slide under without getting electrocuted."

"That would be wise," I said with a smirk.

"Patch." Rexx put his hand on my shoulder and stared intently into my eyes. "This could go drastically wrong."

"Well, might as well get moving before it gets too bright out here."

We walked within sight of the fence, stopping as we passed each post equipped with a solar panel and camera, looking for a fault. Then, some sixty-odd sections in, there it was—a camera dangling from its wire, free from its mount.

"Stay here a minute," Rexx said.

Before I could say anything, he was off and running, clearing the wild brush easily between the fence and where I stood. He was already holding a large branch and looking around for a rock of some sort. He pulled one up from some tall grass and kept going, barely slowing down as he carried the rock and the branch to the fence. Then, as he showed me, he put the rock down, about two feet from the fence, and balanced the branch on top, aligning one side with the bottom of the fence. He wiggled and pushed until the branch was caught underneath. He shot me a look that said, *This had better work or we're dead*, then pushed on the other side of the branch. To my relief, the fence gave to his pressure and rose.

He put his knee on the branch to steady it, and waved one hand in the air, signaling that I should come over. I grabbed everything and headed in his direction. When I approached, he whispered, "Wedge your backpack under the fence. Careful not to touch the wires." I set it up as tall as it could go, hoping the contents inside would be sturdy enough to support the fencing. Rexx slowly let go of his hold on the branch. Pleasantly, the wedged backpack performed admirably.

"Okay, go, go," Rexx whispered. I dropped down to my stomach, did a quick assessment to make sure that my head and butt would fit underneath the wire—it was going to be close—and began to wriggle my way under the fence, holding my breath the entire time. As soon as my shoes cleared, I inhaled.

I turned around and watched Rexx. It was just as tension-filled watching him as it was doing it myself, but he made it look easy as he swung his legs to the side and completed the mission in half the time it had taken me. Rexx then motioned for me to back away from the fence, and in one fluid motion, he grabbed the bottom of my backpack and pulled it out from underneath. I had to hand it to him; it was a brilliant plan.

Once we'd moved far enough into the zone, Rexx began messing with his clothes, tucking in his shirt and rebuckling his belt. He was so concentrated on putting himself back together that it took him a moment to notice what had already arrested my attention. When he finally looked up, his lips parted slightly.

I had had a feeling that Zone 36 could be in worse shape than other sites we had visited. No matter what I expected, I was not prepared for the scene spread out before me.

It was simultaneously a ghost town and a near replica of the backdrop to many of the international disaster zones I'd seen on television. An old city outside Portland, clearly evacuated in haste, as abandoned vehicles riddled the streets, pointing this way and that. Buildings in disarray surrounded us, some still standing, maintaining at least a shadow of their former glory, while others were nothing but large piles of debris. Off in the distance, towering over the buildings in the foreground, was a tangle of large metal equipment. Actually, *large* was a gross understatement.

The ground beneath my feet felt off-kilter, and I looked down to see that it had split. The sidewalk and the asphalt of the road that ran parallel to the walkway rose and fell. Large fissures between the asphalt plunged deep into the earth.

"Well," I said in a shaky voice, "I guess we start walking and put some space between us and the fence."

I began picking my way through the wreckage one carefully placed step at a time. Rexx stood for a few moments more, watching me. Then, once he was ready, he scrambled up and down the shattered sidewalk on his long legs until he was right beside me—his footing surer than mine.

Each step confirmed that the area had indeed been evacuated in haste. Houses lined the main street, interspersed with "diners," "wineries," and "art galleries," identifiable only by their weathered signs and the long-forgotten items within. Glass lay in drifts on the sidewalk. I wondered whether the windows had been broken by the same disaster that had destroyed the roads, or if the damage had been inflicted by human hands, after the fact.

A front porch was broken into a V, with bleached patio furniture clogging the break in the sagging wood. Clothing of a uniform brown color, desiccated from exposure to the sun, hung stiffly from a line in a backyard. A pair of children's shoes sat next to an empty upside-down kiddie pool in a front yard.

"How does something like this happen?" I muttered. "And how have we not heard about it? I mean, this looks like the scene after a major earthquake."

"I just hope that they were all able to get out before it happened," Rexx said, his eyes fixed on the same pair of children's shoes that had caught my attention. The image of a child small enough to fit into those shoes imprinted itself in my mind. She had sat in her pool and screamed for her parents as the ground began to shake and the water sloshed across her little legs. I shook my head to dislodge the thought.

I put my hand on Rexx's arm to steady myself and noticed that his hands were shaking. With fear or rage, I couldn't tell, and I dared not ask, not yet. But seeing his reaction gave me strength. We were in this together.

I searched for the cameras that were otherwise ubiquitous in our universe, scanning the tops of the buildings still standing, the lampposts whose lights had long since shattered, and for drones in the sky above, but I saw none. They were likely removed after the shutdown—resources better allocated elsewhere. A common story. Other things were missing as well. The town's parking meters, charging stations, recycling compactors, solar panels, and wind turbines had been removed. That, or they had never been there.

"How long ago do you think this happened, Patch?" Rexx asked. His voice shook. "This town, even without the damage, it looks nothing like ours."

I racked my brain, diving deep into the edges, for the minute amount of history I'd been taught.

"This is an old fracking site, right?" I began. "Well, the practice was abandoned more than four decades ago, to my knowledge. So that would mean this town was evacuated sometime after the late forties."

The Board liked to boast about how its ingenuity has made us the cleanest nation on earth. If that's true, then our planet as a whole must be sick and exhausted.

"Why hasn't it been cleaned up, just a little bit?"

We kept walking, and sometimes climbing, down the broken street.

I saw a fire truck up ahead. As we approached it, I noted that at some point something had gone terribly wrong with the emergency vehicle. It was tipped over on its side, and the doors had been extracted from its body. Scattered among the weeds growing through the asphalt were medical utility scissors and discarded needles coated thinly with rust. Moldy, dusty blankets had been piled in bunches next to the fire truck. My stomach turned when I saw the dark stains, a rich brownish color. For a split second I saw a mother and her two children writhing on the ground as others attempted to help. Blood pooled on the freshly clean blankets. Then, as quickly as the images came, they disappeared. I closed my eyes and took a deep breath before opening them again.

We turned onto the next street, and I was relieved to see that the roadway and the buildings flanking it were comparatively undamaged.

"Which way do you want to go?" I asked.

No reply.

"Rexx?" I asked. When he still didn't answer, I turned to find him. Then, suddenly, an arm was around my neck, and a large, calloused hand was on my mouth. A bitter, rancid taste filled my airways, and before I had time to attempt a scream, everything went black.

CHAPTER 12

Mother's arms are made of tenderness, and sweet sleep blesses the child who lies therein.
—Victor Hugo, *Les Misérables*

I MUST HAVE been three or four years old. I was lying on my mother's chest, gasping for breath in between sobs. My long red curls cascaded in every direction. Her strong heartbeat rhythmically whooshed in my ear as she stroked my hair. She was trying to calm me, reassure me after something had frightened me—I couldn't remember what. At first I struggled against her embrace, pushing her away with fingers scrunched into fists, but she held me close and her large, reassuring fingers found the edges of my tiny face in just the right way. "It's okay, Patricia. Everything is going to be all right," she whispered. My small body melted like wax into hers as her thumb caressed my eyebrow and deliberately stroked the side of my temple. She repeated this motion and soon my sobs subsided. Someone walked into the bedroom. A tall, dark figure. Its arms reached out toward my mother. She stood, keeping one hand on the back of my head, still pressing me to her chest. Then she extended her arms with me in them and handed me over to the dark figure. My screams woke me up.

Marble, all I could see was marble. A vast cream-colored marble room with a high-reaching domed ceiling. The silky, smooth pillars supporting the central dome rose at least twenty feet above my head, and the dome itself climbed higher than I could estimate. I sat at the base of one of the marble pillars, its surface cold against my back, unable to move. I tugged at my hands, telling them to come back to where they belonged in front of me, but they didn't obey. Restraints held me tightly as I squirmed. Something covered my mouth.

In the middle of the massive lobby was one large, legume-shaped desk. Behind the desk was a man. His thick, shoulder-length ebony hair was disheveled, and a dense beard covered most of his honey-bronze face. Voluminous, naturally lined eyes stuck out against his scruffy facial hair and framed his prolonged, thin nose. He was perhaps a decade older than Rexx and me; it was difficult to tell.

His clothes were unusual. Clearly not a uniform, but they didn't resemble civilian clothing either—color-shifting fabrics made with thermochromic technology that fit the contours of any body. This man's citrine-colored shirt fit slackly and was covered in bright, vivid patterns that looked as if they had been painted on by hand; his baggy tawny pants were ripped at the right knee.

He was hastily opening and closing large drawers, searching for something. Suddenly he stopped what he was doing and inquisitively cocked his head in my direction, watching me resurface into consciousness.

Frantically, I looked around for Rexx. There he was, tied to the pillar next to me, unconscious. I said his name, but only a low, muffled sound emerged. Fear and panic rose quickly like floodwaters. *What do I do? What do I do?* I kept asking myself, but no answer was forthcoming. The man still stared.

I peered down at what was keeping me contained. Nothing more than a length of rope, not even one inch in diameter. As I struggled, the frays dug into the skin on my arms, which were sufficiently pinned to my sides in three places. There was nothing I could do. I was completely at the mercy of the man in front of me.

I stared back. He wore a disturbing smile on his face. I could feel sweat beading on my forehead. He continued to observe me quizzically, his large forehead pinching where it met his nose. I felt like one of the insects we kept in the terrariums in our lab, which we observed to discover the impact of living in contaminated soil systems.

My mind bolted from one eventuality to the next. *No. No. No. We made it; we actually made it, against all the odds. We made it to Zone 36. This can't be happening. No one's supposed to be here. This zone is empty.*

I tried to yell, but again only stifled sounds emerged.

Who was this person? Was he simply holding us until Compos came to retrieve us? Or were his plans more sinister?

Our possessions had been dumped on the floor by my feet. Nothing was missing as far as I could tell, but it'd obviously been rummaged through. How long had I been unconscious? Bright light shone through the windows. I strained to look at my hand, pinned at my side slightly behind my hip, and saw the bandages had been removed. A rough scab covered the area where Rexx had cut out my chip.

This man had gone through our stuff and had seen that we'd cut out our chips. Did he know who we were?

The man left his desk and started to walk toward me. I instinctively shut my eyes, bracing for an impact of some kind. When I reopened them, I saw instead that he'd stopped about two feet away. Then he squatted in front of me, grabbed the piece of fabric covering my mouth, and pulled it down so it hung on my neck. I filled my thirsty lungs. The acrid taste of whatever chemical he'd used to knock me out still coated my lips. Then he walked over and did the same to Rexx, who was starting to stir.

The man sat down on the floor and crossed his legs, then leaned back on his palms as if he were settling in for an hour of television. What was he going to do to us? Why were his pants ripped, and why was he in an evacuated zone? Was it possible that we hadn't ended up where I thought we had? Or could he possibly be the exact type of person we were looking for?

"Mr. Moreno and Miss Collins," he said.

As my name passed from his lips, I felt the color seep from my face. The man shook his head, and an invisible force kept my eyes trained on his mouth, terrified yet hungry to know what he would say next. "Well, you two have been quite busy, haven't you? Yes, very busy." He cracked a smile oozing with amusement. My muscles tightened, and I tried to straighten myself up but I couldn't. I was confused and ensnared, like a fly in the web of a spider. The man's tone was not authoritative in the least. Was it my imagination, or was it almost friendly?

"Who are you?" Rexx croaked next to me, the dryness in his throat clear. I felt instant relief that he was awake, though neither of us could do anything to help the other. The man ignored Rexx's question, jumped up, and ran out of the room.

"Rexx, Rexx, are you okay? Can you move your hands?" I asked.

"No, the rope's too tight. I'm okay though. I think if we just—" Rexx was cut off.

"My name is Oliver Shelling," the man declared as he sauntered back into the room holding two glasses of water. He slid to a kneeling position in front of Rexx. "Here. Here. Let me help you take a sip."

Rexx stared daggers at him as he knelt there, holding the glass of water out in front of him, but then his thirst won out and he put his lips to the glass and let the man help him drink.

Something about his body language was foreign. The way he sat on the floor and the way he skidded to a kneeling position on the ground. His motions were youthful, unguarded. My fear started to give way to mild trepidation.

"I want to untie you. Oh, I hated tying you up. Didn't hurt you, did I? I wasn't sure who you were at first. . . . Well, until I saw your hands. Brave, very brave of you. Pictures and footage have been sent to the higher tiers, of course. The latest is, well, you're likely hiding out somewhere in the wilds of Arizona. They're looking for you there." I felt my shoulders lighten. At least part of our plan had worked. Up until now.

He scooted over and held the other glass of water up to my lips. I took a sip.

"Anyway, we need to talk," he continued, "and I needed to be sure you wouldn't try to run away. You aren't going to run, are you?"

Rexx and I shared looks of dejected resignation. There was nowhere else to go, even if we did run. This was it. Zone 36. This was our goal. The empty zone we were aiming for was not in fact empty at all. We now had a man, whoever he was, who knew exactly who we were and could report our last-known whereabouts. Hope of finding clues that could lead us to the rescue of my father was a candle flickering in a rainstorm.

I looked back at the man who called himself Oliver. There was softness in his eyes, but it was accompanied by a disarming, erratic stare.

"No," Rexx and I both uttered in unison.

Oliver beamed at this. He set the glasses of water on the ground and leaned toward me. I felt myself flinch but tried to hide it as he reached around and untied my hands. My stiff, sore arms dropped to my sides and I rubbed my aching shoulders. He scooted over and untied Rexx.

Rexx immediately jumped to his feet and walked in front of me protectively, then reached his hands down to help me off the cold marble floor.

"Won't you please make yourselves comfortable?" We watched as he went around the desk, then pulled out two chairs and dragged them over, patting them eagerly. Rexx kept his arm on my back as we walked toward them. "Oh, I'm so glad you're both here! Not a lot of company in these parts. Welcome, welcome. Can I get you anything? Oh dear, I haven't even introduced myself, how rude of me. Or did I? Oh, I can't remember. Anyway, my name is Oliver Shelling, Tier 2. But, of course, you can call me Oliver. Sit, sit."

We did as he requested, sitting cautiously in the two abnormally thick and sturdy chairs. Their surface was made of something I'd never felt before, smooth like plastic but softer. My hand, needing something to do, caressed the supple covering.

There must be a reason he isn't just holding us tied up until the authorities arrive, I told myself as a knot started to form in my stomach. *Who is he, and why is he here in this building, in a quarantined zone? And why does he look like something out of a vintage newsreel?*

Oliver was all smile and eyes. His teeth were large and bright and didn't quite seem to fit his bedraggled appearance. He was of average height—compact, yet muscular. As I watched him move around the room, I wondered if he was completely sane. I was still afraid, but my overwhelming emotion was one of bewilderment. Rexx and I looked searchingly at each other from our soft chairs, both disappointed to see that there was no answer in the other's eyes. I shot my glance to the entryway in the distance, asking without speaking, *Should we run?* Rexx shook his head slightly. What did that mean? Not yet? Not at all?

I looked back to Oliver. However odd the person in front of us, one thing was obvious—we'd walked into an unconventional situation and we were about to see where it took us.

"Well, we've found ourselves in quite a pickle here, haven't we? The two of you, showing up here." Oliver let out an awkward laugh and ran his long fingers through his thick, unkempt hair. "How'd you do it? How on earth did you do it?" Another awkward laugh.

I swallowed my apprehension and asked the one question I needed answered before any kind of two-way conversation could take place. "Oliver, are we under supervision?"

"No. No. No, we're not. And there is no one else in this zone, no one but me. Alone." The way he said this, punching the last word, wasn't exactly reassuring. "This particular site, the very one you're in right now . . . Well, I mean you saw it; you walked down that wretched street. Anyway, this location, Zone 36, represents the worst of the fracking disasters. The waste injection into the wells triggered significant seismic activity in this region."

I thought about the broken streets we'd been walking down before everything went black.

"It'd happened before," Oliver continued, "but never anything on this scale. Never anything that could be so clearly, so unequivocally, linked as cause and effect. You, Miss Collins, and you, Mr. Moreno—can I call you that? What should I call you? Slow down, Oliver; you're getting ahead of yourself."

Rexx and I both opened our mouths to answer Oliver, but he continued before we had a chance.

As he spoke, I couldn't help but look around and take in the interior of the building. The column aligned with his desk was a veritable bulletin board covered in drawings and clippings from what looked like a myriad of sources. More loose paper than I'd seen in one place in my entire life. I squinted to read some of the text, but my vision wasn't sharp enough. Some of the larger drawings were visible, but they didn't mean anything to me. They appeared to be sketches in charcoal and marker, repetitive images suggestive of the national emblem. I recognized one item, approximately a third of the way up the column: a government flyer, with a similar appearance as the metal sign we'd found in the van in the state park, with handwritten notes strewn over the face of it, though I couldn't see what they said. With renewed unease, I turned my attention back to Oliver.

"You're standing in the last natural gas drilling site before the entire practice was shut down on American soil forty-two years ago," Oliver was saying.

I'd been unabashedly staring with my mouth open as if I'd frozen in the middle of a sentence. No one talked this freely, and definitely not in front of two people they didn't know. No one. There could only be one of two reasons for Oliver's candor: we really weren't under surveillance or Oliver was entrapping us. He knew our names. Perhaps he knew we were coming; perhaps they'd been watching us the entire time. I mean, who did we think we were? How could we have been so naive? Was Oliver tasked with getting us to talk? I glanced to my right and saw Rexx shifting uncomfortably in his seat. I wanted to reach over to him, to grab his hand, but our chairs were too far away from each other. Oliver, for his part, apparently remained oblivious to our anxieties.

I stared at the pile of clutter shrouding his desk, a mess of paperwork and personal effects. Heaped almost a foot high in some sections, spread thin in others. Physical paperwork was almost unheard of, and bringing personal items into the workplace was forbidden, at least in every office I'd ever been in. My workspace in Arizona housed a computer, a shelf for digital resources, a desk, a chair, and not much else. There was no computer on his desk. I saw no digital devices at all. No screens, no cameras. I quickly scanned the sprawling room. The absence of the screens was weighty, like a fourth person in the room.

"This zone was originally part of the Portland Urban Center," Oliver continued, "but when it was rendered unfit for habitation and in need of a *shit ton* of time to recover, a mass evacuation took place. Everyone was relocated, whether they wanted to leave or not, and all surveillance equipment was redistributed. The only surveillance devices in the whole zone are installed on my computer equipment in the other room." Oliver pointed across the large oval expanse, to the corridor. I could vaguely make out a few doors lining the edges.

Why was he disclosing so much? It didn't make any sense. "I don't spend much time in there. No use for it." I wondered if his voice was low enough, but Oliver didn't seem concerned. "Wouldn't want to have to replace those expensive town cameras! They cost more than I'm credited in six months." He barked an awkward laugh, triggering my chest to tighten. I forced an uncomfortable smile.

Oliver stood and started pacing back and forth on the other side of the desk from where Rexx and I sat. If he was sincere—a big if—how long had he been waiting to share his thoughts with someone? He promptly provided me with the answer.

"I've been here for the past five years, relocated from another Tier 2 position, and as of yet, no one's waltzed in with a camera and a toolbox. Thank the lucky stars, or I don't know what I'd do! I wouldn't be able to stand it. Nope. I suppose they think it's pointless—what good are a few cameras if I have the whole zone to myself? No, they would have to rig up the entire zone, and not in a million years would they waste that sort of effort on one citizen. Not cost-effective, not one bit. Especially not for one who could so readily be disposed of at the snap of their fingers, like countless others. I'm sure you both, like everyone else in this forsaken country, have had people ripped from your lives. That's why you did what you did, I assume. No way around it. Am I right?"

I could never answer such a question, yet Oliver's eyes locked on mine, awaiting a response. A tight knot formed in my throat and I nodded, thinking of my father, of Amara, of my neighbor Claude.

"So," Rexx jumped in after clearing his throat. I could tell from his timbre he was nervous, though it likely wasn't perceptible to someone who didn't know him so well. "What do you do here, Mr. Shelling?" Rexx gripped the edge of his chair tightly as he spoke. It'd been confirmed that people were looking for us, we were wanted for treason, and we were alone and listening to someone a tier above us speak in such casual a manner. I didn't believe it. It had to be a trap. But why trap us? There was already more than enough evidence to put us away.

"Well, Mr. Moreno—wait, that's silly. Is it okay if I call you Rexx? After all, we're going to be spending a lot of time together." Oliver smiled eagerly.

I wondered what he meant by that. Rexx nodded, but the expression on his face was hard, skeptical. He looked to me as if he were deciding whether to tackle Oliver. There were a few items on his desk hard enough to knock him out, if I could just sneak up behind him somehow.

Oliver continued: "Great, great. Glad we got that out of the way. What do I do here, what do I do? It's my job to keep an eye on this place! A humble caretaker, if you will. And what a fun job it is, keeping an eye on the trees, making sure the crumbled buildings don't get up and walk away. Gee, I don't know what they'd do if I weren't here watching the rats making their nests in all the unoccupied houses." Oliver stopped and winked, and the lump in my throat grew slightly larger. "I was permitted to leave the zone last year, for a virtual training. Not much has changed out there. Still a shit storm. Couldn't get back fast enough."

Oliver abruptly stopped talking and remained silent for the longest stretch since we'd awakened on the floor. His eyes widened, and he studied my face, then Rexx's, and then mine again. I gathered he was waiting for one of us to say something. He sat down and leaned back in his chair, his gaze alternating between the two of us as he wore the same exuberant and complex smile.

I began cautiously, choosing my words carefully. "Well, Mr. Shelling—"

"No, please, please. Call me Oliver. I beg of you."

"Oliver," I began again, "you've been here five years? As far as we know, the department hasn't determined this site to be safe, so how is it okay for you to be here? We've never met a site contact who lived on the premises before."

Oliver continued staring until the silence became uncomfortable. Then, just as I was about to break it, he chuckled. "You speak as if you're here to work! I saw that in the report, that you two work for the NRD. Brilliant, fascinating. But, as to your question, let's get into that later, Patricia, shall we? For that, my dear, is a long story. One best saved for another day. After all, we have time to spend until we figure out what to do with the two of you." Oliver loudly clapped his hands and rubbed them together eagerly. "As you can imagine, it can get pretty dull."

What possible explanation can there be for his on-site residence? I wondered.

"So . . . you're not going to turn us in?" Rexx asked guardedly.

Oliver stared for a minute, seeming to be thinking of the right words to say. "I've never met two people who've taken such a risk. Heck, I've never been brave enough to even consider running. I want to know everything. It's not every day I meet folks who could possibly despise the Board as much as I do. I'm not letting the two of you go anywhere. I'm going to help you."

CHAPTER 13

AFTER OUR TALK, Oliver offered to take us on a tour. He didn't protest when I put our supplies back in my backpack and slung it over my shoulder. Rexx stayed right beside me as we walked out the front door. He wasn't convinced, and neither was I. We needed to stay on guard and be prepared to bolt.

"So," Oliver said, swinging his arms out wide, "Zone 36 in all its glory. The entire zone's enormous, close to eleven square miles in total. Whew! Right now we stand at the southeast corner. A few miles that way, just about an hour's walk, is the river." He pointed off in the distance, where I could make out a patch of dense Oregon foliage. "And over there, that hideous piece of equipment protruding from the ground is the old fracking equipment and the epicenter of the quake."

I looked at the tangle of equipment. "Wait, why is it still there? Did they send a hazard mitigation team?"

If there really had been a fracking disaster of the magnitude he suggested, harmful levels of methane, ethylbenzene, and other dangerous compounds would be present. They'd been linked to neurological disorders, cancers, and birth defects. Even forty-odd years later, they could still be a concern. Especially if proper cleanup measures hadn't been taken at the time. If there had been a quake, the chemicals likely hadn't stayed where intended.

Oliver did not answer my question. Instead he continued. "Twenty-seven people lost their lives in the quake, and once the call was finally made to fully evacuate, thirty thousand citizens, give or take a few dozen, had to be reassigned. The closest urban centers were directed to absorb them, and many families had to be split apart. Never parents and their minor children, but they didn't think twice before reassigning elders to locations hundreds of miles away from the rest of their family. Jackasses." I stifled a gasp at his candor. I wanted to trust him, to think that he was someone who could help. But I'd also trusted my mother. I'd also trusted the Board. If there was one thing I was learning, it was to question everything.

At one point, when Oliver was walking ahead of us and pointing out something, I turned to Rexx and whispered, "What do you think? Genuine? Or should we be getting out of here?"

Rexx shrugged in response. My thoughts exactly.

"Let's just let him do the talking for now," Rexx said. "He might have the right connections we're looking for, or know something that could help us find your father." I knew Rexx was right. We were both eager to hear what else Oliver had to say. Wasn't that the whole goal? To learn something that might lead us to my father? Here in front of us was an opportunity that might help us. A bristly, bright-eyed, slightly manic opportunity.

It could be possible that Oliver himself was a surviving member of the Veritas Ring. It was equally possible that he was cornering us. I couldn't escape the feeling it might all be a test. That, or he was a sociopath who planned on murdering us later.

"Let's just see how we feel about the whole Oliver situation by the end of the day," I said. "If needed, we'll figure out a way to sneak off and find somewhere to regroup."

Oliver wanted to know the details of our escape, what prompted it, how we avoided capture. Even though our pictures had been circulated, the details of the incident with the van were not making the rounds. The Board didn't hand out details lightly, even when they needed eyes on alert.

Rexx and I provided superficial answers to his prying questions—mostly parroting back information he already knew. The intensity with which he watched us made me self-conscious. It became increasingly evident that Oliver spent a great deal of time alone and was thirsty for human interaction.

"So, what are things like out there in the 'real' world?" Oliver asked in a tone that made me wonder if the question was rhetorical or if he wanted an answer. "Unlikely that my one-week training excursion gave me a full picture, but it gave me plenty for my taste."

The real world. I turned the phrase over. On a normal day, I'd be just getting to work, walking carefree into the morning meeting, ready to receive the day's assignments. Blissfully unaware that everything I believed was built on a mound of lies. Unaware there were details, details that led to the remains of seventy-five people being stacked like dirty dishes in a chained-off building. Details that led to Rexx's great-grandparents disappearing, whether beyond the Walls or into a similar pile, who could say. I thought about Jordan and Lydia and felt a painful tinge in my chest at the thought of never seeing them again. I thought about my mother but stopped myself. Even a taste of the pain that awaited was too strong.

I hesitated answering Oliver out loud, but Rexx jumped in. "How long have you been here? Five years? You know more than we do, probably, but things in Arizona are basically the same as they've always been, at least for us. Excessive thought filtering before speaking, avoiding the compliance officers at all costs—all that everyday stuff. I've watched a few locals I knew by name carted away in recent years, but not any more than in the five years before that. Patch and I are lucky—or were lucky, I guess. We had more freedom than most." I watched Rexx as he spoke, shocked by the words flowing out of him. So much for our wait-and-see approach.

I grabbed Rexx's arm and gave a firm yank, indicating I wanted him to follow me. As Rexx complied with my wishes, I glanced at Oliver, who was sitting, stirring the dirt on the ground with a stick, a broad smile spread across his face.

"What are you doing?" I asked once we were out of earshot.

Rexx rubbed his shoulder dramatically, letting me know I shouldn't have been so rough.

"Sorry," I muttered.

"Okay. I see two options here. Tell me if you think I'm wrong," Rexx said. "One: Oliver is sincere, and he's just a goofy guy who has a bone to pick with the people who wronged him and is aching for someone to talk to about it. And, possibly, he has information that can help us. Two. It is a trap. A very real possibility. But, if that's the case, we're already done. You know as well as I do. So, if we want him to tell us about the Veritas Ring and about everything he knows about the Board before we get out of Dodge, then he needs to think we trust him. I didn't give much away, really, just enough to build some rapport."

The brutal honesty and resolve in Rexx's voice frightened me, but he was right.

"You wanna know something strange?" I said, not knowing what prompted me to talk about it just then. "I wasn't surprised when my mom reported the van. Shocked at first, I guess, but the more I thought about it, the more it made sense.

She never felt sorry for those who were taken; she just talked about how they should have been following the rules, should have been fulfilling their patriotic duty. She nodded in agreement when they aired stories about heroic children ratting out their parents. That day I led them to the park, it must have been a big betrayal for her. I don't think I was any better. I never questioned it all before. Even when Amara was taken, I didn't understand why she couldn't just follow the rules. Now I know how wrong I was."

Rexx put both arms around me, squeezed me tight to his chest, and sighed loudly.

"What, what is it?" I asked.

"I've just been waiting a long time for that, Patch."

Yeah, I guess I had, too. Neither of us spoke for a few minutes; we just stood there, quietly acknowledging we'd crossed a threshold. Then Rexx let go and we headed back to Oliver, who hadn't moved from where we'd left him.

"Sorry if I struck a chord," Oliver said as we sat down next to him, with possibly convincing smiles plastered on our faces.

After a tour of the part of the town in which Oliver spent most of his time, our host walked us to his house, where he said there was plenty of room. At the mention of dinner, any hesitation I'd been feeling decreased exponentially. I was starving, and we were down to dehydrated meal pouches. Having food served to us was beyond anything we could have imagined for that evening.

"If we're about to be murdered, at least we'll have a real last meal first," Rexx whispered in my ear as we walked. I smiled. Rexx always seemed to know what to say to cut through the tension.

"In addition to the office building you saw earlier, they fixed up this place for me," Oliver said. "It's not much, really, but it's my home."

He headed to a quaint tiger's-eye-colored one-bedroom on what looked like it used to be a charming cul-de-sac. It was the only home in the vicinity remaining relatively intact. Others were flattened into piles of rubble or split and left open like an unpacked box.

Flowers bloomed alongside vegetables out front in a lovely garden surrounded by a knee-high fence, each picket painted a different color. At first look, it was clear my garden paled in comparison. The fragrance was refreshing compared to the underlying rancid smell of Zone 36. A lovely expanse of purple bloomed underneath his front window. Lavender. I decided in that moment I wanted to like Oliver. But those I'd put my trust in had deceived me before.

Oliver saw me looking, and jogged ahead on the stone walkway that wound to his front door. He returned a moment later with a bundle of fresh lavender and placed it in my hands. "Smell it. It's delightful," he said with a smile. Rexx walked toward the lavender and bent down to inhale the sweet aroma. It was the first time he'd left my side, I realized. He must be feeling more comfortable.

"I know—I grow it outside my apartment. Or, well, I did." I inhaled the comforting fragrance of the bundle of herbs I held in my hands.

"I get a delivery of food, bottled water, and other essentials once per week," Oliver said, "at which point someone picks up my list for the next week." At this I instinctively looked over my shoulder. "Don't worry," Oliver continued. "They just came yesterday, and they don't come inside the zone, just meet me at the gate. Not a super-exciting system, but it works. Since I have no other way to spend my credits, I make sure I at least have healthy food." Saliva started to fill my mouth at the thought of fresh vegetables.

We followed Oliver through the threshold into his home, and it became clear his residence was unlike any I had stepped into before. "Wow," I exclaimed.

The word that came to mind was *whimsical*. We entered through the kitchen. The table and chairs were painted with similar colors to the fencing outside, each a unique blend of pinks, reds, oranges, and yellows. Past the kitchen, through a wide-set archway, was a small living room. The walls were covered from floor to ceiling with paintings; some were hung, and others were brushed right onto the surface. Some were beautiful. Paintings of landscapes, or the up-close view of a flower. Others depicted gruesome images and I flinched before looking again. I took a step closer. Bodies, some of children, lying bloody in the street; a classroom full of children, their brains appearing to evaporate into the air above them; an up-close image of the eyes of a Compo. A chill ran through my spine. I didn't know what to think.

Stacked on the floors, leaning against one wall were more paintings in frames.

A blush spread across Oliver's face. His eyes remained on us as we took in our surroundings. "I find myself with a lot of extra time, a lot of hours to kill, you know, not really having much of a job other than supposedly keeping an eye on the place. So, I started scouring around town and making things out of whatever I could find. I also grab artwork when I find it and bring it here to protect it." He motioned to the artwork stacked on the floor. "Some of it's actually in pretty good shape." His arms were folded across his chest, his body language guarded. He seemed tuned in to our reactions, worried we wouldn't like the things in his home. "It fills the time, anyway."

He pointed out the pillow on his couch that he'd covered with fabric from a home a few streets over. The table in the living room was assembled from the fragments of two broken tables from a restaurant downtown. We learned it took two weeks of scavenging to track down an oil finish, which he eventually located in the basement of a house a mile away. I was in awe as he guided us through his home, showing us how he spent his hours. Any doubt I had about this man's sincerity started to diminish.

I didn't know anyone else who made things the way Oliver did; everything I knew was mass-produced. Sure, a few antiques that passed inspections still occupied some apartments, but for my generation, almost every home merely affected an air of uniqueness rather than embodying it—one of a few nominally altered variations on the same model. That was what I was realizing, looking at all those things crafted by Oliver's own hands.

In his bathroom, the walls were covered completely with an array of cracked tiles, creating a piece of art unlike anything I'd ever seen. I made up my own mind to trust Oliver. If it was a hoax, it was quite the elaborate one. Rexx admired the tiles one at a time, touching them with his fingertips—countless pieces of broken homes and shattered futures had been carefully and thoughtfully pieced together to form an exquisite mosaic. I pictured Oliver rummaging through empty residences, collecting pieces that suited his vision. As I backed out of the bathroom, the picture clicked. "Oh my Board," I said unintentionally as I realized what it was. Rexx stepped back and, a second later, saw it too. He gasped and wrapped his fingers around my forearm. The darker tiles, when viewed as a whole, formed a symbol.

∞

The infinity sign. The symbol used by the Veritas Ring. My heard stopped in my chest. Was Oliver a member of the Veritas Ring? Was he in contact with others? Or was the Veritas Ring ancient history and he was just someone who had heard of them and took an interest? Or maybe he just had a fascination with symbolic shapes.

I stood there, frozen, wondering what to do. Were we supposed to tell him we recognized the symbol? That it appeared on the map that had led us here? That my father used to be part of the movement?

Rexx leaned in to whisper in my ear. "Let's just pretend we didn't notice. Let's see what unveils itself, all right? Oliver might tell us something on his own, and we don't want to mess this up."

We backed out of the bathroom. Oliver was already in his living room, waxing on about another piece of art he'd created, not seeming to realize we weren't right behind him.

We sat down in Oliver's living room. I leaned into the corner of his sofa, against an intricate patchwork quilt folded over the armrest. I let the stillness envelop me as I stretched out my neck, side to side, feeling the heaviness of the preceding days sink through me and into the armchair. Rexx sat down next to me, unusually close, and stretched his arms to either side of him, leaving one resting behind my head, disturbing my tranquil moment. I looked at him, ready to motion for him to scoot over a bit, but his eyes were on Oliver, analyzing him.

Oliver sat across from us, smiling again, and began rocking in a wooden chair.

"So, let me guess," he said, "your heads are just spinning off into space right now. You aren't sure whether or not to trust me? Plus, you've never seen anything like this before, have you? The broken streets?"

Before either one of us had a chance to answer, Oliver continued. "That's how I felt when I first got here. I was in the same field as you: disaster recovery, resource evaluation, except one tier up, privy to all sorts of classified government information—though not all of it, no, definitely not all of it, they made that clear. I dispensed assignments, wrote up those confidentiality agreements you had to sign when entering a new zone—a veritable ringleader if you will—determining what took priority but ultimately given access to only the information needed to do my job correctly, nothing more, nothing less. Well, you two obviously know the routine. The sheer quantity of cover-ups I took part in on some level or another—and keep in mind, I was never privileged to see the entire picture, which is probably for the best . . . You know, mostly natural disasters and their true roots. It would blow your mind what was actually behind some of them. And keep in mind these cover-ups were just in our field! Imagine what else is going on out there."

I thought about the site of the 2029 bombing and of everything we had seen and experienced over the past week. Oliver shifted in his chair, his eyes wide, making odd movements with his hands, and Rexx and I glanced at each other. "Oh, oh, sorry, that's my puppet master gesture. But, yes, of course, the puppets you're familiar with don't have strings at all, so I'm clearly making no sense. Never mind that."

Oliver rose from his seat and paced back and forth. "I started asking too many questions, not the forbidden ones, but too many questions nonetheless. They don't look too kindly on questions; it makes them uncomfortable. Do your job and do it well—that's the motto of the upper tiers. Curiosity is not looked upon with admiration or approval. Nope, nope. I asked things like 'What's their job?' or 'Hey, what do you suppose they're doing in that room?' The nerve of me! So, they finally got tired of me. Tired of my questions that didn't officially cross any line and give them an excuse to get rid of me for good. They shipped me out here indefinitely, the bastards." I started to worry about Oliver. If authorities were ever to search his house, well, what would happen to him would likely be unthinkable.

A whistle called from the kitchen and Oliver jumped up to attend to it. He returned a few moments later with hot tea and cookies that appeared homemade. He smiled broadly and intently examined our reactions as he set the tea and cookies down on the table in front of us. A social man forced to live a solitary life, with no friends to entertain or play host to. I wondered how old he was and how much his time here had aged him. After spending a little bit of time with him and hearing him speak, I guessed that underneath all the scruff was a man in his mid- to late thirties.

Sensing his need for approval, I offered him the only thing I could at the moment: my gratitude.

"Thank you so much, Oliver. We haven't eaten much other than protein bars and dehydrated meals for three days."

"So no questions yet, my dear? None at all? As I said, I know some stuff. Why, yes I do, and I have no intention of keeping my mouth shut any longer, even once I am out of this purgatory."

I wondered what that meant, and if we truly had a new ally and someone who may have information that could help us. If the infinity symbol in his bathroom really meant he was someone we could trust. Rexx wore a contemplative look and remained silent, likely tossing around the same thoughts that I was. All the questions that had occupied my mind for days were suddenly irretrievable. Then I looked down at the cup that was warming my hands.

"Okay, Oliver. Do you happen to know where tea comes from?"

CHAPTER 14

AFTER A DINNER of fresh garden tomatoes and basil over a bed of mixed grains, which put most meals I'd had to shame, Oliver set us up with some blankets and pillows in his living room. I turned down his offer to let me have his room but didn't say it was because Rexx and I wanted to stay close in case we needed to bolt. Rexx insisted I have the couch while he took the floor.

I slept harder than I had in days and woke before anyone else. I had a renewed sense of determination. I lay there staring at the ceiling, thinking about what the day would look like, how to move forward. How the safety I felt now was relative, and I couldn't let myself become too comfortable. I thought about my father, how he was likely in a redemption camp, possibly already started with his training. I wondered what his mornings looked like, and what he was doing that very moment. We needed to find him. I needed to right the wrong I had caused. Oliver was the answer. I could feel it.

"Morning," I said as Rexx stirred on the ground next to the sofa.

"Wasn't a dream, huh?" he said as he propped himself up on his elbows.

Oliver emerged from his room seconds later and walked toward us, and Rexx and I both stared in awe. The man approaching hardly resembled the jumbled individual from the day before. Oliver's once-disheveled hair was sleeked back and tied into a bun. His beard freshly trimmed and uniform. Even his eyebrows looked newly tamed. His eager eyes and smile were the only constant.

Oliver made some tea, then joined us in the living room. We wasted no time before we started asking questions. Wading in with some that seemed rather benign, such as:

"What do you think was behind the tsunami of 2079?"

"Do you know where monkeys live?"

And, working our way up to others:

"How many American authors had their books banned in the beginning? Do you think there are any still out there somewhere?"

"What do you think the Board headquarters look like?"

Oliver offered tidbits about the inner workings of the upper tiers from his personal experience as a Tier 2 official. Board members and most Tier 1 employees operated in heavily guarded headquarters centered in a few select parts of the country. No one knew their exact location. I thought back to the four empty states I'd noted when looking at the map.

Oliver confirmed the Board, consisting of 30 members, made all the major decisions for the country. As Oliver said, "They write the reality the rest of us live."

The Board was a faceless yet all-consuming entity. "They aren't used to their methods falling short; that's a big thing you have going for you and probably why you haven't been found yet," Oliver explained. "They rely too much on their shortcuts—you know, mass surveillance, tracking, chips. They're pretty impotent without 'em. They've built this whole system where no one really knows how to do anything other than their assigned role, and now even if they needed hundreds of Compos to come after you, they're left with people who barely know how to function outside the grid of the cities. It's insane if you ask me."

I wanted to tell Oliver everything. About the books, about Wildcliff. I wanted to ask him directly about the Veritas Ring, but something was still holding me back, and each time I opened my mouth, something else came out instead.

For lunch, Rexx, Oliver, and I had fun in the kitchen as Oliver brought in vegetables from the garden and portioned them off to each of us to chop. A sliver of self-reproach accompanied each cut of the knife. I was enjoying myself when my father had been ripped away from his life because of me. *You need to regroup. That's all you're doing. You won't do anyone any good trying to go after him without a plan.*

Oliver was gracious and appreciative, obviously flattered someone was enjoying his space. When I asked how he felt about growing food in the contaminated soil, he reassured me he only planted in enclosed, aboveground beds with soil specially delivered from outside Zone 36. Despite the adverse environmental conditions, Oliver had managed to produce a cornucopia, and it was hard not to wonder what could be accomplished in society with the benefit of a few more like-minded individuals.

After lunch, Oliver wanted to take us on a hike. The sun was high in the sky and the shade of the forest beckoned. Oliver knew it well. He wanted to show us one of his favorite places. No reason we can't hike and talk, Rexx and I decided.

"It's right this way, guys," Oliver said as we headed away from the houses and buildings and toward the patch of green he had pointed out to us the day before. "Oh, I'm so excited to share this with both of you. Close your eyes! No, wait—that's ridiculous. I can't lead you on a dangerous hike with your eyes closed. Okay, just follow me." He waved in a wildly large arc, gesturing us onto a rather tidy trail, considering the dense foli-age that surrounded us. I wondered if he'd been maintaining it.

As we entered the comforting umbrella of the forest, the air changed. The uplifting smell of pine filled my nose, a blend of butterscotch and subtle notes of citrus.

We crossed a short, old wooden bridge, home to bright moss and lichen climbing its posts. A carpet of thicker, denser mosses rolled on the forest floor around the tree trunks, inter-rupted only by the occasional fern.

Splashes of pink appeared here and there, released from the recently blooming dogwoods.

Rexx dropped several paces behind Oliver and me, a behav-ior I'd grown used to from our days at work sites. He would often get distracted by the scent of a flower or the look of an unfamiliar plant and then stop to explore it further. He stepped off the trail.

I jogged ahead a few steps, knowing Rexx would catch up when ready. "It's really beautiful out here, Oliver. The plant life's so green and opulent compared to Arizona. I can't believe you have this all to yourself." As soon as the words came out of my mouth, I immediately regretted them. I was sure Oliver was lonely. "Do you make it out this way often? It's pretty far from your house."

Oliver smiled, and as casually as if we were old friends, he wrapped his arm around my shoulders. "I come out here every week when the weather is nice. I found this trail a few months after I arrived and, well, I just fell in love with the place. You'll see! We're almost there! Come on!" With that, he dropped his arm and picked up his pace.

I was already falling in love with it, and I was excited to see what else he had in store.

I turned around to look behind me, and the view arrested my attention. Oliver noticed I'd stopped, and he stood beside me. The town's devastation was even clearer from up here, pinned against the beauty of the forest. The fracture line from the earthquake permeating out from the tangle of fracking equipment couldn't be mistaken. It split the view in two, and something about seeing it from this angle caused the anger to well up inside me.

"Just imagine the looks on their faces when they saw what havoc their allegedly safe drilling process could wreak," Oliver said. "The epicenter of the seismic activity was near the waste-injection site, but the disruption progressed outward in a radius of approximately ten miles, resulting in a massive chemical spill at the drilling site and heavy contamination of both the groundwater and the Willamette River. All this time later and we're still cleaning up the mess."

It was worse than anything I'd ever seen. Rexx caught up with us as Oliver continued. "As you probably know, the country underwent a massive energy crisis right around that time, having to convert rapidly to alternative energy. Yup, since they had royally butchered their relationships with the nations they used to depend on for oil, and their backup plan wasn't working out so well, what with the poisonings and the earthquakes and all, they were shit out of options. Whoops! A little ironic, really."

At that he turned and continued up the hill. I took one last look at the scene before me and then followed.

"Which chemicals are still present?" I asked as we hiked. "Benzene? Lead? Mercury? Methane? Are you testing regularly?" Oliver didn't answer, and I found myself wishing we had access to testing equipment. If Oliver were experiencing symptoms, would he tell us?

We wound through a small trail as sunshine cast speckled light through the ash, spruce, and white oak trees, onto the ferns growing next to a stream skipping along the forest floor. My hand moved to pick a leaf off an elderberry plant. We headed up a hill that dipped abruptly ahead. I expected it to be just a slope we'd follow down to the river. I was surprised when Oliver and I were suddenly standing on the edge of a cliff overlooking the water below. It was spectacular—the awe-inspiring green Oregon foliage, the rushing water reflecting the light of the sun, and Oliver's impossibly wide smile. Wider than I'd seen on anyone in my entire life.

Eager to enjoy the view for a moment, I started to sit down on a rock face, but I was quickly lifted back onto my feet by Oliver's strong hand on my elbow.

"What are you doing? No, no, there's more!" he said as Rexx appeared out of the woods and sauntered up behind us.

"Wow, this is absolutely incredible!" Rexx said. I knew he'd need more than a few seconds to admire the scenery and would be slightly annoyed, though he'd never admit it, if rushed into something else.

"Better not sit down," I whispered. "I think our friend has bigger plans for us up here."

Oliver walked parallel to the cliff edge for a few yards, then disappeared behind a tree. I strained to see what he was doing, but he was out of view. Rexx and I shrugged and then walked around to explore our immediate vicinity.

Before long, Oliver reappeared holding what looked like a harness and two very long lengths of rope. One end of each of the ropes was secured to the tree Oliver had just appeared from behind.

"Ladies first," he said as he held out his hand. Our hike had taken an interesting turn. I looked at Oliver's hand, then over the edge of the cliff as he gestured. Finally the dots connected. Was he crazy? That must be at least one hundred feet down.

"This isn't why we're here, Oliver," Rexx said. "We're close enough to getting ourselves killed without throwing ourselves down a cliff!"

"Don't worry, don't worry. I have the proper equipment. You don't want to miss it—believe me," Oliver said.

I shook my head. "I don't think—"

"I'd go first if I could," continued Oliver as he placed the harness in front of me and motioned for me to step into it, "but you're gonna need me up here."

Before I knew what I was doing, my heart was beating with exhilaration and I was shimmying the harness up and pulling the straps on my legs and waist to tighten them. Oliver double-checked, threading his fingers between the harness and my hips as he pulled, and then doing the same around my thighs. I looked over at Rexx. He was standing unnaturally close behind Oliver, watching the scene unfold, his arms crossed over his chest. Is he annoyed or nervous?

"I have to make sure it'll stay on if you flip upside down," Oliver said matter-of-factly, as if the words that just came out of his mouth were completely ordinary.

He gave me a quick overview of how the process worked, having me lean away from the tree and practice feeding one of the ropes through a metal contraption he called a descender until I was sure I had the hang of it. It was tricky at first, but after a couple of tries I had it down well enough, or at least that was what Oliver said.

"Okay, are you ready?" he asked. His smile was catching. "Are you ready to have the most fun you've ever had in your life? I'll have the other rope right here. See, it's connected to your harness too, so I can catch you if you start to fall."

If I start to fall? I took a deep breath and resolved to be brave. I had a strong feeling if I backed out, I'd regret it for years to come.

"Patch," Rexx said, "are you sure you want to do this?"

"Yes." I realized I meant it as the word came out. There was no turning back. I wanted to do it, maybe more than I'd ever wanted to do anything in my life. Rexx gave me a reassuring pat on the shoulder and then stepped back and watched, his face pale. If I went, so would he.

"Okay," Oliver began, "just walk up to the edge there, turn around, and lean back until your feet are straight out in front of you. I've got you."

As I turned around on the edge of a cliff and creeped slowly backward until my heels were suspended in midair, I realized I'd done it: despite my reservations, I had just put my life in Oliver's hands. I also realized that what I'd been doing up until that point in my life may have been many things, but it certainly wasn't living.

The sensations coursing through me as I rappelled down the cliff to the riverbank were incomparable. Consuming fear heightened my senses, and tears of joy welled up in my eyes. They may not have been the most *graceful* minutes of my life—my knees buckled as I bounced from foot to foot, slowly making my way down, using my shaking hands to maneuver the rope—but it was an extraordinary experience nonetheless.

About two-thirds of the way down came the realization that I'd been so focused on my hands and not plummeting to my death, I hadn't taken a moment to enjoy the scenery. Looking in all directions, I was faced with a view that took my breath away—quite literally, in fact: I had to remind myself to breathe several times. The river, sparkling with sunlight, rushed below me. At one point, I passed a large nest mounted on a ledge and found myself at eye level with five eggs, speckled pale blue, awaiting the return of their mother. Moss, untouched, in varying hues grew on the rock faces on either side of me.

Rexx came next, and then Oliver, who apparently had done the trip many times before, astonishingly without the assistance of anyone else. I wondered if the adrenaline surged for him each time, if he felt afraid. He looked confident in his movements. As I watched them come down after me, I knew I'd never felt so alive.

CHAPTER 15

*His brain was in one of those violent, yet frightfully calm,
conditions where reverie is so profound that it swallows up
reality. We no longer see the objects that are before us, but
we see, as if outside of ourselves, the forms that we have in
our minds.*
—Victor Hugo, *Les Misérables*

THAT EVENING, I fell asleep with the book lying open on
my chest. My father frequented my dreams, alternating from
warm memories to vivid nightmares depicting torture of many
forms. My sleep was interrupted by the sound of a door opening and closing. I awoke confused, looked around, and in my
drowsy state confirmed all was well and then tried to go back to
sleep, assuming the noise was part of my dream. Then I heard
something else.

The sound was unmistakable. A door opening and closing.

"Rexx. Rexx, wake up," I whispered.

"What, what is it? Is everything okay?" He sat up from his
blanket on the floor and rubbed his eyes.

"The front door. I think someone came in. I thought it was
a dream."

We both jumped up and Rexx switched on the lights. The front door was closed and there were no signs anyone was inside.

I felt foolish, realizing it must have been the dream after all, and guilty for waking Rexx for nothing. Then I looked down the hallway. Oliver's bedroom door was open, just a sliver, and I was certain he'd shut it the night before. A light emanated from the crack. It was the middle of the night; what was he doing awake? I walked carefully down the hallway.

"Oliver. Oliver, are you okay?" I whispered as I placed my hand on the door and slowly opened it wider. He wasn't in his room. It was empty, and a small light beside his bed was still on. Lights ran with automatic shutoff timers, so this meant he'd switched it on in the last few minutes.

I checked the bathroom across the hall. Empty.

"He's gone. It must have been him opening the front door. Where would he go in the middle of the night?"

"We're going to find out," Rexx said in a vexed tone. He was thinking exactly what I was. We'd put our trust in Oliver, and something suspicious was going on.

"It hasn't been more than three minutes since I heard the noise, Rexx," I said. "We can probably catch up to him, wherever he went, if we hurry." I walked toward the front door and started putting on my shoes. Rexx did the same, then grabbed a solar lantern off a table of odds and ends by the front door.

The moon was full and the air crisp as we searched the nearby vicinity for any sign of Oliver. Nothing. We ventured out even farther, making wider and wider circles around his house, our eyes and ears on alert, struggling to see by the dim light of the lantern. At one point Rexx tripped on the broken street and gashed his elbow. For a split second, when he first went down, I thought he'd been shot with a pacifier. I dropped to my knees, put my hands in the air, and skipped breathing momentarily until I realized what had happened.

As I helped him back to his feet, I thought about how careless we were being, and how we couldn't let another day end without figuring out a plan. I didn't have any clue how long one stayed in a redemption camp, but the more time that passed, the more likely it was that my father could be sent on military assignment and out of my reach forever.

We were about to give up and head back when we stumbled upon an abandoned park in the middle of town and noticed a light on in the distance. It was coming from an old stone structure.

I felt a familiar knot in my stomach. I halted in my tracks and took a deep breath.

"What do we do?"

"We need to go take a look, I think," Rexx said, but the way he said it didn't exactly inspire certainty.

"It might just be Oliver in there, alone, right?" I whispered. Rexx nodded at my words, a few too many times, then he extended his hand to me.

"You're sure they're not Compos?" I whispered as we walked closer to the light, and the large building came into view. The words COMMUNITY CENTER were written across the top of an archway that framed the entrance. Wide stone steps started at ground level on either end and met in the middle in front of two tall, wooden doors. The whole building was sided in slate-gray stone. It was dark, except for one window on the right side of the building sticking halfway up from ground level. The basement.

The two of us crossed the park and crept toward the side of the building, our eyes fixed on our illuminated destination.

The small glass-paned window sat a foot or so above the ground. As we inched closer, I noticed the light was not from an electric bulb but the soft warm glow of several candles. I reassured myself there were no Compos in there by rationalizing that compliance officers would certainly carry their own flashlights or have the ability to request temporary power.

Rexx turned off the lantern and continued to grip my other hand, a little too tightly, and we walked closer to the window. I was starting to feel queasy.

A shadow crossed between the candlelight and the window, and Rexx dropped to the ground, pulling me along with him. In an instant we were lying with our faces in the dirt. I flattened out my body and squeezed my eyelids shut so tightly, they started to ache. The dry blades of grass nipped at my forehead as I flattened them to the earth. After a moment, I turned my head and opened my eyes so I could see the window once again. The movement ceased, and after several minutes we gathered the courage to move.

Follow me, Rexx mouthed as he slowly rose to his knees and began to crawl forward until he was next to the building and off to the side of the lighted frame.

I followed right behind him and pressed myself against the wall on the other side of window, crossing in front of it, my breath held the entire time. Rexx took the first peek and I followed suit. What we saw was hard to reconcile. Sitting at a round table in a large basement room was a group of older individuals. Elders. From their white hair and wrinkled faces, I would guess they were in their eighties and nineties. From the way they moved, they all seemed to be in astonishingly good health for their age.

Since the average lifespan was mid-sixties, my confusion was warranted. Sure, some people lived into their eighties or even beyond, but it was not the norm—despite all the ways we tried to counteract the effects of age. Mandatory monthly injections provided essential nutrients missing from the

modern diet; carefully designed yearly detox programs aided
in ridding the body of toxic buildup; a slurry of vaccinations
were administered to prevent everything from a case of the flu
to diseases so rare, no one had ever heard of them outside of a
doctor's office. Even after all those efforts, disease still seemed
to cut down people earlier and earlier with each passing year.

Suffice to say, it was a jolt to see so many older people in
one place. The table around which they sat was lit with a circle
of candles at the center, with scattered papers occupying the
perimeter. There, standing in the corner, with his arms gesticu-
lating in the air, was Oliver. *What the hell is going on?* I thought.

I looked back to the table. How had these people gathered
here, without any clearance, in this heavily guarded, gated-off
town? By the way they were all grinning and laughing, I could
tell they were close. By all appearances, their conversation was
nothing but enjoyable. One woman stood out above the others. I guessed by the looks of her she was in her mid-eighties.
She had a magnetic smile that drew you in, and a dark mahog-
any complexion impressively radiant for a woman of her age.

"Look at them laughing. These are warm people," I whispered. "They're all friends."

Then I noticed a detail, as one of the women raised a hand
to brush hair out of her face. A tattoo on the underside of her
forearm. An infinity symbol. I inched closer to get a better look.

We'd found them. They were real. And Oliver was in there
too. My chest ached with the relief of it all. There were five of
them—and Oliver spoke, though we were unable to hear his
words. Some of them periodically touched one another's arms
during the conversation in the way only loved ones do. When
one rose from a chair, another went to help them up. I was
entranced. I imagined myself at that age, still taking risks, still
in the company of trusted friends. Whatever was going on in
that room was truly inspiring.

As I went to lean my head just a little closer, my hand slipped out from under me and my head bumped the window. I buried my head in my hands, unwilling to witness the result of my clumsiness.

"Oh man. They heard us, Patch. What do we do?" said Rexx in an anxious whisper.

Despite my disinclination, I willed the vertebrae in my neck to respond, and gradually I forced myself to raise my head. Fighting an overwhelming urge to run, I looked through the window to witness the hectic scene I'd created. I'd never seen a group of elderly individuals scramble so quickly, and part of me was fascinated by their vigor.

One of the older gentlemen was comforting the woman who had just moments before stood out to me with her bright smile. She was crying with a look of sheer panic in her eyes as she talked to the man. She brushed his hands away as he tried to calm her down. Two men were collapsed at the table, where the gathering had been taking place just a moment ago, in a position of defeat. They each had their heads on the tabletop as they held hands, waiting together to accept their fate. Another woman, the one with the tattoo, quickly stashed the papers that had been strewn about the table into an old dresser leaning against the wall.

Oliver stood tall like a rocky island in the middle of the chaos. I started to feel queasy, seeing the distress I'd caused in these people who seemed so friendly and kind. They knew what awaited those who trespassed on restricted property, and they thought I was here to deliver that terrible fate. I desperately wanted to cease being the source of the dysfunction and despair that was unfolding in front of me. I stood up and, before I could give it any more thought, knocked on the window.

"Oliver, Oliver it's us!" Rexx yelled.

They looked around, relief registering on their faces, and I could see Oliver speaking to the room. Slowly, each face turned in our direction. One of the men, the older gentleman from before, waved the others into a corner far from the window. Even from where I was squatting, I could see that they were discussing among themselves what to do next.

After several uncomfortable minutes, the man walked to the door and propped it open, and then he and the rest of the group sat back down at their table. He scrawled something on a piece of paper, and after a moment he held it up to the window. In big, bold lettering he had written:

BOTTOM FLOOR ROOM 15
BACK ENTRANCE IS OPEN

With a fluttering in my chest, we walked toward the back of the building.

"We might be able to really do it, Rexx," I said. "These people might actually be able to help us. They were alive, Rexx. They were alive during the Seclusion."

"I just don't want you to get your hopes up, Patch. Let's try to minimize our expectations," Rexx said.

"We need a plan, Rexx. We can't just keep staying here as if nothing is wrong, when who knows what is happening to my father right now," I said as we walked around the block.

"We don't even know where he is. We should just stay here as long as possible. We have a good thing going. We're safe. Why risk it?" I was taken aback by his words. Was this the way he'd been feeling the whole time?

"Why risk it? How can you say that?" I stopped in my tracks. "You think we shouldn't even try? Just leave him to rot? To become the face of another dead soldier forced to fight for who knows what?"

"If I thought it was possible, don't you think I would've tried before?"

"What do you mean tried before? We've barely been gone a week."

"Don't you think I would have gone after her? If it's possible to get someone back, then what have I been doing all these years?"

Guilt coursed through me and I stopped talking. Of course. I'd been talking about rescuing my father, and never once had we considered going after Amara. But her arrest wasn't our fault. My father's was. Amara knew what she was doing, I thought. Even thinking that made me feel ashamed. I had to let go of old thought patterns and knee-jerk reactions and separate them from the present. Problem was, I didn't feel like I *knew* anything. I didn't know what to believe anymore. What the truth was. I did know I didn't want to take my anger out on the one person in the world I trusted wholeheartedly.

"I'm sorry." My words hung in the air between us, filling me with tremendous sadness. I looked at Rexx and tried to analyze what he might be feeling.

"Me too," he replied, and then opened his arms to me. I went into them and the frustration I'd felt melted away. I looked up into his sad eyes and he was gazing at me with an inquisitive, uncertain expression I couldn't read. I'd never seen him look at me like that before. He was holding something back.

"All right, let's go," he said, and we continued to the back door to find that it opened easily.

On the other side, Oliver was standing, his arms crossed.

"I was getting to it," he said. "If you'd only waited until tomorrow. I was going to tell you everything." He looked us up and down, then smiled. "They've been waiting for someone just like the two of you for a very long time."

CHAPTER 16

"WE FOLLOWED YOU," Rexx said curtly, cutting to the chase as we stood with Oliver in the hallway. The only light was from the solar lantern we had taken from Oliver's house. "Who are they?" Rexx went on. "Are they part of the Veritas Ring? Are there more? Did you tell them about us? Damn it, Oliver, we thought we could trust you."

Oliver didn't answer right away. His usual exuberance was gone; he was visibly tired and seemed to be contemplating whether to answer the questions.

"So, you know about the Veritas Ring?" Oliver asked after a moment.

"Not much," I said. "Just that they were resisting the changes during the Seclusion, trying to preserve what they could. We saw the symbol in your mural. We wondered if you were part of the group, but we weren't sure it still existed."

Oliver closed his eyes and took a deep breath. "It does. I discovered them a few years back, shortly after I was transferred. They were part of the original effort, yes, but they might be all that is left." My heart sank at this. All that was left of the Veritas Ring was a handful of elders? "The ability to spread messages has become impossible," Oliver continued. "There may be more groups scattered elsewhere throughout the country, but, well, we just don't know. There's no way to know anymore."

He told us they all met there once a week to talk about anything occupying their thoughts, typically topics forbidden to talk about at home—cultural traditions, ancestry, world history, and their true feelings about the state of the nation.

"How long have they been coming here?" I asked.

"Almost forty years; that's what they tell me anyway," Oliver answered.

"Wow," was all I could manage for the time being.

"When was this zone shut down again?" Rexx asked.

"I think just over forty-two years," said Oliver.

"How on earth do they get inside?" I asked, honestly perplexed as I imagined a bunch of eighty-year-olds getting in the same way Rexx and I did. There had to be a different way.

"There's an old sewage tunnel running from inside this zone to a few blocks over, outside the fence."

"But all the sewer entrances and manhole covers are . . . ," Rexx began, then paused for a moment before resuming. "Toilets are incinerator models, and with the gray-water filtration systems, we barely need sewers anymore. And the ones still in use are all guarded. How did they gain access without being seen?"

"After the earthquake, a dear friend of theirs, rest his soul, happened to notice a sewer cover on the outskirts of town was no longer sealed completely. One day he took it upon himself to see where it led. He found this zone. After it was shut down, he led the others here."

We all stood there looking at one another. I thought about how, just a week before, my first impressions of both Oliver and the elders would have been disgust. I would have labeled them traitors and put them in a box to avoid confronting their humanity. The realization was a hard one to swallow.

It was time for me to play my hand. "Oliver. My father was arrested. I need to find him, and help him if I can. I have to try. Do you know where the redemption camps are located? Do you know if anyone has ever escaped the camps? Do you know anything that could help us?" It felt good to say the words out loud, to someone other than Rexx. Oliver didn't look surprised. He simply nodded and looked down.

"I don't, Patricia. No one knows where the camps are. But I still think you need to hear what they have to say. When I told them about you, there was a spark I haven't seen before. Let's go."

I found myself smoothing out my clothes and running my fingers through my tangled hair. Even though I didn't know them, I wanted to look presentable.

Oliver led us down the dark, winding hallway.

We reached a door, indistinguishable from the rest except for the fact that it was propped open. Oliver motioned for us to go inside.

An elderly man with a prominent forehead and a ring of bright white hair sticking out in every direction opened the door. He smiled cautiously at us, then walked back to the table and sat down with the rest.

We entered the room calmly, respectfully, and were immediately offered seats in bright orange, metal-framed chairs tucked under a gray folding table in the middle of the room.

Introductions followed soon after.

The gentleman who opened the door was Noah. He was tall, very tall, with a strong yet approachable presence. Thin glasses framed his nose. The woman next to him was Sophia. She eyed us curiously, and even her forced smile was radiant against her dark features.

The others were Mason, Ethan, and Mia. Mason and Ethan held hands, introducing themselves eagerly. Mia politely offered her hand to each of us in turn after Noah introduced her. She was petite, with bright green eyes and light gray hair that flowed down to the waist of her flowered dress. Mia was the one with the infinity tattoo. Up close they all appeared weathered, older than anyone I'd ever met.

I repeated each name as it was delivered to me, to burn them all into my memory. As we sat down I took in my surroundings. The room was sprawling. Several folding tables leaned against the far concrete wall. Stacks of bright orange chairs lined up against them. Short blue carpet covered the floor wall to wall, where it met floor-to-ceiling shelves on three sides.

After settling in, I asked about the time the Walls were built. Noah answered.

"It was an age in history where there was increasing dysfunction in our society. I was just twenty-two when the second Wall was built." I did some quick math and concluded Noah must be eighty-two years old.

"We were all upset, everyone was upset about something, and the members of our government ceased to be held accountable," Noah continued. "There was no transparency. It decreased for a while, and then one day it was just gone completely. We tried protesting, holding investigations, but the news cycle, it just moved too fast. People couldn't keep up. Some citizens were vocal about their displeasure, but most were complacent. Information came from so many directions back then," he said with a wave of his hands. "People, well, we're all experts at writing off that which doesn't justify our predetermined opinions." At this Noah rose from his seat and started to walk back and forth behind us.

"The government was floundering, hemorrhaging money; it had been for years. A series of votes by Congress happened behind closed doors as we all tried to make sense of what was going on." Decisions behind closed doors were all that the government had ever represented to me, but I tried to open my mind, to imagine a different possibility.

I could tell it was taking immense effort for Noah to keep his voice level. His eyes moved back and forth between Oliver, Rexx, and me for a moment, and then he sighed. "Are you comfortable? This is going to be a long story." I shifted in my seat and crossed my arms.

"They officially eliminated the power of the people, something we didn't even think was possible," Noah continued. "Details, they told us. But once that happened, the climate of the country started to shift dramatically. The announcement of the Board was met with massive outrage and widespread demonstrations. People took to the streets by the thousands. The Internet and free press were abolished until strict guidelines, which they referred to as *information cleansing*, could be enacted. They left an information-saturated society to drown in the darkness. Without their primary revenue streams, many businesses became insolvent. The Board swooped in to buy them up, and within five years every single business in America had merged under the same corporate umbrella, America One.

"Human rights legislation unraveled along with the rest. Protestors were taken into custody en masse, with the most serious offenders being summarily executed in public as examples to the rest of America. People fought back, some even with weapons. But the Board was stronger. When they started gunning down protesters, that's when most stopped showing up. Millions were killed or imprisoned. Participation in so-called traitorous activities as simple as a signature on a petition was tracked with ease. None of us knew where they were holding prisoners. As time passed, we soon began to suspect they weren't being held anywhere at all, instead being purged in mass killings."

I swallowed a large lump down my throat as I thought about the bodies in the Wildcliff library.

Noah continued. "Small-town police underwent stream-lined virtual training and were transformed into compliance officers."

The way he spoke was so different. Not just what he was saying but the way he said it. "He wanted to be a history teacher," Sophia whispered to me as Noah continued.

"The construction of the Northern Wall and the enact-ment of no-fly zones effectively sealed off America from the rest of the world. It was announced as a chance to start over, to build a new country where American values and traditions could flourish free from outside influence and external threats. An ultimatum was given—get out for good or stay in and sub-mit to the new order. Since the Board offered no assistance to those who might choose to leave, no help with relocation, gaining citizenship, or employment in another country, leaving wasn't a viable option for most. Bridges had been burned and doors were quickly closed to American refugees. Those who elected to stay were to abide by the rules of a new America, to leave their own cultures and traditions behind. Those who refused were quickly weeded out. As you can imagine, it was an incredibly frightening time that grew worse with each passing day. Many were arrested for simply misunderstanding the new regulations. The underlying resistance simmered, emerging here and there, but with primary means of communication cut off, it fizzled out. Rebellion only got people killed."

I tried to piece together the information Noah was telling me with what I'd learned from my father and from Oliver, but some of the words and phrases he used were unknown to me. Sophia looked at me and seemed to read my confusion.

"To give you a bit of perspective, dear," she began softly. "In the year 2030, when the Northern Wall was built, things had been unraveling for quite some time, but I was still hopeful. I'd just graduated from college with a degree in cultural anthropology." She clenched her hand on the table in front of her, as if what she had just revealed made the entire situation that much more insulting and unbearable. "I had a lot of plans, none of which came to fruition." The others around the table nodded in sympathy.

"I was going to travel and study different cultures, and I even planned on teaching at a university. One day, oh, I remember it like it was yesterday," she said, and then went silent. The color drained from her face, and her eyes, filled with warmth a second before, were like glass. "One day, I heard a beeping on my smartphone. The tone reserved for amber alerts, tornado warnings, that kind of thing."

"What's a smart—" I began.

"It was kind of like an ideation device," Mia interjected quietly. "You could use it to receive messages, make calls, and browse the Internet, but back then all content was not monitored by the Board. Well, that's a subject unto itself."

"Anyway," Sophia continued, "I checked it. *MANDATORY VIEWING* was all it said. Not being one to click on suspicious links, I did what most at that time did to get the news of the day. I turned to my social media accounts. But everywhere I looked, I saw the same thing. A blank page with only the words *MANDATORY VIEWING*. Beneath them, a green sideways triangle at the center. Thinking it was probably some kind of virus, I decided to go ask my neighbor if they were having the same issues.

"Before I reached my apartment door, I was distracted by loud yelling from outside. I looked to see several neighbors, mostly college students like myself or recent college grads. Their faces were bright red and they were standing in a group staring at their smartphones and looking livid. I saw my neighbor Alex; he violently spiked his phone into the ground and stomped on it until it was broken into tiny pieces on the sidewalk. He marched away and came back out with a firearm. I backed up from my window for a moment, confused and afraid. Guns were a sensitive topic, and until that point I didn't know any of my neighbors owned one. I stood with my back against the wall and listened as four shots rang out. I couldn't watch, so I just sank to the floor, my hands over my ears, shaking. After several minutes my curiosity drew me back. I peeked out the window again."

I squirmed in my seat and looked at Rexx. His nails were digging into the table, his gaze fixated on Sophia. He didn't intend to miss a single word. Oliver was leaning back in his seat, his arms crossed. He wasn't watching Sophia; he was watching us. He'd heard it all before.

"Alex's body was being dragged up the street by four compliance officers. I screamed, but it was lost in the noise of the countless screams outside. People ran out of their houses to see what was going on, though they were forced back by the sounds of gunshots fired into the sky. I didn't understand what was happening. One man ran at the officers. He was gunned down too."

Sophia looked at her hands. I remembered the vacant eyes of the man who had dropped from the sky the day before we left. With every word, I relived her experience.

"That evening, with the second man's body still lying in plain view, I finally worked up the courage and pressed the blinking green triangle. I watched the video over and over again."

At that, Sophia stood and walked across the room, opened a drawer, and pulled out an object I didn't recognize. She then moved her chair so she was positioned in between me and Rexx, with Oliver on Rexx's other side.

"A friend of ours, an original member of the Veritas Ring, he managed to save it. He was able to rip an untracked copy." She opened a device, pressed a few buttons, and then suddenly a video was streaming. A recording of a recording.

A dark conference room, a large table, men in suits. Only men as far as I could tell from the figures displayed on screen. No faces were visible, only suits from the neck down, and in front of each, a set of wrinkled milky-white hands sat folded in front of a microphone. Suddenly a voice, deep and unrecognizable.

"My fellow Americans. Today we have an important message for you. Too long we have been divided. Division of the highest level, clouding our judgment, sowing doubt in those who serve, making patriots forget they're a vital member of the greatest nation on earth. The system that has served us for generations upon generations no longer has the trust of the people. Cyber communication has made it so easy to sling hate, and misinformation has led to confusion and fear. How do we mend? How do we move forward? We do what any broken organism must do: we evolve.

"Our old laws are outdated. They do not protect and serve the needs of all Americans. Seated alongside me are your new leaders. Strong businessmen who have invested to save our collapsing economy. Together we will build a stable America, ready to reclaim its title as world leader. Ready to inspire you to once again become a country full of loyal, proud, united citizens. This is your new Board of Directors, and with their innovation and dedications, our wounds will be healed, and we will be united once more."

The video ended without introductions, without even faces. Then the video symbol was replaced with these words—*THANK YOU FOR VIEWING. INTERNET WILL REMAIN DOWN UNTIL ALL INFORMATION HAS BEEN*

CLEANSED. FACTUAL INFORMATION, CLEARED BY THE BOARD, COMING SOON.

"So what can we do to help? What do we do?" Rexx said as soon as the screen shut off.

Ethan shook his head, but Noah leaned forward on his elbows. "When Oliver told us about the two of you, told us your story, we couldn't help but become excited. Two people who know the landscape better than we could possibly ever hope to. We here in this room, we are some of the last living Americans who know the truth about world history and what was going on when the Walls were built. We're not prepared to leave this earth with that being the case."

"What does that mean? I don't understand what that means," I said.

At this Noah went quiet, and the group exchanged glances I couldn't read. I steeled myself for whatever warranted the looks. Oliver nodded in Noah's direction, signaling for him to continue. Then Noah spoke up again.

"Well, there were some theories in the beginning. We knew we weren't receiving the whole truth. The events of the late teens and early twenties made that obvious. Some even went so far as to guess everything was fabricated. Also, as difficult as it was to build the southern border and tackle changes in terrain, it was nothing compared to the northern border. The northern border, before the physical Wall was built, was the largest international border between two countries in the world. A border that was filled with ravines, mountain ranges, lakes, rivers—"

"Wait," I interrupted, thinking about my topographical map. "So you don't think the barrier is consistent?"

"I'm saying, common sense dictates some spots are weaker than others."

"So, what would that matter? If it were possible to cross, what would be gained?" Rexx asked.

"Well, another theory during the early days was that, outside of the US, people were living peacefully. That what we saw on the news, what we still see, is fabricated or plays up isolated incidents. Some didn't think international leaders had a full grasp of what was taking place in America, and they still might not. If they knew what was really going on, maybe they could help. You ending up here, it can't be a coincidence. The two of you—you're our hope."

"Hope? Hope for what?" I asked.

Noah held out his wrinkled hands toward Rexx and me. "The two of you could change everything. If you could get outside the United States, if you could get through the Northern Barrier, you could be our voice. You could tell the rest of the world what is going on here. You could convince them to intervene. The only question is whether you're willing to try."

CHAPTER 17

I STOOD UP and walked away from the table, signaling for Rexx to join me. I fought the overwhelming urge to run out of the room. They wanted us to cross the Northern Barrier, to risk our lives, to run headlong into a world we'd been taught was full of nothing but terror and destruction. To do what? To beg someone for help they might not be able to provide? What if there was no one out there who could help? Then where would that leave us? What if there really was nothing but violence? Even with everything I'd learned and seen, it was hard to wrap my head around us being the ones who needed help. The barriers were there to protect us. They kept danger out—the real danger. Even if the Board had lied to us, had lied to us about everything, the rest of the world couldn't really be fine.

"No. No, we can't do this. We're supposed to be finding my father. We need to ask them what they know about the redemption camps," I said.

"If they have some way to help, some way to help us cross the barrier, maybe that is the way to help him. This is bigger than us, Patch. We both want to try; we both want to save him. But we need help. Real help."

"We want to show you something," Noah said tentatively from the table.

"What are these?" I asked, walking back over to see the group had spread several papers across the table. Each paper was scribbled with handwritten notes, and several were marked with what resembled maps of some kind. I remembered watching them stash papers away through the window when we first saw them. I was fairly sure they were the same ones.

"These are maps of the Northern Barrier, almost four thousand miles in total. See these areas we have marked? These are the areas where we believe the barrier may be broken."

He moved his finger around one of the pieces of paper, pointing out various regions.

My mind started to race. I'd lived my whole life under the assumption both barriers were impenetrable. If it wasn't true, it changed everything.

"How long have you known about this?" Rexx asked, a bit hostile. "Do other people know? How did you find them?"

"Through what we knew about the Canadian-US border at the time the Walls were built," Noah replied, unfazed by Rexx's tone. "There's no way to be sure how many people have figured it out, but I can't imagine we're the only ones. However, the reality is these are our best guesses."

"I don't understand," Rexx said. "Why didn't you use this knowledge? Why didn't you do something? Any of you? It was up to your generation to stop our country from turning into this!"

Noah didn't seem disturbed by Rexx's outburst. "In the beginning, it was a nightmare," he explained. "The Board saw how easily behavior could be altered when driven by primal human emotions. They decided to use fear to their advantage. It wasn't a new way of thinking, really."

Noah sighed. "We believe the Board concluded that if people accepted the borders as impenetrable and the surveillance as infallible, the fear was already there. The Board realized quickly where corners, and therefore budgets, could be cut. Various members of the Veritas Ring have been working on these maps for years."

I looked at Rexx, whose expression was still steely. "We need more information," he said curtly.

Then I turned to Noah and placed my hand on his. "Tell us everything you know, and then we will decide."

After several more hours, we decided to meet again two nights later. At that time, we told them, we'd have a decision.

The next morning, after a sleepless night of wrestling with my emotions, I awoke to find Rexx and Oliver in the garden and joined them. Rexx didn't look up or seem to notice my arrival as he continued to harvest salad fixings into a pile. Then he absentmindedly threw a clump of soil on top of the heap. When I looked at him, he was staring out in the distance.

"Hey, Rexx. You all right? What's going on?" I asked. He didn't answer, and I realized he didn't hear me. Concerned, I looked over at Oliver.

"Rexx. Hey, Rexx. Are you okay, buddy?" Oliver asked in a louder voice.

"What? Oh right, sorry." Rexx brushed soil off the lettuce he was holding. "Yeah, I'm fine. Just a lot on my mind, you know? Of course, you know."

"Yeah, do I know," Oliver said. I knelt down next to Oliver. "That look," he continued, "the one you just had on your face? I am pretty sure I wore that look for at least a year, oh yes, I did. It gets to a point where the information overload is just too much to handle, and you go a little nuts. At least, well, I did when I first started in Tier 2." Oliver was crawling over next to Rexx as he spoke.

"You hear all of these things, and all of this information just . . . it just comes at you. It piles on, and you feel like you're gradually being buried alive. You are suffocating, and you wonder how anyone could live in this society and not feel this way. And then you start to feel crazy because some people out there, they're doing just fine. They're enjoying their movies, shopping, they're playing with their children, they're living the American dream—or coma, as I call it. Everything is taken care of, so long as you don't have an independent thought in your head. So, you start to ask, 'What is wrong with me if I can't feel that way?'"

A knot started to form in my chest at his words. Oliver slammed the ground with an open palm, then stood up and started pacing.

"So, you know, you just decide to shake it off, like it's not that bad. You're making something out of nothing. But you can't, man; you just can't. The feeling you have swallowed a grenade that is eventually going to be activated, that could explode at any moment, will not go away. There is a rage inside you."

I was thrown off by Oliver's rising emotion. He was reliving something, dissociating as he spoke.

"So you try to brainstorm these big plans, potential ways to combat what's going on in our country, or possibly get some word out there, or figure out what the hell is happening in the rest of the world. I mean, there's got to be some way out! No one even knows what the rest of the world is doing right now! I mean, it's been over sixty years! They have to be doing something!"

Oliver was almost shouting at this point. He stared at Rexx with such intensity, it seemed as if he might strike out at him any moment. Rexx was drinking in every word, not breaking his gaze for one second.

"And then it just hits you—whammo, none of your plans will work. Or even if they might, you are too scared to try." Oliver had a beaten look on his face. "You can't do a thing.

Then, just to show you how powerless you really are, they stick you in a zone so toxic, it's a miracle at all you've made it this far without dying. It just makes you feel so small, man. It makes you feel so damn small."

As he said the words, for the first time I wondered if Rexx and I were the first. If previous attempts had failed. I was afraid of the answer.

"I won't accept that," I said loudly. "If everything we have heard is a lie, how do we know none of our plans will work? How can we be sure?"

"But how, Patch?" Rexx asked, his voice cautiously optimistic. "We're talking about crossing a barrier that's been there since before we were born."

"No, but think about it," Oliver jumped in. "You made it here, already more than halfway without being caught. There are even fewer residential areas up north. The elders have figured out some of the shortfalls in the surveillance cameras. We will focus on that the next time we meet—yes, we can do that. You have a water filter; you are good there. This river here flows north for a good while. We can get you enough food. We will also be more specific about spotting the most likely places to be able to cross, where the border might be weak or built of fencing, where natural erosion may have occurred—ummm, let's see—rivers, ravines, mountain sides . . . Yes, we will talk about that next time. . . . You both know how to climb, so you're good there. You know how to spot landslide risks, places to avoid . . ."

"Patch, you know how this is going to end," Rexx cut in.

I turned to look at him. "I know," I replied with firm resolve. "I've known since we left Arizona. But I think we have to try."

In the afternoon, the three of us went on a long walk. We asked Oliver questions that had come up after digesting our conversation from the evening before. He answered a few, but frustratingly said, "I'd rather you heard it from them," to most.

To distract us, Oliver pointed to a building across the street and said he had something he wanted to show us. He led us up a winding walkway to a beautiful old building wrapped in long, thin expanses of wood, once a bright white but dulled over the years. A giant wooden cross was mounted on the A-frame rooftop.

Oliver heaved open the large wooden door by its oversized handle. The latch was broken, and I wondered whether this was Oliver's doing, or if it had happened before his time here. We stepped inside. The dark colored-glass windows and lack of electricity made for a rather dim interior. It took a moment for my eyes to adjust, before the room started to come into focus.

I looked around, taken aback by the vastness of the space as my vision sharpened. The ceiling was at least thirty feet above me and met the walls in spanning, white stone arches. Narrow, ornamental chandeliers hung from the ceiling, suspended by gold chains so thin, they almost appeared to hover in the air.

Oliver jumped ahead of us and spun around while spreading his arms as if unveiling a magnificent surprise.

"What are we doing in here, Oliver?" I asked.

"Oh, I just wanted to show you one of my favorite things to do!" He practically skipped up the aisle between rows and rows of long wooden benches.

Rexx and I exchanged intrigued looks, and I found myself shaking my head in amusement. As we followed Oliver's ready footsteps, I half expected him to start scaling the walls. When we reached the end of the aisle, I saw he had seated himself at what looked kind of like a gigantic keyboard. I had seen musicians on television play something similar before.

"This is a grand piano! Isn't it grand?"

Music was highly regulated, forbidden to be created or performed by those outside the entertainment industry. And like the rest of us, musicians were started on their paths as teenagers. Compositions were heavily synthesized and often used as a backdrop for other media, such as films or video games; any lyrics centered around love of country. For most of us, music was simply part of the background, like the plastic trees outside our homes, or the billboards advertising the Board.

Oliver started to play us something, and the sound that filled the room radiated in my chest. I found myself drawn to placing my hands on the back of the piano, feeling the instrument's vibrations resonate through me. The tune Oliver played was haunting, like nothing I had ever heard before. There was a quality to it that took me some time to place. The sound was rich and real, without the tinny electronic repetition that radiated from my car and my television set outside of Zone 36.

Oliver continued to play pieces of music as Rexx and I sat on one of the benches. After a few minutes or so, Rexx turned to me, his most charming smile on display.

"Would you like to dance?"

I laughed. "Dance? I wouldn't even know how to dance to this style of music if I tried!" Rexx grabbed my hand anyway and pulled me to my feet. I had seen other people dance on television, but other than occasionally catching myself swaying in time to music on the radio in my car, I didn't know the first thing about it. We did our best to try to imitate dancers we had seen. He placed his arms around my waist and I rested mine on his shoulders. I tried to follow his steps, but the result was nothing short of a disaster. I imagined the toes within his shoes had turned various shades of purple and blue at that point. We couldn't stop laughing.

Oliver stopped playing and walked over to us. "Allow me," he said, and Rexx took a step back.

He placed his right hand in mine and his left hand on the small of my back. Though the music was no longer playing, Oliver hummed the recent melody. He danced with confidence, and I found if his hold was firm, I could easily follow his motions. As we made our way across the floor, I wondered where Oliver learned this, and if this was what dancing used to be like. There was something so simple, charming, and romantic about it. I looked at Oliver and his eyes were fixed on mine and his face was decorated with the same goofy smile I was starting to adore. I smiled briefly and then directed my gaze over his shoulder at Rexx. I wondered if the elders in the community center used to dance like this, and my smile broadened. After Oliver brought our dance to an end, he stepped back and took a bow. He then walked back to the piano and resumed his playing.

Rexx and I continued attempting to improve our dancing skills for much of the evening. We even tried our hand at playing the piano, though I decided I preferred the dancing. Rexx held me the way Oliver did and, slowly, we improved.

Oliver's dancing was more polished. Rexx's hands, and his body against mine, felt comfortable and familiar, safe and solid. I realized as we danced I had never been that close to Rexx for such an extended amount of time. I could feel his heart beating against my chest. His hair smelled of cinnamon, and when the melody slowed, I let my head fall to his chest. I felt safe.

The happiness I felt was a new watermark. Dancing. I never envisioned the joy that could come from something as seemingly frivolous as dancing.

Oliver continued to play until the room grew too dark for him to see the keys. Then, yawning, he announced he'd meet us back at the house. I walked over to the closest bench and sat down, my feet sore from all the dancing. Rexx came and sat down next to me and put his arm around my shoulders. I let my tired head fall into the crook of his neck. I was exhausted, mentally and physically. But it was a blissful, contented exhaustion. I couldn't stop smiling if I tried.

I inhaled Rexx's familiar, comforting cinnamon scent. His hand moved from my shoulder and found the side of my head. His thumb brushed my temple. We sat there for several minutes in silence, Rexx's hand brushing my face, charging something deep and dormant between us.

I was afraid to look up, to meet his gaze. I knew if I did, I wouldn't be able to hide it any longer, wouldn't be able to pretend the feelings weren't there. I looked up anyway. Even in the dim light, I saw it, reflected in his eyes—an urgent longing, sad and sweet.

He leaned forward, his eyes closing—

Before I could rationalize any more, I was kissing him. A long, searching kiss fueled by the need to discover the unknown within the familiar. When it was over, he moved his lips back but kept his forehead pressed to mine, his hand still on my face. "I've wanted to do that for a long time," he said softly.

My hand reached up and tangled itself inside his curls and I pulled him in closer, kissing him again, deeper and with more passion than before, savoring his taste, in wonder of how natural it all felt. How different than any kiss I'd ever experienced before. I was flooded with relief, and fear. Relief of no longer fighting the unspoken between us. Fear that crossing this threshold gave us so much more to lose.

"Patch," he said, and the world fell away. My free hand grasped his shoulder, and he ran his fingers down my spine, wrapped his arm around my waist, and in one fluid motion moved us to the floor. Instinctively, I opened my eyes and looked around for the America One cameras that had captured every intimate encounter I'd ever had. They weren't there. No one was watching. Everything I thought I knew about intimacy, about desire, fell away. It was only us, and the feeling between us.

CHAPTER 18

WHEN THE SUN rose, we wandered back to Oliver's house. He was already outside, tending to his garden. Upon seeing us walking toward him, hand in hand, he smiled widely. Rexx kissed my head, then wandered inside.

Oliver jumped up and handed me a basket. "Come on over here; you can catch these," he said as he walked back and knelt on the ground. I watched as he grabbed large clusters of garlic scapes and twisted to remove them from the rest of the plant, leaving the bulbs in the ground to thicken. He then gave them a slight shake and tossed them to me. They spread out in the air, and I maneuvered the basket to catch them, laughing as I did.

"Oh, Patricia, Patricia, these are going to be just fantastic later with dinner. Many people don't realize you can cook this part of the plant, you know. But they're delicious. Just you wait," Oliver said. "So, now that we're alone. All, all alone. How are you doing? I know it was a lot to process last night. Are you prepared for this evening?"

"Well, to be honest, it's been a lot. I feel like we're spending too much time sitting still, while my father is, well, who knows . . ." My mind was still on the night before with Rexx.

I felt guilty for my happiness. "Everything's just changed so much."

Oliver came and sat next to me. He studied my face as I ran my fingers through the rosemary growing nearby. I picked a sprig and brought it to my nose. Its green needles tickled my upper lip.

"In my experience," said Oliver, "it is hard to go backward, yes—that has never worked for me. I tried that for a few years, tried to act like everything was fine, in fear of what would happen if I didn't. Suppose I still do in many ways."

I contemplated his words. He'd done so much to set himself apart, things I would have never dreamed of before coming here. But only by sacrificing other parts of himself and accepting this life of near solitude. What actions would Oliver be taking if the fear that handicapped us all wasn't residing in him as well? I realized there was still so much I didn't know about the man sitting beside me.

"Do you have any family, Oliver?" I asked gently.

He solemnly focused his attention on his gardening.

Then, finally, he said, "Mint! Mint. We need mint. Could you grab some, my dear?" as if my words had never been uttered.

I picked a single rosemary needle and placed it on my tongue, then went over to pick some mint. Maybe he'd tell us something about his life eventually. I secretly wondered what the Board had taken from him. Family, friends, a lover? They'd taken something from all of us.

That night, back in the community center, five pairs of anticipation-filled eyes tracked us as we walked through the door. They were waiting for our decision.

"Don't worry—we've decided we're going to help you," I said as I pulled out a chair. Exhales of relief filled the room, and hugs and handshakes soon followed.

Over the next several hours, we studied hand-drawn maps of the world Noah had loosely organized into a makeshift geography lesson, while four other voices inundated us with what they believed to be points in history that would be immoral to take to the graveyard. We attempted to swallow as much of the information as possible as it came at us from five different directions.

The eight of us brainstormed potential methods for getting across the border. Noah and the others had obviously given it more thought than we had. When I showed them the department-issued topographical map I had in my possession, Noah was almost giddy with excitement.

"Well, you're not alone in this anymore," I said. "We're here now, so let's keep going."

"You need to be ready to go at any time; we must act like every time we meet might be the last," Noah said. Though there was some trepidation in his voice, there was something else—relief. Perhaps relief at someone else picking up the baton he had been carrying for most of his adult life.

When the lesson came to a close, Sophia asked if we had interest in walking them home—she was offering to show us how they entered Zone 36, thinking it might be of use to us. I exchanged glances with Rexx and Oliver.

"It's up to you, Patch," Rexx said after a long, awkward silence.

Despite my apprehensions, I nodded, curiosity tipping the scale against my better judgment. I had a pit in my gut, but I ignored it. Everyone rose from the table, and I could see the thrill in their aged eyes as they walked to the door. We slowed our natural pace to match the elders', offering them assistance on the stairs when needed.

They led us outside, and I was shocked when they stopped just one block away.

"It's right here," Noah said as he leaned over to lift the heavy metal sewer cover. Rexx and Oliver sprang in to render assistance.

They peeled off the cover, revealing a ladder inside. I was genuinely interested to see how our new friends could manage it, given their advanced age. But they all looked terrific and healthy, fitter than many people I knew in their fifties and sixties. Perhaps having something to live for had helped them to stay fit.

Noah climbed down the ladder first, followed by Mason, Ethan, Mia, and Sophia. "Are you coming?" one of them called out from below once they had all descended.

The sewers had been drained a very long time ago, well before I was born. Compact zero-water incinerator toilets were the norm for human waste disposal and installed in every household, leaving a fine, disposable ash. Home gray-water filters ensured all household water made its way back to the home water supply—riddled with chemicals, but wasting nothing. Still, even after all the years, the sewers harbored a dank, musty smell that could not be ignored, and I found myself bringing the neck of my shirt up to cover my mouth. Rexx and Oliver seemed in agreement based on the looks of disgust on their faces. The others appeared unaffected, presumably used to it after so many years traversing the sewers.

The community center was close to the edge of Zone 36, and I was starting to understand how they managed the journey on a regular basis—the entire walk spanned the distance of only a few city blocks—a mere ten minutes once we were all down the ladder.

"That's it straight up ahead, the ladder that goes up to our town," Noah said. "To a dead space, obviously. That's how this whole thing really got started. Once we started coming down here without getting caught, it proved the Board isn't as omnipresent as it claims. And here we still are, forty years later. Now we're going to start testing some of the other dead spaces more thoroughly."

"What do you mean 'testing' them, Noah? What are you going to do?" I asked.

"Let's talk about that more in a few days, at our next study session, shall we? I'm getting tired."

I had only known these people for two days, but I couldn't bear the idea of them putting themselves at risk, especially when we were willing to take up some of the slack. I really hoped we lived up to their expectations. Or was it enough to simply know their knowledge was passed on and they had played their part?

They were not the end of the line anymore.

We were.

After we said our good-byes, Oliver, Rexx, and I turned back the way we came, and the elders slowly started to climb the ladder. I was eager to get back up to fresh air and was already imagining my first sweet inhalation.

We hadn't made it very far when a rough, craggy voice up ahead stopped us dead in our tracks.

"I think they went this way." It was a man's voice. "You, check over there," echoed in my direction.

Rexx grabbed my shoulder. Through the reverberation of the tunnel, it was hard to pinpoint how far away the voice was, but it sounded like it was getting closer.

"Shit, shit, shit, shit, shit. Oh, shit," Oliver muttered under his breath as he spun in a circle, like a compass struggling to settle on a final direction. He turned around and pushed us ahead of him, back toward the ladder the others had just ascended.

"They must've spotted you with a drone. No. No. No. Hold the door," he said roughly, though trying to keep his voice as low as possible, just as the last foot, Sophia's, was disappearing through the hole above. Thankfully, they were not the fastest climbers.

We scrambled up the ladder. I heard heavy footsteps approaching, and I climbed as quickly as I could. When I made it to ground level, I reached down to help Rexx up behind me. Rexx was pulling Oliver up to the street when I caught the faintest hint of a light shining on the sewer floor and heard the echo of footsteps drawing nearer and nearer. Noah was waiting at the top to help replace the grate, but the others had already dispersed, the instinct to split deeply ingrained.

"Go! We'll take care of ourselves. Get out of here," Oliver said.

Noah nodded in sorrowful understanding, and before any of us had the chance to say good-bye, he slipped into the shadows. With a sinking feeling, I realized that could be the last time I would ever see Noah or the others.

"What do we do, Oliver?" I asked, my voice shaking. "They'll be here any minute." Rexx and I stared intently in his direction, waiting for him to tell us what our next move should be.

"Oh shit. Okay. Give me a second. Okay, so we know this area where we are standing and the area just around it is a dead zone. That's what Noah said. If we leave this area, then we'll be under surveillance, and it isn't dark yet, so that's no help. Okay. We need to hide." We inched away from the sewer grate and scanned around for anything that might serve as temporary concealment.

Oliver took a deep breath, seeming to prepare himself for something. "Go. Go right over there, not too far, right there in the shadows. Go duck there in that alley. It's okay, really, guys. It's okay. I'll be fine. What's the worst that can happen?" Oliver smiled, and I had the impression he was assuaging himself and not us. "I have a hunch things are about to get shaken up around here. So, if I am not okay, then, well, maybe this is how it ends. And, to be honest, I'm not quite prepared to live out the alternatives."

I stared at him in confusion. Wasn't he coming too?

"If it all works. If you get out. Figure out a plan and come back for me, okay? If you can." At that, Oliver placed one hand on each side of my face and quickly kissed me on the forehead, then did the same to Rexx. Rexx started to leave, but I just stared.

"Don't you make me regret this," Oliver said. "Go!"

Before we could stop him, he was off and running in the opposite direction. I watched, shell-shocked for a moment, before following Rexx in the direction we were pointed.

As Rexx sprinted, he removed his shirt and strategically held it over his head, so it was angled down in the front. It took me a second to realize he was trying to hide his face from the cameras, preparing for the completely possible scenario the others were incorrect about their reach. I quickly messed with the dial on the bottom of my shirt, turning it to its darkest color setting, then held my backpack over my head.

We sprinted into the alley Oliver had indicated and hid in the darkest spot we could find. The instinct to look up and search for cameras was overwhelming, but I fought it, focusing my attention on Rexx. From there, we watched as three armed Compos emerged from the sewer grate. Fear began to escalate.

"What are we doing? They are going to be here any moment. We can't just sit here," Rexx whispered.

"Oliver had a plan. We have to trust him." We watched as the officers surveyed the area opposite the sewer; they would soon round to our side. As the seconds ticked by, the chances of us going unnoticed were slimming rapidly. For all we knew, Noah could have been wrong, and a team could be monitoring the footage at that very moment.

I wondered if they knew it was us, had spotted from above like Oliver had suggested, or if they were only expecting the elders. After all, they'd gone from sneaking into Zone 36 once a week to twice in one week.

"We could keep our faces covered and try to make our way around the fence, find some other tracks," Rexx said. At first, it sounded good. One reasonable option given the circumstances. If we could make our way around the city without being observed, we had a chance. It was a big if.

"I don't know if that's going to work, Rexx." I whispered, "Whatever we do, we have to do it fast." We'd dug ourselves into a deep hole that seemed impossible to climb out of unscathed. I contemplated our next move. I considered trying to revert to the sewer, or just giving myself up and ending it right then. Oliver's voice in the distance interrupted my train of thought.

"They went this way!" he yelled.

Suddenly the group of officers was off and running in the opposite direction.

"What was that? That was Oliver. That was Oliver. What does he think he's doing?" I whispered fiercely, my voice shaking.

"He's buying us some time to get back, Patch. He knows we can't leave this area. He's driving them away. Let's go."

Rexx and I started sprinting. After a minute we both halted when we heard an unmistakable sound. A terrified shriek, from the direction the officers headed, stopped short. A scream induced by only one thing. The pacifier. It was Oliver. There was no doubt in my mind.

I couldn't move. I felt as if wet cement were creeping up around my ankles. Rexx was holding my hand and pulling me, and suddenly I was running again, in a trance. The next thing I knew, we were climbing the ladder back down into the sewer.

The minute our descent was complete, Rexx ran to the opposite wall and vomited at his feet. Tears started to stream down my cheeks as the reality of what had just happened sank in.

"Let's go!" I cried. "We have to go back and help him. This is our fault! First my father, now Oliver? What are they going to do to him, Rexx? What are they going to do?"

Suddenly Rexx pulled me close and held me tightly, steadying my shaking body against his.

"Patch. It's okay. It's okay. He made his choice. He did this for us, and if we try to go after him, we could wreck everything. We have to trust him on this one. We have to go."

I willed myself to calm down.

"We have to go now, Patch," he said gently. "A search drone might have spotted us sometime over the last couple days. Or spotted the elders. The drones showed up for a reason. They'll be coming back through and sending more to search Zone 36 any minute. Listen to me." He lowered his forehead to mine. "It's time to leave. Do you understand?" He stared at me, the look of desperation on his face having transformed to one of resolve.

"We have to leave," I repeated back in a hushed tone. As I started to walk away I added, "It shouldn't be this way, Rexx. Running, hiding, being punished for asking questions, for wanting to know the truth. It shouldn't be this way."

Rexx stared at me with an expression I couldn't quite read, and after a split second he kissed me lightly on the lips and grabbed my hand, then together we started to run again. Once we were on level ground in Zone 36, Rexx stopped. "Patch, you wait here," he said, his voice detached. "There's something I have to do."

"But they could be here any minute," I said, grabbing at his sleeve as he started to walk toward the community center.

"I'll be fast. Just grab our stuff and meet me down at the river." He shook his arm free then sprinted away. Meet him at the river? The plan. It was happening. We were enacting the plan.

I stood for a moment surrounded by the increasingly heavy darkness, staring in the direction Rexx had run. Then the light in the basement window reappeared, the slight flicker of a candle. The flicker spread, spread rapidly, until it reached an unnatural brightness. Suddenly I knew what Rexx was doing. He was protecting Noah, Sophia, Mia, Mason, and Ethan. He was destroying the evidence.

CHAPTER 19

I STOOD ALONE at the top of Oliver's trail, gazing out over the river. The moonlight cast a rippling silver sheen on the water. In the distance, it wound its way around a bend and into the unknown. Maybe if I dove, I could let it carry me, let it rock me to sleep.

I thought of the last night I'd spent in Tucson. Of the man who jumped. I closed my eyes and I saw him, his vacant eyes, as real and powerful as they'd been that day. *I will not go with them. I will go on my own terms.* Scribbled on his arm. So much had happened since that day. I did some quick math in my head. Nine days. It had only been nine days. It felt like a lifetime.

I peered into the enticing heart of the river. I could give myself to it entirely; then the nightmare would end. The weight of society's future on my shoulders would dissipate, along with my breath.

The night sky wrapped itself around me like a veil and I crossed my arms and rubbed them to warm myself. I thought about the task before us. About how we'd likely die or be imprisoned. That was how this would end. The Board was too strong, too omnipresent. We didn't stand a chance—not a real one anyway. If we'd just left the damn van alone, we'd never be in this mess. We wouldn't be on the run for our lives. We'd still be blissfully ignorant. That was better, wasn't it? Was I happy before? I didn't know anymore. I was different. At the core of my being, I was different, and now I was involved in something infinitely bigger than myself.

Our entire nation had been lied to for decades. Millions murdered to fit a narrative. We had no idea what was taking place outside the Walls. Whether we were being protected, as we were told, or caged. We lived lives guided primarily by fear. I stared at the river. The sweet release it promised. If I aimed just right, I wouldn't feel a thing; it would be over before it began.

No, I thought as I took a step backward. *I have to try. Even if I die along the way. I'm going to try to cross the border, to find someone who might offer hope. Hope for my father. Hope for Oliver. Hope for countless others. And if on the other side there is only terror, or someone waiting to chop my head off, at least I'll have seen it with my own two eyes. At least I'll know once and for all what the truth is.*

I paced at the top of the hill, firming up my resolve, but after several minutes Rexx still wasn't there. I put myself to work rearranging the backpack. I realized I didn't have the book, *Les Misérables*. I had no idea where I'd left it. Had it fallen out of my pack? It was too risky to go back and look for it. I would probably never find out what happened to Eponine or Marius. I would just have to add it to the list of things lost, relationships left unfinished.

My mind jumped to the worse possible circumstances and played them out in my head like a movie—Rexx burning himself alive in the community center, Rexx falling down the mountain, Rexx cuffed and shoved into the back of a Compo car, Rexx pacified for a second too long and lying on the pavement, a lifeless heap. Fear, no matter how much we resisted it, could paralyze the body in an instant. I had to be stronger than fear; I had a feeling there was more fear ahead. But I didn't want to do this without him. I couldn't do this without him.

Rexx emerged from the foliage, holding the climbing ropes and harnesses.

"Sorry, I got turned around on the trail in the dark," Rexx said as he ran up to meet me. His ruby-red shirt, an extra of Oliver's, was drenched in sweat as I wrapped my arms around him. He looked down and saw that not only had I been there awhile, but I'd taken it upon myself to lay out and start organizing our possessions. Rexx dropped the ropes and set the solar lantern next to the contents.

"Right, well, it could be worse," Rexx said, and started to laugh. And he kept laughing, with increasing severity. A nervous, contagious laughter. The kind that emerged when the grief was too much to process. Oliver's absence hit like consecutive crashing waves as Rexx doubled over, gripping his sides. His sweaty curls hung in front of his face, and in the dim light of the solar lantern, I watched him with concern. I placed my hand on his hunched shoulder and rubbed in a circular motion. After a minute or so of laughing, it started to subside.

"I don't know how it could be worse, Patch!" Rexx said once he finally caught his breath. "I just set a building on fire! Oliver is headed who knows where." Tears came to Rexx's eyes. "We just ran away, with only a vague plan, to try to make it to a border that is, for all we know, impassable. Even if we get through, we'll then enter a foreign country where we could be killed on sight. Who knows how long before someone finds us." Rexx wiped his eyes with the back of his hand. "We're probably going to die."

"We're still together," I reminded him. "At least there's that." As I said the words, I realized how terrified I was of it being otherwise. I'd lost almost everything that used to define me, and yet I'd never felt like I had so much to lose.

He nodded. I turned my attention to the maps. We didn't have time to procrastinate; we could feel sorry for ourselves and come up with a plan B along the way.

"We need to get up north, within walking distance of one of these parts right here that Noah marked," I said. "These are the spots where we'd most likely be able to cross the border and have decreased surveillance. Now, we can't follow the river the whole time, because up here it's going to pass through these major towns, including Portland soon." I pointed out the circles on the map found in the van. "We have to circumvent those somehow. We have about three hundred and fifty miles to cover, more because it won't be a straight line. It's possible for us to do it on foot, but it will take forever. We can't go back to the tracks; they'll be monitoring them now. They must have figured out that's how we got here. The river here flows north, and it's not too deep, so we may be able to use it to guide us around the city."

"Good plan. So we're really doing this?"

"We're really doing this," I said as I started to fold the maps back up. "We still don't know if they showed up after us or after Noah and the others. And if they're here for us, they still might think we ran with Noah and could be looking in the city. They'll probably search the city and Zone 36 first. That should buy us some time, I hope. We just need to keep an ear out for search drones and stay hidden as best as we can."

We gathered up our possessions, stuffed them into my backpack, and then looked at the climbing ropes lying on the ground.

"Do you remember how he did it? How he did it solo?" I asked, my voice catching, and Oliver's bright smile agonizingly flashed through my brain. Oliver wasn't with us. I'd let myself care for him, given him my trust. I thought about how just weeks before, Oliver would have been the type of person I shunned as a traitor. A person I would have cataloged as "other." Put him in a box to never think highly of again. But I'd been wrong. I thought about the cooking, the dancing, the rappelling, the artwork. About how at his core, Oliver was someone who wanted to share joy with others. He was good. He was caring. He was selfless. He led the Compos away to save us, and soon he'd probably be imprisoned, or dead. How many more out there were like him? How many people labeled as radicals were really those searching for the truth and refusing to be guided by fear?

Maybe there was a way he talked himself out of trouble. Maybe he could convince them he was going after us or the elders, that he was just doing his job. If not, maybe he'd end up with my father, tell him I was sorry. Tell him I was trying in the only way I knew how.

"I think so," Rexx replied in an unconvincing tone, snapping me out of it. I walked to where Oliver stashed the harnesses and the other equipment, then tossed one harness to Rexx and put on the other.

"I think he used this one when he went by himself," I said as I held up a metal contraption slightly different from the one we used. "I think you thread it through like this. We better get on with it. I'll go first; you hold the light. Then, once I'm down, you can clip it to your harness and you can pull this thingy back up for yourself." I looked down to the river's welcoming arms again.

I got to work setting it up exactly the way I remembered Oliver doing it. While I was distracted, Rexx startled me by wrapping his hand around my arm. "That's a long way down Patch, if we don't do this right." He stopped talking and we both took a simultaneous breath.

"Well, then at least it will be quick. Here, what do you think?" I asked. Rexx held the lantern close and studied the setup. As he did, I tried to commit every feature of his face to memory. If I started to fall, I'd need an image to hold on to.

"I don't know. I think it's right. I don't know," Rexx said.

Rexx reached up and brushed his fingers through my tangled, unkempt hair, then leaned in and kissed me. My heart sunk as I kissed him back. I knew what the kiss meant. It was a good-bye kiss, a good luck kiss, a *Hope I have the chance to kiss you again but in case I don't* kiss. If the descent didn't go as planned, or anything that followed in the hours and days to come led to our separation, he was preemptively saying good-bye. I dropped what I was doing and kissed him, wrapping my hands around the back of his neck as I balanced on my knees. When our lips parted, I looked at his eyes. There was so much I wanted to say. I wanted to tell him how I felt. Tell him that he was a piece of me, and that if something happened to him after everything we had survived together, I didn't know how I would keep my head above water. Instead I nodded and went back to work.

We made it down without Oliver's support. In the dark. My heart stayed in my throat for the entire descent, until my feet found solid footing at the bottom. My eyes remained glued on the small light that was Rexx as he came down after me, hoping he'd threaded the metal carabiner correctly, hoping he didn't slip on the slick rocks. He made it down too. Then, together, using the matches Rexx had in his pocket, which he'd swiped from the community center, we set fire to the ropes and watched as they slowly burned. About halfway up, the fire went out, or it was simply too dark to track anymore. We turned and started walking northwest; there was nothing else we could do.

We walked all night, following the compass northwest to try to bypass Portland. We tried to stay in the protective cover of trees, but there were fields as well. Those we ran through as quickly as we could in the dark, clutching to the hope that it wouldn't be the moment a drone arrived.

When morning came, we estimated we'd covered only ten miles. At that rate, it would take us over a month to make it up north. We had enough food for about ten days, give or take. We were exerting a lot of energy hiking and wouldn't be able to spread our rations as thin as we had on the trip to Zone 36. But we continued on, in the same fashion for a second night as we had the first. During the day we found overhangs to shelter ourselves from overhead surveillance.

Part of me couldn't believe we were back on the run. I guess we'd never stopped really, but Zone 36 had started to feel safe and natural. Oliver had almost been like family, but suddenly Rexx and I were on our own again.

On the third afternoon, Rexx was crouched beside a stream, scooping up water with the portable filter and letting it run into our water bottles. I was underneath a nearby overhang, centering ourselves in the maps and repacking our supplies in preparation for heading out, when the sound reached us.

The crunch of boots slowly making their way over the blanket of dried pine needles. Making their way toward us.

Oh shit. Shit.

A Compo was slowly descending the hillside toward Rexx. He hadn't spotted me. I stopped myself from yelling Rexx's name in warning. I held my breath as I hastily peered over one shoulder, then the other, trying to assess if the Compo was alone, if there was one approaching me from behind as well. No sign of anyone else. Compos often traveled in pairs; there could be another nearby. Rexx still hadn't looked up. Did he hear him too? Did he assume they were my footsteps? *Distract and disarm*, I told myself, remembering a conversation with the elders about such a situation. The Compo's pacifier was aimed directly at Rexx's head as he slowly walked toward the water's edge.

"On your knees," he ordered. Rexx startled and dropped the water bottle and filter, and they headed downstream. My stomach churned at the sound of the Compo's voice.

Think, think, think. I reached to the ground next to me and wrapped my fingers around an object.

"What are you doing out here?" the Compo demanded.

"Working," replied Rexx thinly, with only a slight tremor in his voice as he turned his head toward the Compo. "I'm with the Natural Resources Department," Rexx added, his voice becoming more confident with each word. "I was assigned to collect soil samples upriver from Zone 36 to see if the levels are evening out away from the zone."

"Why would the levels even out upriver? Wouldn't that happen downriver?" *Damn, he's a smart one,* I thought. I wondered how a Compo knew such things. It wasn't that advanced, but again, citizens were generally taught the skills needed to perform occupational duties, and not much more.

"Right. Right you are. Yeah, they want both. Upriver and downriver. Trying to isolate the markers, you know. Figure out exactly where the parameters are when it comes to elevated chemical levels in the riverbed."

"Mmm-hmm. Well, we've had some trouble within the zone. I'm going to have to scan your chip and call in about this." He stepped toward Rexx, switched the pacifier to his left hand, and maneuvered his right hand to grab the chip scanner from his uniform. But before he could do so, I brought the stone down on his scalp as hard as I could, and the blow sent him sprawling to the ground, unconscious.

Rexx lunged for the Compo's pacifier, which had landed alongside his legs, and tried to shoot him, but the weapon didn't work in his hand. He flipped it around, inspecting it. On the side, in jet black against a metallic finish, was the national emblem, and above that, PAC-21. I assumed this referred to the specific pacifier model. I then spotted a small rectangular pad beneath the barrel.

"It's biometrics. Biometrics. You need his fingerprint!" I hissed.

"Right." Rexx fumbled and took the officer's hand, positioning it so he was holding his own weapon. The pacifier's tip emitted an emerald glow. Then, together, they pressed the button that triggered the shot to the Compo's chest. He'd be out for several more minutes now. The whole ordeal happened within twenty seconds, and then Rexx and I both fell to the ground.

I looked at the Compo's face for the first time. He was older than we were, maybe in his mid-forties. He was tall and thin, with raven-black skin and hair cut short against his scalp, which now bulged at the top where I'd struck him. I lifted his head gently and straightened it out so it was arranged in a more natural position. Then I glanced at his badge:

COMPLIANCE OFFICER
ROBBIE WEBB

Rexx carefully unattached the ID from the Compo's wrist and chucked it in the river. We both watched as it floated downstream. It could buy us some time if someone was tracking him.

"Nice work, Patch. I didn't even hear you," Rexx said. I was still in shock over what I'd just done. The ease with which I brought a rock down on a man's skull was all at once empowering and frightening. My hand trembled in the aftermath. After a second we each grabbed an arm and dragged the officer over to a nearby tree and propped him against it. We searched through the pockets on his uniform and took out everything we could find. Some of the items I didn't recognize—official tools of some kind or another. Others I did—sunglasses, and one of the torch-like tools I'd seen the Compos using on the van's contents in the state park. I pressed the button on the side and was pleased to discover biometrics were unnecessary.

"This could come in handy," I said as I turned it over in my hands.

We sat facing the Compo. I held the torch, and Rexx pointed the pacifier in his direction, though neither one of us could fire it even if we wanted to.

"Now what?" I asked. "I don't think he's going to be exactly happy when he wakes up. He could also have a partner searching nearby."

Rexx didn't answer; his eyes were fixed on something and they grew wider by the second. I followed his gaze up the bank until I saw what he was staring at. The Compo's car.

It wasn't far away at all, just through a few trees. I wondered how it had approached so silently. Window tinting rendered the glass almost as dark as the body. Thin strips of red, white, and blue lights skirted its flank. The glow was the only thing one saw when the vehicles bolted down the road in the dark. Truth be told, there'd always been a part of me that wondered what it would be like to drive one.

"There must be surveillance in there, though, right? I mean, that seems too easy," Rexx said.

"We could give it a try," I said, "even if it's just to cover a bit of space. We could take the main thoroughfares in a Compo car. People wouldn't even look twice. And with the lights off, they're almost impossible to spot. How many times have you been caught off guard by an approaching Compo car? Too many to count."

Whatever decision was to be made, it needed to happen fast. He nodded, then scrambled up the bank in the direction of the car. "I'll go check it out; you stay here." I sat cross-legged, torch pointed in the Compo's direction. We knew one thing about the effects of the pacifier that brought some comfort—waking up was not a quick process. The bump on the Compo's head continued to swell. I felt guilty. He was only doing his job.

A few minutes later, Rexx came down the hill a bit too fast, slipped, then jumped up and brushed himself off. "I looked in the windows and the panels look similar, but it's chip activated."

Of course it was. I felt foolish for thinking it'd be otherwise. All vehicles were. Just like mine, the Compo's car would only operate when the assigned user's chip was detected.

"Guess Officer Robbie Webb is coming with us," I said.

Ten minutes later, with the unconscious Compo tied in the passenger seat, we pulled onto the road in the compliance vehicle. As I looked in the rearview mirror, there she was. The Compo's partner. Emerging from the trees, ID held in front of her mouth. *Shit.*

"We have to put distance behind us, and then we need to get out of this vehicle," Rexx said, his voice quaking as he spoke. The irreducibility of what we'd just done sinking in. I drove silently, and Rexx sat in the backseat directly behind the Compo, leaning forward, our knife at the ready. I held the torch in my lap just in case. We drove for about twenty minutes. Occasionally I reached over and checked for a pulse, just to make sure we didn't need to add murder to our growing list of crimes.

It was surreal, and part of me wasn't fully convinced I was living in reality. It felt more as if I were existing inside a video game. The kind that Rexx, Amara, and I used to play in my parents' living room. Part of me expected Amara to sideswipe me off the road.

"I didn't ask for this job, you know. I wanted to be an engineer." Officer Webb was conscious. He spoke in a craggy, resigned tone from the passenger seat, his face angled so he was looking out the window. I didn't know how long he'd been awake. He hadn't made a peep until that moment. I wrapped the fingers of my right hand around the torch on my lap.

"The first time they put a weapon in my hand," Webb continued, "I told them. I said, 'I want to be an engineer.' But they didn't care." Neither Rexx nor I answered. I continued to drive in silence for about twenty more minutes. The Compo didn't yell, didn't try to escape, just sat there and didn't say another word.

I thought about what he'd just said. Though I knew how our job system worked, for some reason I assumed Compos were special and loved their jobs. The sedition I'd seen in the eyes of most Compos in the past all but confirmed it. But they were probably thrust into their positions in the same way the rest of us wound up in our own, because of an aptitude test, and if they were lucky, a mild interest in the work.

"How's your head?" Rexx finally asked him, leaning over in his seat to get a good look.

"You know, at first it made me sick," Officer Webb said, slurring his words. He sounded drugged, still suffering the aftereffects of the pacifier, which I'd heard could lower inhibitions. "I would go home afterward and just feel disgusted. But eventually I started to enjoy it, started to crave it. I was doing the Board's work. I loved it. I couldn't get enough. I felt powerful. One day I came home and my daughter, she was five at the time, she said, 'Daddy? Will you shoot me if I say something I'm not supposed to?'" He stopped talking. A chill ran down my spine, and I felt as if I'd been dipped in icy water.

After a while I couldn't hold my tongue any longer. "None of it's true, you know. None of what they tell us."

"Patch! What are you doing?" Rexx said hotly. I shouldn't have been talking to the Compo like this, but I was past caring.

"America isn't the best or the brightest or the safest. There's a whole world out there. Hundreds of countries, possibly thriving, and the Board's lying to us about all of it. The others moved on without us, and you know what I think? I think they might be succeeding while we are failing."

The Compo didn't say anything, didn't jump to the Board's defense; he just replied in a monotone voice, "I know who you are. I put it together. You're those traitors from Arizona. They'll find you. They find everybody. And once they do, there's no going back."

We turned a corner in the road, and there in the distance they were waiting. The entire width of the road was covered—two Compo vehicles, the same style as the one we currently occupied, and an armored transport vehicle that slightly resembled the incinerator vehicles used for raids. Several officers stood in a row, pointing their weapons directly at us as we approached. Drones circled overhead.

No.

I put the vehicle in reverse, turned my head, and started to back up, but two more weapon drones dropped to eye level, blocking any escape. I careened the car over to the left shoulder of the road.

"Get out, get out, let's go!" I shouted to Rexx. We scrambled out of the vehicle, leaving Officer Webb tied in the passenger seat, and started to run into the brush. As I ran, I threw my backpack into some tall grass. When Rexx saw me, he did the same with the multi-tool. If we were going to be captured, we could at least try to avoid handing over our maps and other possessions. We ran until a drone lowered itself right in our path. We turned, trying for another direction, but we were no match for its speed. It blocked our path again, shining a blinding light in our eyes and reporting information back to its master.

I dropped to my knees. Rexx puts his arms behind his head and stepped in front of me. Then five uniform-clad Compos stepped out from the glare of the drone's spotlight. The scene from hundreds of my nightmares over the years had finally come true. It'd only been a matter of time. My father, Oliver, the elders. It had all been for nothing. We had failed.

I wish I could say I faced them with strength and pride like I told myself I would. Wished I'd been stronger than the fear. But at the sight of six weapons pointed at me, five hand-held and one drone-operated, an animal impulse overtook me. I jumped to my feet and, of all things, I tried to run.

The excruciating pain started in my spine, and I quickly lost all motor skills and muscle function. My skeleton felt caged in electricity. Everything in my body went rigid and I collapsed to the ground, unable to break my fall. The front of my body hit first, and I felt as if someone had kicked me hard, square in the face. All I felt was pain, a pain so immense that it seemed to push me out of my body.

In the bleary sky, a dark shape circled, getting lower with each passing. An eagle. I could clearly see its face, much larger than its body. It screamed a call of alarm. Then it flew off in the direction we were meant to go, toward the unknown, toward freedom, leaving us behind.

CHAPTER 20

I AWOKE DISORIENTED. My cheek and left eye pulsed with pain, each throb like a knife in my skull. I tried to raise my hand to my face to inspect the damage, but it wouldn't budge. My arms were locked behind my back. I then remembered how I came to be unconscious.

I tried to look around, but my head was bound tightly by something cold and unyielding, securing me in an upright position that strained my spine. My throat was raw when I swallowed, and a metallic taste filled my mouth. My only functional eye rotated from one periphery to the next, but there were no details to my surroundings. I was in a nondescript room, and it was unclear whether I was aboveground or below. Rexx was nowhere in my line of sight.

The room extended about ten feet to my right and seven to my left. The white walls were coated liberally with a waxy varnish that made them appear sticky and unwelcoming. On the wall in front of me was a door, with the same varnish coating as the walls. The only defining characteristic, if you could call it that, was the national emblem that stretched from floor to ceiling. About two feet from my knees was a large maroon office chair that currently sat empty. It was the only furniture in the room as far as I could tell, other than what I was sitting on. I had a feeling its position was not coincidental.

"Rexx," I whispered. I then listened with all of my might but didn't hear a sound. It was unclear if I was seated against a wall or had been left vulnerable in the middle of the room. I scanned the tops of the walls within my field of vision but didn't spot the cameras that were generally prolific in corners and seams.

"Do you know why you are here?" A low, baritone voice interrupted my train of thought, rattling my spine. The ache in my throat intensified. The voice spoke calmly from behind me. I didn't respond. Bile started to rise, stinging my dry throat with its ascent. Then the tramping of shoes, and a man passed by my right side, brushing my aching shoulder with his hip.

"I'll ask you again. Do you know why you are here?"

I opened my mouth to speak. The metallic taste lingered on my sandpapery tongue.

"Yes." The word came out scratchy and raw.

The man stepped into full view. He didn't look like he belonged in the room, recoiling from his surroundings as if they were beneath him. He wore black from head to toe. Suit, tie, shirt, shoes. All black. His hands he kept in his pockets, and when he sat down in the chair across from me, he did it ever so carefully, as if the chair itself should be so lucky to accommodate him. I put him in his mid-forties.

"Enlighten me," he said as he leaned forward and made eye contact. The dark bags under his eyes bulged, like someone had injected a pocket of air under his skin, while his cheeks and forehead were taut. His brown hair was thick but superficial looking. The strands each too robust and shimmery to be natural. He'd clearly been the recipient of one too many cosmetic surgeries. His freshly shaven skin showed blotches on his chin and neck. He clasped his hands together. "Don't be disagreeable now, or we will have a problem."

"Who are you?" I asked, though I thought I already knew the answer.

"I am a member of the Board. Which one is not important. But I think I'll be the one asking the questions from here on out, Patricia. Play it," he commanded.

The last words were not directed at me, but at someone else who could hear our conversation. Then, where the emblem had been on the wall a moment before, footage started to stream. I watched my parents climb out of our work vehicle a block from their apartment. Then footage of my father wearing the same clothing he wore on the day we visited the van, pinned to the ground by multiple Compos. I watched Rexx climb into my car and the two of us drive out of city limits. I watched the drone footage of Rexx and me on the cargo flat in Nevada. Then a still image of the crushed drone on the tracks. Then Noah and Sophia walking hand in hand down the street with the words *LIVE FOOTAGE* flashing in the corner of the screen. Then Oliver in a dark room. His hair and his beard were gone, and a strip of black fabric covered his eyes. Then myself as I tried to run from the drone, then being sent to the ground by the debilitating sting of the pacifier. Rexx tried to get to me, only to be simultaneously shot by two Compos. The footage ended on a still of Rexx's unconscious, twitching face.

"Where is he?" I asked hotly.

"I said I would be asking the questions." Something landed on my lap, but I couldn't angle my head down to see what it was. "Victor Hugo. We found it in Zone 36, Patricia. Your DNA is all over it. Now this is a preview of what you'll experience if you don't cooperate."

Out of his pocket he took a small device and placed it on his knee. Then pain. Pain that ran from my wrists and up to my elbows, as if someone were slicing into my carpal bones with a knife. Whatever was binding my hands behind my back was connected to the device on his knee. Tears came without invitation, salt water rolling down to my chin. The man before me cocked his head, reached out a finger, and wiped away the trail of moisture. A shudder ran through me at his touch.

"You have committed treason, Patricia. There is no reason to keep you alive. You have turned your nose up at the bounty we have provided you. And why? We take care of you; we take care of all of you. You've never wanted for food, for shelter, for comfort. Have you?"

"No," I answered through gritted teeth.

"We have you on camera in Nevada. That was over a week ago. Tell me, Patricia, what have you been doing all this time?"

I didn't say anything. Then the screen was replaced with another image. "We will give you a chance to redeem yourself," the Board member continued. "But you know what happens when you don't cooperate."

On the screen was someone from my past, barely recognizable as her emaciated body lay crumpled on the floor of a small, dark room. Her once long hair was shaved almost to the skin. Her eyes were vacant of the mischievous spark they'd once held.

Amara.

Part of me had always known she wasn't still out there, living the life we imagined for her. Part of me knew she was dead. But knowing that was one thing; seeing the dead body of my friend on-screen was another feeling entirely. "What did you do to her?" I demanded, fighting against the bonds that held me to the chair. My words were no longer choked. In that moment I wasn't scared; I was angry. I thought of Rexx. Was he being shown the same footage at that very moment?

"A friend of yours, right? I considered having the guards exterminate you, like we exterminated her. But I don't think you should get off that easily. You and your friend must spend some time atoning for your bad behavior." The way he said "bad behavior," punching the *b*'s as if he were reprimanding a child, made my skin bristle. "But first, tell me. Did this end the way you wanted it to? Your search for the truth?"

I looked at him more carefully. What had he been taught to believe? What vision was he convincing himself he was upholding? "Our history is toxic, and the outside world is dangerous," he continued. "Even if you cooperate, you will spend the rest of your life in here, paying off your debt to society. Was it worth it?"

I swallowed the lump in my throat. "What about redemption?" As I spoke the words, the answer became clear. It was all a lie. I should have known. A smile widened on his face, satisfaction at seeing that at least in that one regard, the Board had continued to fool me.

"You surprise me, Patricia." He looked at me quizzically. "Most of our citizens are sheep, content to live without questioning, as long as their needs for entertainment and security are met. But not you. You had to keep looking."

A voice told me not to say what was on my mind, but I ignored it. "How many did it take before the scales tipped?" I asked, thinking of the piles of decayed remains in Wildcliff. "How many people did you murder?"

His eyes widened, but the smug look on his face grew. "Most don't dare to speak to me that way. How thrilling." He leaned closer. "I wouldn't call it murder, per se. More like"—he waved his hand in the air as if he were trying to conjure the right expression—"removing the toxins. Starting fresh. For the safety of the people. Mob mentality must be squashed, and the Board took care to protect those who would come next.

They needed to ensure that only true patriots, those with a deep-seated love for our country and respect for our leaders, remained. The rest of the world is in ruin. You've seen it. We are the last survivors; there is no room for compromise. But I am ever so eager to hear what you know."

I didn't break eye contact. "I know that those before me conformed because they were afraid. They were afraid of you, afraid of a government that was supposed to protect them." As I spoke, his eyes narrowed into slits. I was backing myself into a corner, but again, I did not care. "I know I believed you. We all believed you."

He looked at me inquisitively, as if I were a lab animal and he were mentally compiling notes. I waited for the blowback, but he just said, "And now?"

I continued, "I know the Board was behind the bombing in 2029. That you used it to suit your narrative." I didn't actually know this, but the smile creeping across his face all but confirmed it.

"Fear of the unfamiliar has always existed in our country, Patricia. Since long before you were around. People have a strong capacity to hate; we simply redirected that capacity, channeled it to our advantage. We did it so you didn't have to. We did it for your protection. You people, you don't know what's good for you. With your limited education. Someone has to make the hard decisions. You should be thanking us." I wondered why he was telling me this. What benefit could it possibly serve? I then realized he reaped pleasure from it, from their manipulative accomplishments. He was proud of the role he played, and he liked bragging about it.

"Now, from the beginning, dear. Tell me everything."

"No."

The pain began again.

It intensified to a level I had never felt before, and I watched as his blurring figure got up and left the room, his shiny black shoes the last thing that faded from view. The pain escalated until it enveloped my entire body and I could see nothing but black.

When I came to, he wasn't in the room, but there was someone else there. In my disoriented state, I couldn't get a good look at him.

"She's awake," the unidentified person said. There was something familiar about the voice. At that, the door opened and the Board member came back into view wearing a smug smile.

"Bring him in," the Board member sad. The pit in my stomach expanded into a black hole as I ran through the options of the "him" he could be referring to. The person walked out of the room. "I want you to tell me everything you discovered on your little trip. The names of everyone you talked to, every single person involved. I want to know how you got so far without being detected and how you survived." He never mentioned the Veritas Ring by name, but I had a strong hunch it was the well he was trying to dig.

"We just rode the flats. There was no secret to it. It was just us. You have both of us. We didn't talk to anyone else," I said, my voice shaking, afraid of what was coming next and wanting to avoid an encore of the pain I'd just experienced.

"I don't believe you," he said. Of course he didn't. Why else would he have shown me footage of Noah and Sophia? Of Oliver? He'd been carefully studying my reaction as the footage played, and I wasn't fooling him or myself.

The door behind him opened and a guard came into view. I realized at once why the voice had sounded familiar. It was Officer Webb. My heart sank. He was dragging someone behind him, someone whose head was covered in a black bag.

I could tell from the mystery person's skin tone that it wasn't Rexx or Oliver. Whoever it was, their badly bruised arms were secured in front of them, and they looked malnourished. I had just seen Noah a few days prior; he couldn't have digressed that quickly. I looked at Officer Webb, hoping to receive some clue. He did not meet my eyes.

"I'm going to give you one more chance, Patricia. I want you to tell me who else you talked to. Who else doubts the Board. Redemption isn't a complete fabrication. There are many paths to reclaiming your patriotism. Help us find others, and we won't make your time in here a nightmare. Don't help us, and . . ."

He reached over and pulled the hood off the person kneeling on the ground.

At the sight of him, I felt as if my heart had been crushed in a vice. His red hair was shaved close and he looked bedraggled, abused, and skinny as hell. But it was him.

It was my father.

CHAPTER 21

"NOW, I BELIEVE I asked you something, Patricia," the Board member said. I stared at my father, and he stared back at me.

"What have they done to you? Are you all right?" he asked me. *What had they done to me?* I could hardly believe he was asking me that after looking at him. He had obviously been through more than I had. Though my swollen face and eye probably told a different story.

Before I could answer, the Board member spoke again.

"Tell me where you went and who you talked to. I want names and locations," repeated the Board member. I looked at my father and thought I perceived a slight shake of his head. Was I imagining it?

"I told you, we just took the flats. We avoided the cities. We had knowledge of the landscape due to our line of work. There was no plan. We just knew we were in trouble and ran away. Please. We saw others in Zone 36, but we didn't interact. They didn't see us. We kept to ourselves until we ran into the compliance officer, but you know that part."

"Yes, that part I know," he said, and looked sternly at Officer Webb, who was still standing at attention next to the door.

"Officer Webb," he said. At that Officer Webb pulled a pacifier from a clip on his uniform and stepped toward my father.

I didn't take my focus off my father. His eyes, usually bright and glassy like my own, were dull, bloodshot, and listless. I still didn't know what had transpired the evening after we'd taken him to the van. Was it simply my mother turning us all in? Or was there more to the story? Then, of all things, I smiled. We had more in common than I'd realized.

He then spoke. "Patricia. Don't worry about me. Don't tell them anything you don't want to," my father choked out with great effort. At that the Board member nodded to Officer Webb, and Webb stepped forward and pointed his weapon at my father's neck.

"Now, I am going to give you one more chance. What Officer Webb is holding right there, it is not your standard pacifier."

Webb shifted uncomfortably on his heels.

"There are many settings," the Board member continued, "and it is now set to lethal. I know your incident with Officer Webb occurred not far from a closed-off zone. I know you arrived at the zone by flat. I know you spent time in that zone and interacted with an Oliver Shelling, and a Noah and Sophia Feldmann. We know that Mr. and Mrs. Feldmann have somehow been accessing the zone and partaking in illegal activity and that you were in their presence on the night Mr. Shelling was arrested. Now, I will ask you one more time to tell me everything you know. What were Mr. Shelling and the Feldmanns up to? What did they discuss?"

"I've told you everything I know. Please—" But before I could finish, the device's energy crackled into my father's skull. Within a split second he was a lifeless heap on the floor. I felt myself screaming, and again there was immense pain. But this time I couldn't differentiate the physical from emotional. The room started to spin. Everything became blurry, just one long scream filled with anguish swirled with flashing memories of my father. Two people closed in on either side of me, something was jabbed into my arm, and then everything went black.

I awoke. It was completely dark, no windows, not even a sliver of light through a crack under a door. I wiggled my body, disoriented and still under the impression I was sitting with my hands behind my back. But they were free. I wasn't sitting in a chair at all, but lying on a cold, hard floor. I lifted my hand to my head to find that it was free as well and that someone had bandaged my wounds, though the aching continued.

It was so dark. The kind of darkness that made me feel as if I'd been disconnected from my body and set adrift in the void. I lay on my back, feeling the floor with my palms. It was cold and damp, like I was underground, though the room could have been on the top floor of a building for all I knew. I had no idea how large my current cage was. I wondered if Rexx was on the same floor.

I felt numb, my brain unwilling to fully acknowledge my reality. I lay there for several minutes, staring into nothingness, listening for a clue, letting my other senses heighten. The room had no airflow and smelled of wet laundry left too long before drying.

I raised myself to all fours and started to feel around with my hands, spreading my fingers out to keep my balance as my aching body protested. I felt more of the same, cold concrete, and I slowly started to crawl, reaching in front of me every time

I moved forward. About six feet from where I started, I felt a wall. I followed it until I reached a corner, then started to trace it back the way I came.

I deduced I was in a room about ten feet long. I kept going, trying to determine the width, and then stopped when my hand touched something. It was a grate of some kind, even colder than the concrete enclosing it. I felt around some more and when I realized what it was, what was installed in the floor of this small cement cell, bile once again began to rise in my throat, burning my esophagus as I struggled to keep it from coming up. What I had felt was a large toilet drain.

I crawled back to the corner and curled myself up against the wall, letting the numbness wash over me until my bruised body and brain gave in to the darkness once more.

A loud blaring sound woke me up. And suddenly there were figures moving on the wall across from me. The whole surface was a television screen. The bright figures were blurry, as my eyes had not adjusted to the light. The audio was instantly recognizable as screams, the screams of someone experiencing horrible pain, followed by the sounds of gunshots, explosions, and more screams. Once my eyes adjusted, the picture came into focus. There were words on the bottom of the screen:

THESE ARE YOUR ENEMIES, PATRICIA.

Foreigners were on the screen, torturing and killing young women and children. Groups in black masks burned the American flag and sliced the necks of American military men and women. Similar scenes unfolded for hours on end. Other messages appeared on the screen.

YOU HAVE BEEN LED ASTRAY.

YOU CAN MAKE IT UP TO US. LABOR IS HOW YOU REPAY YOUR DEBT AND SERVE YOUR COUNTRY.

FOREIGNERS WANT US DEAD. AMERICA IS THE ONLY SAFE HAVEN IN THE WORLD.

I had seen similar images and video footage on *America One*, interjected in other media throughout the day, and built into childhood lessons. But watching it for hours straight made me want to sink into the concrete below me and never emerge. The volume swallowed the entire room; it was so loud, I couldn't hear myself think. No matter where I turned my head, I couldn't look away from the images. I was hungry and hadn't eaten in over a day as best I could tell. There was no way to keep track of the time. My throat was dry and becoming drier by the minute.

They are lying, I repeated over and over to myself, even though the scenes in front of me told a different story. Leaders of other countries begged our powerful and righteous leaders for mercy.

I didn't know how much time had passed before an object was slipped through the hole in the door. The streaming footage ceased, and instead the words *PUT THEM ON* flashed on the screen. I inspected what came through the door and saw that they were cuffs, though thicker and heavier than any I had seen before. Their silhouette resembled that of a butterfly. I took them, hoping it was a sign I would soon be led out of the forsaken room and integrated into the general population. I placed them onto my wrists and heard an instant fusing sound as they shut themselves. A light on the side of each wrist blinked red. I tried to open them again but found that operating them was out of my control.

BACK UP AGAINST THE METAL WALL, the screen blinked.

I looked around and noticed that the wall behind me was, in fact, metallic. I did as instructed and then my hands were jolted into an upright position above my head. The cuffs fused with the wall behind me, twisting my shoulders into an unnatural position. Magnetized handcuffs.

The door opened and someone walked in carrying some kind of bag. She wore a mask, and I could not see her face. She started to remove tools from her bag, and then picked up what looked like a medium-size set of shears. I began to hyperventilate. But she did not hurt me. Instead she inched forward and began to cut off my hair. She came back for a second pass with another tool, taking all but the last inch. I watched it fall to the floor around me.

She then took another tool from her pack and started to slide it up my leg. She was cutting off my clothes. The cool material left a trail of goose bumps across my skin as she did so. Tears of fear and humiliation started to fall down my cheeks as my skin was slowly exposed. She removed every last piece of fabric, then stood back and examined me. She removed something else from her pack and then stepped next to me. I felt her hand on my fingers above my head. A snipping sound, then she stepped back into view. The remnants of my grandmother's ring lay in her gloved palm.

I was left naked and shivering, still fused against the cold metal wall.

When she shut the door, the handcuffs unfused and opened again. I was prompted to put them back where I found them. I stared with disgust at the camera in the corner of the room and crawled over to the door as sobs racked my body. I put the handcuffs back on the shelf in the opening of the door. They disappeared, and a few seconds later a pile of clothing appeared in their place. They were similar to the scrubs my parents wore at the hospital, and I put them on as quickly as I could, imagining the Board member who murdered my father watching every second.

Then the propaganda began to play on a loop once more, and the hours started to trickle by. Disturbing questions dug themselves into the recesses of my brain, though I tried to ignore them. I also wanted to ignore the stimulus in front of me, and focus on grieving the death of my father. But the questions returned nonetheless. How had it been so easy? Why did we believe the lies we were told? Then an answer presented itself—*to accept that everything you believe is a lie is to also accept that your entire identity was built upon falsehoods.* At that point, who were you? How did one deprogram an entire nation?

Two days later, by my best guess, the screen went dark and a robotic voice spoke through the speaker in my ceiling. "Ten minutes." My cell door slid open.

CHAPTER 22

FOR THE FIRST time in over two days, I stepped out of the dark room and into an empty hallway. Lighted arrows on the floor pointed the way I was to go, and I followed them, until after several turns I was led out into an open yard, surrounded by fencing.

There was a crisp bite to the air. I rubbed my palms against my exposed upper arms as I walked around slowly. I wondered what state I'd ended up in. I wondered what day it was. I realized I had no idea how long it had been since I'd been shot with the pacifier and had woken up in the room where my father was killed. I could be somewhere near Zone 36, or somewhere else entirely. The difference in climate made me think it was the latter.

The yard was covered in a mix of grass and weeds sticking up indiscriminately through patches of worn dirt. In the distance, I could see mountains. There were about thirty other people wandering around outside. Their gray faces showed their lack of sunlight. Given enough time, I was sure I would look the same.

I moved though the prisoners, searching for signs of Rexx or Oliver. I was painfully aware that the one person I had set out to search for was dead. Killed right in front of me. When my vision adjusted to the bright light, I spotted a familiar face. Not who I had been looking for, but someone else—Officer Robbie Webb. He stood alongside the interior fence, his weapon held against his chest. Anger and defeat bubbled to the surface as I watched him. The man who had murdered my father. I imagined grabbing his weapon and firing it into his eye.

There were several other Compos lining the fence at regular intervals. I didn't know why, but I started to walk over to him, over to Webb. Was I right in my detection of a guilty, nervous shift in his stance as I approached?

There were two security fences, the second encircling the first, with about ten yards between them. There were also dividers that split the outdoor area into pie-shaped wedges. No person could wander the entire yard.

On top of the exterior fence was a thick metal material of some kind, which added about a foot to the fence's height. Connected to this were several large metal rods spaced equidistantly, each about twenty yards apart, by my estimation. The question must have been written on my face.

"Lightning rods," he said matter-of-factly, in a not unfriendly tone. I stopped when I'd reached him, not making eye contact. I stood straight and looked at the fence. I wanted him to know he didn't scare me. That he couldn't rattle me. "For harvesting electricity," he continued.

"We've had a surge in the number of lightning storms up this way in recent years. They don't catch all of them, but when they do, it's a sight to behold, that's for sure." He backed away and gestured as he continued his explanation. "The surge travels down those metal spikes and then out either side, shooting down the length of the fence, lighting it up as it goes. I always hope I'm on shift when it happens. Sure is something." I then remembered what Officer Webb had said in the car, that he wanted to be an engineer.

A loud buzzing sounded, and I knew my ten minutes were up. I turned and followed the arrows back to my cell and sat in the corner, unsure when the doors would open again.

Several days passed, marked only by the ten daily minutes of yard time and delivery of food at regular intervals. If you could call it food—the thick gruel they served us was made out of protein powder and cheap grain as far as I could tell. It stuck to the roof of my mouth and wasn't washed down easily. I made the mistake of drinking my entire tumbler of water before eating the first time the gruel was delivered and regretted it for hours as I gagged and swallowed, trying to dislodge chunks from my throat. From then on, I choked down the entire bowl before reaching for my water.

I often closed my eyes and counted, seeing how long I could go without watching the screen, but distraction of the information (if you could call it that) was somehow better than being left alone with my self-deprecating thoughts.

I felt a sense of relief the first time a familiar tune started to play. The opening to *America One: Helping Our Nation Succeed.* "Welcome, Americans!" Aelia's voice was like an old friend's. "Today we are presenting a very special episode of *All One: Helping Our Nation Succeed.* As you all know, next week there is a very important holiday. We, as a unified nation, celebrate Unification Day on the first Monday in June. It marks the anniversary of our nation's investors taking a challenging but essential step to protect America's future by breaking ground at the Northern Security Barrier, thereby embarking on the journey that ultimately eliminated the continuous threats posed by immigrants, terrorists, and the unpredictability of non-American nations."

On-screen, a reel of form after form being signed, in front of a backdrop of the national emblem, by what I assumed was supposed to be a member of the Board at the time of the Seclusion. I was starting to think everything I'd ever seen was fabricated. What was the footage really of? An actor in a cheap suit signing his confidentiality agreement?

"Their thoughtful, selfless actions continue to provide us with a secure, unified country in which each and every one of us is afforded housing, nourishment, and education," Aelia continued. "A nation in which we are free of the threat from international terrorism. Our beloved leaders bear the tremendous burden of toxic historical information, so we don't have to, allowing us to focus on moving ever forward, marching toward a brighter future. On Unification Day, show your appreciation for the hard choices a select few had to make for the good of the masses, and for the choices they continue to make to preserve this great nation. After all, our happiness is their prime concern!"

Internally, I laughed. It was so light compared to everything I'd been forced to watch since arriving. But my amusement turned to a quiet rage and my eyes started to narrow of their own accord. *Our* happiness. *Our* happiness is their prime concern. The words played on a loop in my brain, drowning out the words of the broadcast.

"How are we supposed to show our appreciation, you ask?" Aelia continued. "Well, we have made it simple! Select one of many prewritten thank-you messages to be delivered to the top—straight to the Boardroom itself! Remember, this is the only time of year that you can contact the Board directly. They will be so thankful to read your messages! Simply follow the instructions on your screen after this broadcast. Board Bless America."

The camera tracked away from Aelia, and I imagined the personalized message I'd like to send to the Board.

Later that day, as I paced back and forth in my small cell, trying to shake out the cramping in my legs caused by poor nutrition and my new sedentary existence, unfamiliar footage took over the screen. It was an instructional video.

The video explained how to input one very specific part (unnamed but shown in detail) into an ideation device, and then close it back up properly. I was thoroughly confused why the video was being played on a loop, or why I was watching it. But it was better than watching children blown to bits, or soldiers being scalped.

The next morning I received my answer: a tray of unassembled IDs and a pile of the aforementioned parts waited in the slot in my door when I awoke. The video played again, and I got the picture. This was my job. This was what I was expected to spend my days doing. This was where our omnipresent surveillance technology was assembled. This was what "traitors" did day in and day out. They didn't join the military or defend our borders or make propaganda. Instead they provided slave labor for the Board. It all made sense.

The entire corrupt picture came together. *Well, screw that,* I thought. I hadn't resigned to spending my life in here, and I certainly wasn't going to be a slave. I left the tray where it was, determined to make a point. Within about three minutes, two large Compos pushed open my door and immediately constrained me. I did not recognize either one of them. One pushed me to the ground, his palm jammed into my chest, and his large fingers spread to each side of my neck.

The resolved, indignant anger and confidence I'd felt a moment prior was instantly replaced by a consuming fear. I was ashamed of myself for it. The other Compo aimed his pacifier right above my navel, and before I had a chance to protest, he pulled the trigger.

When I awoke, my stomach screamed with pain and my neck was tender. The screen turned on and again played the instructional video. I glanced at the camera in the corner of the room. Message received. I slid the tray closer, hating myself as I did so.

It was ironic that I, supposedly one of the only citizens in history to cut out their own chip, would spend my days building the technology used to enforce the surveillance of others. Then again, everyone was in here for a reason. I didn't suppose the irony was lost on the Board. Maybe it was some sick form of psychological torture. Assignments dealt according to crimes. Proving that, once and for all, we were powerless.

The pieces were weighed when they came into the cell and weighed when they went out. If the weight didn't match, a humiliating and painful strip search was conducted. My fingers were tender and bled for the first two weeks as I struggled to meet my enforced quota, until callouses formed.

Then they started to deliver double the workload.

I lived for the ten minutes of outside time when I could again try to spot Rexx, or maybe Oliver. I never did. Each time I went out into the yard I looked at the cameras, remembering some of the shortfalls of surveillance the elders had pointed out during our lessons. I would study one in short bursts, careful to fixate for only a few seconds at a time. Then I would try to work out the angles that might result in an unmonitored space.

I daydreamed about intricate escape attempts, holding on to the hope that it was still possible. That my life would not end inside of that compound.

Sometimes I would lie on the cold floor, eyes closed, imagining once again being in Rexx's arms. I replayed memories of him swiveling in a conference room chair, smiling at the sight of me. Of him dancing, of him climbing trees in the forest. What I wouldn't give for a chance to say yes to climbing trees with him.

I imagined making it to the Northern Barrier to find Rexx already waiting on the other side. I would tell him the words I so desperately wished I had said before. I would tell him that I loved him.

But I didn't know where I was. I didn't have my maps or any of my tools. Even if I could escape the prison, using what I knew about the surveillance, then what? They would be after me within minutes.

Officer Webb was often standing by the fence when I went outside. Sometimes he would nod, a guilty, cautious nod. I hadn't approached him since that first day, though. In my cell, I thought about what I would like to do to him if I had the chance.

Other Compos were not gracious, and I became used to being pushed around, barked at, and demeaned. Still, I looked forward to those ten minutes a day of being in the open air and in the presence of other living human beings, the only ten minutes not spent in my cell in isolation. Once a week we were permitted to shower. A female guard stood watch and I was given three minutes. Laser barriers separated each showering area so that physical interaction between prisoners was impossible.

When it rained, people huddled under a small overhang, not willing to part with their ten minutes of fresh air. When it rained, I watched Robbie Webb. I thought again about what he'd told me, how he hadn't wanted the job. He had wanted to be an engineer. He hadn't wanted to murder my father. He stared out at the horizon, waiting for a lightning storm.

One rainy day, it hit me. Though he had been the catalyst, though he had pressed the button that had ended my father's life, it wasn't him I was angry with. Webb was the answer; I just didn't know how yet.

The days dragged on. I tried to keep track, but the tallies tangled themselves up in my mind. I worried about Rexx and wondered what he was doing. If he was in the same prison as me, if he was doing his work and obeying orders.

After a month, maybe more, I was fairly certain I'd narrowed down a camera blind spot within the yard. Over twenty-three hours a day of isolation was getting to me, and I could feel my brain turning to mush. I knew that my time was running out and soon I would resemble the dead-eyed masses that surrounded me. Though I'd been stretching, exercising a little bit when I could in my cell, I was weak. I was starting to crack, and I had to act.

So, one day, after the lighted arrows led me into the yard, I made my way straight for the area I'd calculated. It was approximately two feet in from the interior fence. Officer Webb was standing at his post a few yards down, and he smiled his usual wary smile. I waved him over.

"Is there a problem, Miss Collins?" Webb said in an authoritative tone as he approached.

I didn't respond audibly, simply nodded. He stared at me quizzically, with a hint of frustration.

That was my chance, and I had to take it. "I need to finish what I started, and I need your help," I said it as quietly as possible. "You're our only hope."

Webb did not say anything, but the bright whites of his eyes widened as he studied my face.

Though I'd thought about what else I might say to Webb hundreds of times over the long, solitary days, something else entirely came out next.

"My father, he liked to kiss my hand before he dropped me off at the dormitories when I was little. When I got scared or missed him, I could put my hand to my cheek and it would be like he was with me. That's what he said."

The officer's eyes widened even more.

"Collins, you are out of line," he said, but the words were flat, inauthentic. I continued. "His favorite flowers were daffodils; he loved how they signified that spring was on the horizon. In February, he'd wait for the daffodils kept in a pot on the patio to shoot up."

Tears came to my eyes as I talked. "He loved baseball. He'd talk about it like he was on the team himself as he sat on the edge of the sofa. 'We won,' 'we were almost there,' things like that. He snorted when he laughed, but only if something was really funny. He never carried an umbrella when it rained in Arizona. It was so rare, he would say he didn't want to miss it, that he wanted to feel it on his face before it was gone again."

Five things. Five *details* about my father, Geoffrey Collins.

Webb raised his head slightly as if he was digesting what I'd just said. Then, without a word, he turned and walked back to his post.

Several days passed.

Then, one day, when the gruel came in through the slot, there was something in it. A note, tucked alongside the edge of the bowl. I recognized the writing, because it was my own. My own scratchy notes alongside drawings of cameras and camera angles. It was a testament to how dry the gruel was that it was still legible.

One thing became clear—Webb had found my backpack. He saw us throw our packs into the brush that day. He must have gone back for them. Had he gone back after our conversation, if you could call it that, in the yard? Or had he had them this whole time?

Below the notes and the drawings were other words in someone else's handwriting.

I'M GOING TO HELP YOU. WAIT FOR THE NEXT STORM AND MEET ME AT THE FENCE. BE READY. EAT UP.

CHAPTER 23

I PUSHED THE piece of paper down into my bowl, letting what little moisture that existed in the gruel saturate it. Then I took a large bite, paper and all, and swallowed. I immediately started to gag on the dense mass and took a small sip of water from my tumbler. Gagging and choking in reaction to the dry gruel probably wouldn't raise any red flags, considering it happened almost daily.

For the first time in weeks, I seriously thought that perhaps my life wouldn't be spent in that cell watching videos of rape, murder, and torture, or working until my fingers were raw. I just had to wait until the next storm. In that moment, I just hoped that if this plan didn't work, they would kill me. If I couldn't make it to the border and carry out Noah's plan, then I didn't deserve to live. I wanted it all to be over. One way or another.

We didn't receive morning weather reports. There was never notice if a storm was coming.

So I waited. I took my ten minutes in the sun, then went back into my cell over and over again. I inserted my small part for the ID over and over again, two hundred devices a day. I watched bloody scenes of foreign torture, and of Aelia Ramey spouting nonsense, and willed myself to hang on to my sanity. *Just one more day,* I would tell myself over and over again. *There is more out there, you will see, you will see,* over and over and over again.

Then, one day, I stepped out of my cell and followed the arrows with the other prisoners. They had bags under their hollow eyes, and skeletal frames—just like me. But then the door to the yard opened, and my face was hit with a blast of wet drops.

Rain. It was pouring rain. Pouring large sheets so that it was hard to see more than a few feet ahead. Everyone huddled together under the overhang.

I took a deep breath, and I walked through the rain and toward the fence. The yard was empty as I crossed. I squinted through the downpour, searching for a sign. There, waiting by the fence, was Webb. Confused, I looked at the camera that was mounted above us, about five feet from my left. It dangled from its cord.

Webb leaned over, held the hand sporting his ID as far away from his body as he could, and shouted into my ear so that I would hear him above the rain. "They will think the storm knocked out the camera, at least at first. Rexx will be waiting at the tree line. There's no time to lose."

Rexx is still alive! I thought. *He's alive and at this prison too.* Webb disconnected something from his uniform and swiped it near the fence. A break in the metal fence started to open, and my heart raced. *It's actually happening. This is it.*

I thought he would leave me to go through myself, but instead he grabbed my elbow and started to run, pulling me alongside him in the pouring rain. We were both drenched, and I looked over my shoulder to see that the gate had closed behind us. We approached the exterior fence, and I was surprised that there was a camera loose there as well. Had Webb dismantled the cameras in preparation for my ten minutes of outside time? It would appear so. Had he done the same thing in Rexx's wedge of prison yard as well?

He swiped again, and soon we were completely outside of the compound. We were almost home free, when I heard a gruff voice behind us.

"Where are you going with that prisoner, Webb?"

Webb spun on his heels and, before I could see what happened, there was a Compo lying on the ground as Webb held a pacifier aimed at his unconscious body.

"Come on," he said, and turned to lead us farther away. After about one hundred yards, he stopped. "You need to go. They will know you're missing as soon as you don't check back into your cell. You don't have much of a head start. The border is fifteen miles north. Here."

He slipped something out of his uniform and tucked it up underneath my prison-issued top to keep it from getting wet. I felt the shape of it and knew instantly that it was the map. "I marked our location. I've seen the worst of what goes on in there, Patricia. If what you said in the car has any truth to it, then . . . well, you better go."

I stared at the man who had murdered my father. "Patch," I said. "My name is Patch. Why don't you come with us?" I asked as the rain poured down both of our faces.

"I have a family. I can't leave them. Besides, there is work to be done here. Just go! Get across the border. I'll be here waiting for a sign from you."

I nodded, and then I turned and started to run with all of my might, through the pouring rain, to the tree line that I could barely make out in the distance. I was weak; I hadn't exercised in over a month and I was tiring quickly. But I forced myself to keep going, pushing through the shooting pains in my sides and ankles that protested with every step.

Several trying minutes later, I crashed through the tree line and arms caught me. Rexx. Though his curls were gone and his eyes were slightly sunken and bloodshot, he still looked like Rexx. In relief, I wrapped my arms around his once muscular body and could feel his shoulder blades protruding.

He leaned his head back, trying to look at my face, but it was buried in his shoulder tightly. I was unwilling to let go just yet.

"I was starting to think I'd never see you again, Patch," he said in a raspy voice, and then he kissed the bristly top of my head. After thirty seconds or so, I loosened my grip and looked into his face.

I kissed him. And it started to heal me. All I wanted to do was stand there, kissing him in the rain until I felt like myself again. "We need to go," he whispered. Reality then began to set in again. We were exposed, and they would be after us soon.

"First, there's something I need to tell you. Something I realized in there."

"What?" He brushed my rain-streaked face with his hand. "What is it, Patch?"

Flashes of Rexx throughout the years raced through my mind. Youthfully exploring the forest for the first time, laughing in the conference room, swimming in the lake, dancing in Zone 36.

"I love you."

His thin, sunken face cracked into a smile. Suddenly he looked like himself again. "I love you too, Patch."

We kissed once more, briefly, then started to run again, through the mud and the rain, toward some rocky peaks out in the distance. Looking behind us every so often for any signs of pursuit. None so far.

"We should find a dry spot so we can figure out where we are," I said through gasps when we had to slow down due to lack of strength.

We found a rock overhang and I peeled out the topo map from underneath my shirt. It had not fared well. My thin scrub-like uniform did not offer much in the way of protection from the elements. I slowly opened the map, careful not to shred the wet sections to pieces. Webb had drawn a big circle around where the prison compound was located, and he was right: we were not far from the border.

"I guess we discovered what the government has been doing in those northern states we wondered about," Rexx said. We were currently in northern Montana. After experiencing firsthand what was taking place, I wouldn't have been surprised if the prison work camps were scattered all around Montana, Wyoming, North Dakota, and South Dakota. Rexx and I had been brought in together, but for all we knew, Oliver could have ended up in a completely different camp.

We needed to make the most of the heavy rain; it would delay or at least impact the search for us. I was thankful that the water was doing a decent job of hiding our tracks.

We walked, climbed, and ran through the rocky slopes for over two hours before we saw it up in the distance, stretching like a black stain across the horizon.

The Wall.

CHAPTER 24

IT WAS IMMENSE, impassable. The sheer volume of it was intimidating. For some reason, unfamiliarity, perhaps, it seemed worse than its smaller twin down south.

You're letting fear cloud your judgment, I said to myself. *You have to look at it objectively.* I studied the map as Rexx climbed up some nearby rocks to get a better look.

"Left, I think!" I shouted over the rain.

"I think so too."

We headed against our instincts to the most challenging route. The ground was uneven, rocky, and surrounded by drop-offs. My feet, clad in thin Board-issued flats, slipped on the wet rocks. I took the shoes off.

The rain started to let up, and the light hum of a drone caused me to freeze. I looked over my shoulder. It was approaching quickly. I watched as it circled the perimeter around us and then headed back where it came from.

"It found us!" I yelled to Rexx, who was slightly ahead of me.

"Keep going!" he replied. I skirted around a large cairn of boulders, trying to find a quicker path to catch up to him. "No! Not there. Those rocks are barely hanging on; you could trigger a landslide." Rexx was right: with the wrong step, the whole hillside could collapse. I felt foolish for not noticing it myself.

I quickly moved horizontally until I was directly behind him, but about three yards away. Another drone, or possibly the same one, again circled overhead.

"I see something!" yelled Rexx. "In the base of the Wall up here, there are multiple cracks. I think we can get through."

As he said the words, it dawned on me. It might actually happen; we might actually get through the Wall. The elders were right: natural erosion had taken place. Nature versus man. We had seen this so many times in our work. No matter the structure, no matter the technological advances in construction—given enough time, nature always won.

Our hope for what awaited us on the other side was still nothing more than that—a hope. But it was a possibility. And possibility was everything. The drone returned; closer this time. It was a quadcopter the size of a ceiling fan, and it lowered itself and hovered above our heads. Its centrally mounted camera alternated between the two of us. I did the only thing I could think of. I grabbed a nearby rock and threw it directly at the drone. It tipped sideways but stayed in the air, and after a split second righted itself again. Rexx threw a rock, and the drone dodged, raising itself a few feet, then dove down toward us quickly. I put my hands over my head in preparation for the blow, as if that would provide any protection. It swung past us, within inches; then, suddenly, it flew away.

"What do you think that means?" I yelled as I pushed forward again.

"I'd say it sent out our location. It was just a search drone, and we don't have much time before they are behind us." The only thing we had going for us was the rough terrain. Land vehicles could not catch us. Anyone who came after us would have to be on foot or in the air. I hurried to catch up to Rexx, ignoring the aching in my bony arms and scraped-up feet as I climbed faster than I had ever climbed in my life.

Before I had covered more than ten feet of vertical climb, the surveillance drone was back once again. I turned my head around, expecting the worst, then having it confirmed. Multiple compliance vehicles were making their way through the muddy valley below, approaching quickly.

"Go, go, go!" Rexx shouted as I stared at the scene unfolding below us. About five armored vehicles were parking before the slope, and officers were scrambling out.

We climbed and climbed.

At that, the drone lowered closer, and a voice was amplified from above. It was the Board member who had spoken to me in my cell, who gave the order to kill my father.

"There is nothing out there, Patricia and Rexx. Turn back now. You will only find destruction and death. Turn around now, and help us keep everyone safe. You don't know the depths of what you are dealing with. If you leave, you place all of us in danger. Come back; we can make a deal."

"You're lying!" I screamed, magnifying all of the anger and pain I had been holding in since the day we'd arrived. The enigma of a man who'd murdered my father, who hid behind his job title, was once again trying to pry inside my head. "You won't even tell us your name! Why should we trust you? It's all a lie. And I'll prove it."

The officers were closing in behind us. They weren't expert climbers, but they were in better shape, well-fed, and quicker on their feet. They hadn't spent twenty-three hours and fifty minutes each day trapped in a cell staring at a screen. There were at least twenty of them, one behind the other. We were getting closer to the Wall, but at the rate they were going, they would catch us first.

Rexx realized this the same moment I did. And he stopped.
"Rexx, what are you doing? We need to go!"

"I'm going to slow them down, Patch." There were tears in his eyes. "But they are going to get me. Get out, do whatever you need to do, and then find me. One of us has to get out."

"Wait, what do you mean? You're supposed to come with me! I need you with me," I said, choking on the words as they emerged. "I can't do this alone!"

"Yes. You can. We made it this far because of you. Now go, please. Don't make this all for nothing. Think of Oliver, of Noah, of your father, of Amara. Please, for me, go!"

Tears streamed down my cheeks as I looked hopelessly from Rexx to the approaching officers.

"I love you, Patch." Rexx scrambled away, partially toward the officers, but his sights were set on something else. Too late, I realized his plan.

It started slowly, just a few rocks, then the whole mountainside started to crumble. I locked eyes with him as he turned back for one last look, knowing what was to come next. I would forever remember the fear and determination in his eyes as he rode a landslide down upon his enemies. Then, in a blink, he was gone. Gone, too, were the Compos and the low-flying drone with the voice of the Board member, buried under a pile of rubble.

I stared at the aftermath. Agony spread through my body and I fell to my knees. The world started to spin, and my fingers spread as I tried to steady myself against the wet rocks beneath me.

He can't be gone. He was just right here. Any second now he's going to climb out of the rubble. Just watch. But there was nothing to see.

I wanted to run to him, to pry off the boulders, to lie beside him and wait for whatever came next. But my feet wouldn't move, wouldn't let me ruin his sacrifice.

We were supposed to do this together. How could I go forward alone? Fear began to wrap its delicate tendrils around my throat as I shivered in the rain. I had to decide. Fear, or hope.

I got to my feet and faced the Wall.

EPILOGUE

I WAS EMPTY, bleeding, wet, dehydrated, hungry, and numb. After finding my way through a slit under the Wall that had been exposed due to natural erosion, I'd collapsed on the other side. I expected that any second the drones would follow me over, that it would have all been for nothing. But as I watched, they halted in midair, as if there were an impenetrable force field keeping them from crossing. Why didn't they cross? I didn't know why, but they stayed on their side. There had to be a reason.

I walked for what seemed like hours until I collapsed in a field. I had no fight left in me. I closed my eyes and, wet and chilled to the bone, drifted off to sleep.

"Greetings," said a friendly female voice. I opened one eye. At first, I thought it was just a mirage, a hallucination caused from a combination of my exhaustion and the heat waves undulating through the drying sky. But it was a vehicle. It hovered over the rough terrain. The words BORDER PATROL were written in a bright yellow-and-green font across the side. I didn't move. Light shot out from the side and scanned my body "You are in distress. Let me help you," the voice said.

The side slid open, revealing three spacious rows of plush bench seats, each with three spots for passengers and harnesses.

I lay staring for several more minutes, my cheek fused with the tangle of grasses beneath it. Unconvinced I possessed the strength to ever move again. Then, one protesting limb at a time, I dragged myself over and pulled myself inside of the hovering vehicle.

Inside it was warm, soft. Soothing music played from speakers overhead. The door closed and the vehicle lifted away.

I raised my head to look out the window. In the distance I could see a city, and a rather large one at that. Vehicles like the one I was in whizzed every which way, at every level of the metropolis.

My eyes widened as I stared in awe. The city made our technological advances look like the tinkering of a child. It was abundantly clear that America was decades behind the rest of the world. The buildings and roadways here circled one another in a symbiotic way. Every single structure, whether short or tall, sprawling or compact, had living roofs and walls, plants growing on their faces and tops. It was breathtaking. I wished that Rexx, my father, Oliver, Noah, and everyone else who had helped me were there to see it too.

Rexx. No matter what came next, I would make sure his sacrifice was worth it. I wiped tears from my eyes. He'd believed in this more than I had, and now he would never get to see it. He was gone, and I would, somehow, have to keep my head above water without him.

Within minutes the vehicle navigated toward a large building. The sun gleamed off the mirrored surface, looking like a waterfall of gold. The border patrol car landed on the roof.

They'd been right. The elders, my father, Oliver . . . they had all been right. Everything that had happened, everything I'd lost, it wasn't for nothing. I was laying eyes on a truth that directly contradicted everything Americans believed. The world beyond our borders, it was alive and thriving without us. A world without walls, open and free. Would it welcome me? Would it turn me away? I didn't know. The door slid open, admitting a breath of warm air.

I got to my feet and stepped outside.

There was work to be done.

AUTHOR'S NOTE

FIRST, TO MY husband, Bart, for his patience and support as I dedicated countless hours to writing these past two years. For his willingness to whip up drawings of maps and government emblems at my behest, and read scenes at the drop of a hat. I never could have done this without you.

To my children, Tristan and Willow, who tried their hardest to wrap their heads around the notion that Mom needs time to work on her book, though no physical book was anywhere in sight. I love you both. It's finally here.

To my mom, Sue Regan, whose support never wavered and who was always happy to be a sounding board when the process got rough. Who campaigned for this book furiously alongside of me to reach that magic number of preorders. Who spent hours on the phone with me, naming characters and playing with plot ideas.

To Matt Harry, my developmental editor, who helped make this story what it is by acting not just as a developmental editor, but as a patient and inspiring writing coach. Working through this process with you has taught me so much. So much, in fact, that I'm optimistic that the next one won't require nine rounds.

To Angus McLinn, Jackie Batston, Mary Pembleton, Bob Kalk, and Ralph Regan, who provided valuable feedback at various stages of the process, and helped shape the book into its final product.

To the author community at Inkshares, who immediately jumped in with their support. So many of you ordered copies on day one, were quick to offer advice and encouragement, and joined forces to get this book selected as book-of-the-month for six separate syndicates on the Inkshares platform. It gave me the courage and the stamina to reach out of my comfort zone and keep going until the goal was reached.

To my copy editor, Kaitlin Severini, who undoubtedly saved me from many a literary faux pas.

To the rest of the Inkshares team—Adam, Angela, Avalon, Thad, and Elena. Thank you for your dedication and hard work.

To authors Robert Batten and K.L. Noone, both for your early support, and for lending names to two of my favorite characters (Officer Robbie Webb and Louise Collins) after winning a character-naming giveaway during the publishing campaign.

To the 570 friends, family members, and complete strangers who helped make this book a reality by preordering a copy (or sometimes several) through Inkshares. All of you took a chance on this book, by a first-time author. I am eternally grateful.

GRAND PATRONS

Allen Ahearn
Andrea Olson
Andrew Gill
Annie Sanbower
Bart Castle
Bob Kalk
Bonnie Squibb
Bryan M. Wood
Carolyn Castle
Christina Vigil
Colin James
Daniel McGraw
Deborah Fincher
Dr. Anna H. Hall
Dyanne Ahearn Ryan
Elizabeth Fisher
Gunars Lelis
Jackie Nasca
Jamie Davis
Jennifer Elizabeth Hall
Jerry Lucas
Juanita Wheatley Breland
Justin Kalk
Kathleen Lelis

Kelly Bricker
Kelly Welch
Kenneth H. Hall
Keon Bates
Lea Ann Capley
Matthew Isaac Sobin
Michael Mallory
Noelle Molter
Patricia Smallwood
Ralph Regan
Raymond W. McClusky
Ryan M. Schwarz
Skye Mallory
Sue Regan
Terry G. Halladay
Tom Castle
Tristan Castle
Virginia Heath Moyer
William Furr
William J. McGuire
Willow Castle
Xavier Gonzalez Jr.
Zachary T. Bidle

INKSHARES

INKSHARES is a reader-driven publisher and producer based in Oakland, California. Our books are selected not by a group of editors, but by readers worldwide.

While we've published books by established writers like *Big Fish* author Daniel Wallace and *Star Wars: Rogue One* scribe Gary Whitta, our aim remains surfacing and developing the new author voices of tomorrow.

Previously unknown Inkshares authors have received starred reviews and been featured in the *New York Times*. Their books are on the front tables of Barnes & Noble and hundreds of independents nationwide, and many have been licensed by publishers in other major markets. They are also being adapted by Oscar-winning screenwriters at the biggest studios and networks.

Interested in making your own story a reality? Visit Inkshares.com to start your own project or find other great books.